More praise for Alyce Miller

"[Alyce Miller's stories] capture that most universal of human long-ing, the one seeking contact with other individuals and the difficulty of that in so much of modern life. . . . Telling probings into our inner lives. "　　　　　　　　　　　—Jere Real, *Richmond Times-Dispatch*

"Miller's thoughtful, original first collection surely stretches the reader's range of vision. "　　　　　—Joan Frank, *Hungry Mind Review*

"What puts the charge into *The Nature of Longing* is the knowing way in which Alyce Miller moves back and forth examining. . . the boundary between white and black America. It's unusual, I think, to find a new writer who can so sympathetically portray both worlds, showing us ample common ground, and who can do it without the schmaltz of political correctness. Whether white or black, teenaged or adult, straight or gay, Miller's protagonists are acutely aware of American racial (and sexual) geography. They're constrained by it, enlivened by it, and made real by it. "
　　　　　　　　　　　　　　　　—Kevin Miller, *Harvard Review*

"In *The Nature of Longing*, Alyce Miller uses everyday detail and dia-logue to illustrate the most universal of longings: the worn, slow-dance desire of soul for soul. "
　　　　　　　　　　　—Elizabethe R. Kramer, *Columbus Dispatch*

"Impressive debut collection. . . . Miller brings psychological depth and a keen sense of moral ambiguity to these finely wrought tales. "
　　　　　　　　　　　　　　　　　　　　　　　—*Publishers Weekly*

"[Miller's characters] all share an ache of longing that affects the reader like the slow release of a murmur wafting up from these richly emotional pages. "　　　　　　　　　　　　—*Lambda Book Report*

"A tough, smart collection of stories. . . . It will be interesting to see the shape of Miller's future work. "
　　　　　　　　　　　—Erika Taylor, *Los Angeles Times Book Review*

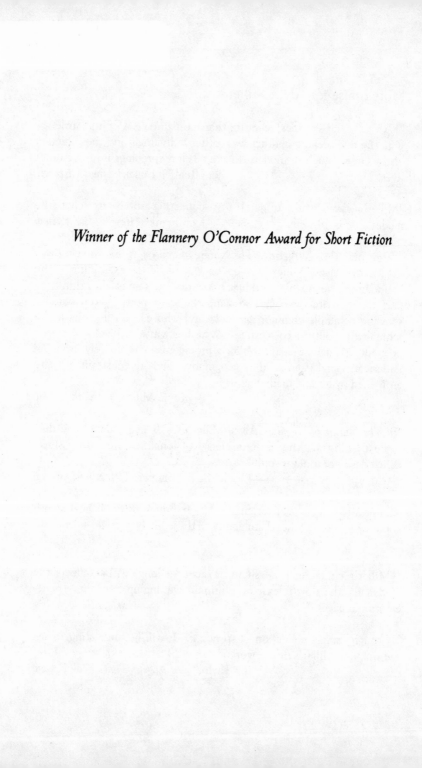

Winner of the Flannery O'Connor Award for Short Fiction

THE

Stories by Alyce Miller

NATURE OF

W. W. Norton & Company   New York   London

LONGING

Originally published by the University of Georgia Press,
Athens, Georgia 30602
First published as a Norton paperback 1995
All rights reserved

Design by Sandra Strother Hudson
Manufacturing by the Haddon Craftsmen, Inc.

Library of Congress Cataloging-in-Publication Data
Miller, Alyce.
The nature of longing : stories / by Alyce Miller.
p.   cm.
"Winner of the Flannery O'Connor Award for short fiction"—P.
preceding t. p.
Contents: Tommy—Off-season travel—A cold winter light—The
nature of longing—Color struck—What Jasmine would think—
Summer in Detroit—Dead women.

ISBN 0-393-31379-4

I. Title.
PS3563. I37424N3   1994
813´. 54—dc20   94-7582

Some of these stories first appeared in the following publications:
"Tommy" in the *Southern Review*; "What Jasmine Would Think"
in *American Fiction: The Best Unpublished Stories by
Emerging Writers,* number 4; "A Cold Winter Light" in *North Dakota
Quarterly*; "Color Struck" in the *Los Angeles Times Magazine*; and
"Summer in Detroit" in the *High Plains Literary Review*.

For Stephen, and for all my families

CONTENTS

TOMMY

There are people who remain connected to us throughout our lives, who seem to follow a similar trajectory, more often through accident than design. It was that way with Tommy Pendleton and me: all those years since we'd both left Fields, Ohio, right up until last week when I got the call from his sister Betty. Strange how quickly I placed her: regal brown Betty Pendleton, four grades ahead, the school's first black homecoming queen. I hadn't seen her in over twenty years. Now, Betty's tone was pleasant and matter-of-fact, with the familiar flattened vowels and slow drawl of our hometown. She'd just flown in to San Francisco, she started off in a chatty way. I knew better than to think this was just a social call.

Her voice softened ever so slightly as she asked if I'd heard about Tommy. That he'd died—this past Wednesday—and his funeral service was going to be held day after tomorrow in Oakland. Did I think I could make it? When I recovered myself, Betty said sweetly, "I'm so sorry, Marsha," as if she'd done something wrong.

My "yes" got lost in my throat. I jotted down the address of the chapel in someone else's shaky handwriting.

"I'm glad you can come," Betty said. "You were one of his best friends. The Lord bless you."

When I hung up, I realized that when I'd asked, "How?" Betty had avoided the word "AIDS." Instead, she said, "Pneumonia." I cursed myself for not having figured out that Tommy was sick. Of course he wouldn't have told me, not the way he was about these things, always so clever about protecting himself. But it would explain his conversion to religion, the final wedge between us that made it so difficult to communicate much at all the last couple of years. "Best friend," I thought bitterly. Tommy and I were never best friends. I don't cry often, but I let myself go on this one.

Back in Fields, all through junior high and high school there were only three of us in the advanced classes. Me, Diane McGee, and Tommy, a regular triumvirate of color, toting around our accelerated literature anthologies and advanced trig textbooks, along with the other college placement kids.

The Tarbaby Triplets, Diane used to joke, loud-talking in her more audacious moods, just to make the white kids turn red. In that snowy dominion, we did manage to quietly flourish, three dark snowflakes alighting on the ivory pile like bits of ash. We ran the spectrum from light to dark—Tommy the color of a biscuit, me cinnamon brown, and Diane bittersweet dark chocolate—handpicked from our 40 percent of the population there in Fields and carefully interspersed among the white kids for that slow-fizzling illusion known in our liberal town as racial harmony. Other than that, we had little to do with one another. Me, Diane, and Tommy, someone's proof of something, all going our separate ways, Diane with the black kids, Tommy with the white, and me floundering somewhere in between.

It was in junior high that Diane indignantly informed our stunned English class that *we* were no longer "colored," nor "Negro," but "*black*." She spat out the word with proud anger that reverberated distantly within a part of an as-of-yet undiscovered me. I quickly seconded her outburst, conscious of the puzzled looks of my white classmates. Hadn't they guessed, I thought, sitting there year after year, tolerating us and taking their own privilege for granted? Hadn't it ever occurred to them that beneath our agreeable demeanors there was more than just a faint rumble of discontent? Diane held out one long, thin ebony arm. "Can't you see?" she demanded. "I'm not colored. Everybody's *colored*. I'm *black*."

The whole time she talked, her voice trembling and passionate, Tommy Pendleton sat stiffly in his seat, never saying a word. I didn't have the nerve, but Diane did. "You too, Tommy Pendleton," she needled. "You too, *brother*." There was a barely perceptible flutter of movement in his left jaw.

The Pendletons owned a small horse farm on Lincoln Street not far from Mt. Zion Baptist Church. There were four boys and Betty, Tommy being the youngest. Mr. Pendleton was a cripple, his body hunched and crumpled like an aluminum can. Years before, he'd been the victim of a horrible riding accident. Everyone said the crippling had affected his mind, as if twisted limbs could spawn a meanness of spirit. You could catch him out back in his icy field in the most inclement weather, staggering among his horses, as if daring another one to kick him.

Tommy's mother was known as "the invisible woman." She was a Jehovah's Witness, spent all her time inside praying. Rumor had it that Mrs. Pendleton was so weak she let Tommy's father padlock the refrigerator so Tommy and his brothers wouldn't eat him out of house and home.

"That man is downright stingy and hateful," Diane informed me once. She lived just down the street from the Pendletons. "He treats those boys something awful. Beats them—those grown boys, too. That's why Tommy's *that way*, you know."

Back then, I hadn't a clue what she meant. Diane knew so much, but I was too caught up in myself to understand.

Tommy never seemed troubled. Every morning he sauntered

good-naturedly up the school's circular walkway with the boys in our advanced classes, or goofed off with white girls at their lockers.

Tommy, never pretending one thing while being another, eventually slipped through the cracks of rebuke and after a while the black kids seemed to forgive him for his betrayal and left him in peace. He was so determined in his position that people quit linking him to the Toms and Oreos who faked it on both sides. It was as if, at least in our minds, Tommy had ceased to be black, or even white. He was just Tommy, handsome Tommy Pendleton ("Mr. *Too* Fine Tommy Pendleton, some of us girls used to concede enviously), even in his downright square clothes: long-sleeve cotton button-down shirts, pressed slacks, and lace-up Hush Puppies from J.C. Penney's in Elyria. When the other black kids were growing their hair, Tommy kept his short and cropped like a newly mowed lawn. You wouldn't have caught him dead with a cheesecutter in his pocket or a braid in his head.

Instead, he walked off with the highest test scores and model essays, posing solemnly for yearbook photos of the Speech, Drama, and Chess Clubs, the only poppyseed in the bunch. His best friend was a white egghead named Paul Malloy.

"The Pendletons must be so proud," my mother used to say wistfully of Tommy's top grades. "Watch, that boy ends up at Harvard."

Big deal Harvard, I grumbled to myself, let him go ahead off with a bunch of peckerwoods and see if anybody cared. Tommy aroused in me all my own uncertainty, about myself, about my awkward friendship with a shy white girl named Mary, about militant Diane acting like everyone's conscience, about my goody-twoshoes boyfriend Phil Willis, and the accompanying push and pull of contradictions. I used Tommy as proof that I was more acceptable.

Though we saw each other daily all through grade school and junior high, we rarely spoke. High school was no different. Even now I can remember only little incidents, like the time he broke a piece off the black frames of his glasses during silent reading and I wordlessly took them from him and repaired them with a piece of masking tape from my bookbag. As the weeks wore on, he never bothered to have his glasses fixed. I derived an odd and private satisfaction from seeing the piece of masking tape there. Too bad, I used to think, too bad he's so fine and so peculiar.

Social divisions run all latitudes and longitudes, and we were all mostly too busy worrying about black and white and on which side of the racial borders romance was flowering to give much attention to what Tommy Pendleton might actually be.

After high school, turned upside down by racial tensions and old pains, I went off to college in the rolling hills of southern Ohio; Tommy predictably left for Harvard on a scholarship, though his father had loudly protested. But our lives, oddly enough, remained entangled long after Diane McGee turned to drugs, my old boyfriend Phil Willis married a white girl named Ellen, and I had moved as far away from Ohio as I could get.

The morning of Tommy's funeral service I canceled my classes in San Francisco and drove over the East Bay Bridge to the Chapel of the Chimes where Tommy's body lay. I took a seat on a wooden pew in the very back of the chapel. It was an odd bunch, to say the least—mourners taken from someone else's life, I couldn't help thinking. Half the pews were filled with formally dressed Japanese business people from a company Tommy had done legal work for. The other half were occupied by mostly well-scrubbed white couples who looked as if they might want to sell me insurance. There was a sprinkling of single men, what Tommy used to in his rare candid moments jokingly refer to as "friends of Dorothy." The front row was packed with a conspicuous group of black women in silk dresses and oversized hats, obviously relatives. There were a couple of men as well, portly and graying. All I could see were the backs of their heads, but I had a feeling Betty and Mrs. Pendleton were among them.

Viewing the corpse was a shock. I had never looked at the dead body of someone my own age, pasted and glued together with heavy makeup, worn out from the ravages of a devastating disease. It didn't look like Tommy at all, too pale, too thin. I turned away, ignoring the woman next to me who was murmuring, "Doesn't he look just wonderful?"

I was both stunned and angered by the simplistic explanation of Tommy's death which, according to the minister, was "part of God's wonderful plan to call his son Tommy home, because Tommy had special business with God." Still no mention of AIDS. It was as if Tommy's "special business" was the reassurance we all needed to pacify us against the senselessness of his death. Easier to believe God chose Tommy than to believe Tommy had slept with many men. I thought about one of the last conversations I'd had with him. I'd accused him of choosing this religion as a way of turning his back on himself. He was smart enough to know what I meant, and he looked pained. Now I wanted to yell, "It's not true!" Somehow, deep inside, I think Tommy might almost have approved.

I kept waiting for someone else to object. I looked to the front row; not so much as a feather on those wide-brimmed hats trembled. As the minister talked on about Tommy's talents (he'd directed the church youth choir), I wondered which one, if any, of those starchy looking white men present had caused him to grow sick and die. I studied the bowed heads, the impassive faces, the soft "Praise the Lord's," and I knew that no one here, except maybe me, was really part of Tommy's past.

The gravesite was three blocks away up a green hill. I parked my car and stood on the periphery, feeling anxious. An overly polite white couple in shades of gray and black and moussed hair accosted me. "We're Bill and Cynthia, friends of Tommy's from church. Are you a *relative?*"

I shook my head. "We grew up together, back in Ohio."

"Oh!" they cooed, "isn't that nice?" I was suddenly being introduced around to strangers. "This is Marsha. She grew up with Tommy in Ohio."

In a way it was true, I thought, truer than anyone could imagine, the growing-up part, I mean. The words rebounded unexpectedly like a heavy fist. I moved back along the edges of the mourners. As the preacher prayed over Tommy's casket, I wandered a ways up the cemetery hillside and looked out over the Bay, the stunning view from Tommy's gravesite, which he would never see, now that his eyes would soon be six feet underground.

The Christmas dance of 1969—such a silly thing, but a turning point of sorts. Tommy and I had never talked about it. Not when we ran into each other one summer on Harvard Square, not when we stumbled on each other in the Cleveland Art Museum one wintry afternoon during Christmas break. And not even when Tommy moved to San Francisco and shared my apartment for six months, shortly after I'd finished graduate school and he was studying for the California bar exam. I knew better than to think Tommy had actually forgotten. Perhaps it was why he felt comfortable inviting me as his "date" to subsequent law office parties and events, even holding my hand sometimes when we were among strangers.

Tommy could be so peculiar about his private life. I mean, one minute he and I would be laughing about the baths and red rooms and glory holes and the games boys used to play, and the next he'd draw back, like a crab in its shell, and say disapprovingly, "MAR-sha," as if I'd said something too personal for him.

Even when Tommy shared my apartment and I'd go to tease him about one of his occasional tricks I'd passed that morning in the hallway, he'd tell me sternly, "It isn't what you think."

"Then what is it?" I'd ask him.

"It's too complicated," he answered. "Don't try to figure it out."

Actually, one night I did broach the subject of the 1969 Christmas dance. Tommy and I were sitting around the kitchen table eating fried egg sandwiches and laughing about the old days in Ohio. We were laughing about Fields, about Diane McGee, about the time gay Terence Lords put on makeup and ran down the school hallway shouting, "I'm ready for my close-up, Mr. DeMille!"

"Tommy . . ." I began, still convulsed with laughter. "Tommy, do you remember that stupid dance we went to?" It slipped out before I knew it.

He looked up at me in such a way that the laughter died on my lips. And then the phone rang. Tommy went to answer it, and from the other room I heard him say cheerfully, "Hi, Jeff." A pause, followed by a low soft chuckle, and then the door of his bedroom closed. A terrible pang cut through me. I had underestimated, as I often did with Tommy, the ways I could offend him.

The 1969 Christmas dance happened like this. In tenth grade I broke up with Phil Willis because, in my teen arrogance, I decided he was a nobody. His only future was to inherit his father's bakery, one of two black-owned businesses in town, and I couldn't picture myself behind the counter for the rest of my life wearing a white baker's apron and serving up dozens of oatmeal cookies to local kids. His parents were what we used to call "siddity." They were extremely fair people, with pink skin and curly sandy hair, the kind of "good Negro that, oh, if only the others could be like, we wouldn't have such problems." Mrs. Willis headed the Boy Scout troop, composed mostly of little white boys, Phil being the exception. Oh, how people like the Willises kidded themselves! Black is black, no matter how white.

I myself had found this out the hard way when, the summer after tenth grade, my friend Mary's family became "concerned." They thought Mary ought to be relating more to her own "peers," and stopped finding it convenient to have me over. Finally, when confronted, Mary's mother informed us gently that we were too old now to continue our friendship, that there would be too many problems. I knew exactly what Mary's parents believed to be in store for Mary: tall, jet-black friends of my boyfriends with hair like tumbleweed sidling up to their front porch asking for porcelain Mary in silky whispers; parties on the east side of town where Mary might dance a hairsbreadth from dark-skinned boys in Ban-Lon shirts and smelling of hair oil.

I started hanging out with other black girls, Camille Hubbard and Monica Pease, who lived on streets named for presidents. We'd meet after school for our singing group and practice in the choir room, and then accompany one another home. I now bypassed the streets named for trees, avoiding the route Mary and I used to take.

Just after Halloween, Camille and Monica and I sneaked into a college dance on borrowed ID's. It was that night I fell in love with Calvin Schumate, a student majoring in political science. Calvin was the kind of boy who gets under your skin and keeps you restless every second of the day. He was, in the opinions of Camille and Monica, just about the *finest, toughest, bossest* thing that ever set foot on the college campus, *ooooh, girl*. Tall and chocolate brown. His hair was thick and wild, and added softness to his angular face. He was a full three years older than I, an abyss I leaped with pure frenzy.

That first night I danced every record with Calvin. He danced New York, I danced Detroit. "You've got some moves there," he said admiringly. Afterwards, dripping sweat, we wandered into the moonlight, fanning ourselves with paper napkins. I suffered from that delicious exhaustion when one is beyond caring. Calvin clasped my hand in his, walked me out to the square, and kissed me so deeply I thought he'd sucked my heart out.

I accepted his ring. My parents heard about this through the grapevine and confronted me immediately.

"He's a full-grown man," said my father, "and you're still a young girl. He's much too old for you."

"He'll pressure you," worried my mother. "He'll expect things of you. I don't understand for the life of me why you broke up with Phil. Now those were nice people, the Willises, whatever could you be thinking?"

I could explain it: Calvin came from the mean streets of Harlem, which was about as exotic as you could get for a sheltered middle-class black girl from a tiny Ohio college town. And he was brilliant and tough. He had grown up in a neighborhood where streets were numbered, where everybody had a hustle, and junkies shot dope in the alleys. He'd shot it himself, he told me, and gambled, and hung around prostitutes until his fed-up father finally dragged him around to the nuns at a Catholic boarding school and insisted they and their God "do something with my wild boy before he gets himself killed."

I thrilled to these stories of the precocious street hood turned scholar, wise and sassy beyond his years, full of himself, and not fooled for one minute by me and what he called my "bourgeois thinking."

My parents and I fought terribly about Calvin. Raised voices and slammed doors were not acceptable at our house, yet the subject of Calvin provoked both.

"He's not even Catholic," my mother fretted.

"He went to Catholic school."

"Not the same," said my mother. "Phil's Catholic."

"I don't love Phil!"

"You don't love this boy either. You're too young. You'll thank us later," my mother went on. "We have only your welfare in mind."

My father warned me, "I want to see you go on to college and get a good education. A boy like Calvin could get you involved in things . . ." His voice trailed off at that intersection of truth where what he really wanted to say lay well beyond what a man can comfortably say to his own daughter.

Little did my parents know that their cryptic, anxious warnings came too late. I did not mean to be careless, but Calvin had a man's ways and a man's ideas. He told me the most compelling things a man can tell a woman, and I was a foolish, lovesick girl with my nose open a mile wide.

We pursued a ritual of clandestine meetings in his dorm room, dangerous and heated congresses, where under sagging fishnets suspended from the ceiling a red strobe light whipped over our bodies with the force of fireworks and stern-faced posters of Malcolm X and Huey Newton observed our tussles grimly. Jasmine incense burned ceremonially in a small ceramic holder by the bed. Now, I was still cautious about certain things and refused Calvin the final token of romantic commitment, but we played at everything else, tumbling around in his sheets, even showering together after in his yellow-tiled shower stall, with me soaping up his thick gorgeous hair. He'd lie naked in bed and read me Harlem Renaissance poetry and essays by Baldwin. We listened over and over to the Last Poets, memorizing together the rhythms of our own lives and talking about "the struggle," Calvin explaining to me earnestly what it meant to be part of a revolution. When he was out on the town square, megaphone in hand, railing against "the Man," I stood on the edge of the crowd, reading his passionate appeals as a secret message directed to me.

At Calvin's urging I took the straightener out of my hair and grew a curly 'fro. I talked more and more about the Revolution, and took to wearing dashikis and brass bangles and the African elephant-hair bracelet Calvin gave me. In my sophomore speech class I expounded on such subjects as "The Role of the New Black Womyn" and the necessity for black students to bear arms. I was Calvin's mouthpiece, his right hand. I was frightening even to myself, uncovering decades of rage my parents had covered over with their prosperity.

"Girl, where the hell do your folks think you are all the time?" Camille wanted to know as she waited for me outside Calvin's dorm room one afternoon.

"Aren't you afraid of . . . *you* know . . . ?" Monica asked.

"Calvin and I don't do that," I informed them self-righteously. Virginity was still a big deal back then, and I wore mine like a badge. "I love Calvin and he loves me, but *that* is out of the question."

I believed what I offered Calvin was enough for any man. I believed Calvin when he said we were two lost halves who'd made a whole, destined to leave our mark on the world together, and that our grapplings in the dark were a natural extension of the sublime communion that passed between us as two exceptional lovers.

And so the Christmas dance approached. I was crazy with wanting to bring Calvin, just long enough to stroll through the door with him and let everyone who'd ever snubbed me, black and white, see me with my fine college brother on my arm. I wanted to set their ignorant tongues to wagging.

It was out of the question.

My mother began pestering me about making up with Phil. She even went so far as to drop hints about having seen Mrs. Willis at Sparkle Market and letting me know that Phil had looked longingly at her when she stopped in the bakery to buy a pie. "You need a date for the dance," she pressed.

And that's when I seized on the idea. In a moment of pure inspiration I became the architect of a crafty plan: I couldn't stand Phil, but I could, yes, I would, invite Tommy Pendleton. The perfect camouflage. My parents, content to think I was finally out with a "nice boy," would extend my curfew, and after I'd pleaded the flu and rid myself of the unsuspecting Tommy, the remaining hours would be spent in rapture with Calvin.

Camille's only comment, when I told her, was "You might as well invite a white boy as invite Tommy Pendleton."

Frostily I approached Tommy outside of English class a day or two later. It felt more like a business proposition than a party invitation, but I said my piece in a casual, upbeat tone I had rehearsed in front of the bathroom mirror.

Tommy studied me a moment, fingering the masking tape on his black-framed glasses. For a moment I thought he might say no, a possibility that had not occurred to me. "Okay," he said simply, as if it were about time a black girl like me showed interest. Perhaps it was relief I saw in his face, more than expectation. "Thank you," he added. I walked off feeling strangely sad.

I bought a new orange minidress and matching fishnet stockings and T-strap, sling-back heels. I even roamed the lingerie department and selected a silk bra-and-panty set, with Calvin and Calvin alone in mind. This would be the night, I thought, my entire body radiating the heat of anticipation. I would be sixteen in the spring; it was time.

"Why doesn't Tommy pick you up?" my mother asked over an early dinner.

"He doesn't drive," I explained, which was conveniently true. "You know how weird and strict the Pendletons are, with that crippled dad and all their crazy religion that's gone to their heads."

"Now that's no way to talk about folks," said my mother, the devout Catholic. "Make sure you two stop by here so your father and I can get a peek."

They were suspicious of my sudden interest in Tommy Pendleton, but I could read the one word in their minds: *Harvard.*

I drove my father's blue Buick LeSabre across Main Street to Tommy's house. When I pulled into the dark driveway and honked, the headlights picked up Mr. Pendleton's twisted silhouette out near the small barn behind the house. He might have been a crooked, leafless tree. A shiver ran through me as though I'd had a premonition. Then the porch light flashed on and Tommy's father vanished into wintry darkness. Mrs. Pendleton stood foregrounded on the porch, her arms clasped across her chest to ward off the chilly December night. She motioned me to come in. Reluctantly, I cut off the motor and got out of the car.

It was the first time I'd ever seen Mrs. Pendleton up close. She was a plain woman, but not severe. She wore her hair pulled back in a loose bun, and a long, brown flowered housedress. She had been pretty once.

"Hello, Marsha," she greeted me with warmth and drew me by my arm into the stale house. "I've heard so much about you. Tommy says you're in all his classes."

"Except P.E.," I clarified nervously. The house was over-heated and the smell of cooking grease hung in the air.

Mrs. Pendleton offered to take my coat and insisted I join her for a cup of tea. I had no choice. The house was uncannily silent. Tommy was nowhere in sight. I took a tentative seat on the sofa under a triple portrait of Martin Luther King and the Kennedy brothers. Just knowing they hovered above disturbed my conscience.

"So, Tommy tells me your father teaches at the college." She seated herself across from me, her eyes bright in that smooth, serene face.

"Administration," I corrected her. "He works in administration."

"Isn't that wonderful!" She asked me all about my mother, my brothers, and the exact location of our house. "Of course," she said, "that lovely big white one on the corner of Pine. And I know who your mother is too. Pretty woman, has all that nice thick hair."

She prattled on, appraising me with her eyes as if I were an article of clothing she was assessing for a good fit. Guilt made me overcompensate. I had what folks call good home training, and I didn't hold back. Each courtesy seemed to please her more, until I realized my politeness would be my own undoing.

Her smile was broad now. "I'm just so pleased you two are going to this dance. I don't normally let Tommy go to such things, but I know what a nice girl you are."

I glanced nervously at my watch. When I looked up, Tommy was standing in the doorway in a dark brown suit, his hair parted on one side. We exchanged cautious hellos.

Mrs. Pendleton had a camera ready and she insisted we pose before the fireplace. "Turn this way, you two," she cooed. "Now, give me a big smile. I can't see your eyes, Tommy."

Tommy removed his glasses and held them behind his back as he squeezed awkwardly beside me. We stared dutifully into the blinding flash.

"Oh, the flowers!" Mrs. Pendleton disappeared into the kitchen and I heard the refrigerator door open and close. Too quickly, I thought, for her to have undone a padlock.

She'd seen to it I had a corsage, something frilly and white, with perfume and ribbons, which she pulled from the chilled box. She handed the corsage to Tommy and then photographed him pinning it to my chest ("Oh, I wish I'd known you were going to wear orange!"), cautioning him when he came too close to my breasts ("Careful now, you don't want to stick your little girlfriend!"). I could see how hard she was trying, how important this moment was to her. She wanted to make things right.

Tommy was flustered under the pressure. Beads of sweat broke out over his forehead.

"Now put your arm around Marsha's waist," insisted Mrs. Pendleton. "There, now don't you make a lovely looking twosome? Praise the Lord."

The flash went off three or four more times. I finally pleaded sensitivity to bright lights.

"Look at me keeping you all to myself. I wish the others were around. I'm so sorry Tommy's father wasn't here tonight to see you two off."

I was still at an age when a lie from an adult startled me. Mrs. Pendleton followed us to the door, her eyes bright as a child's: her son Tommy was off to a dance with a girl, and a black one at that, and now she had the pictures to prove it. She stood on the porch clutching the camera as if she'd just photographed Our Lady of Lourdes.

"My parents want us to stop by," I explained dully to Tommy as we came down the driveway.

"*Quid pro quo*," he said agreeably, but I had no idea what he meant.

Fortunately my parents seemed satisfied just to have us stand in the living room and be viewed. Tommy was not Phil, but my mother made over him just the same. Coatless, she and my father braved the cold and followed us onto our front porch.

"So, will it be Harvard or Princeton?" my father asked Tommy, already joining the two of us in his mind's eye.

"Let them go, Ralph. Have a nice time," said my mother. "Don't worry about hurrying home. Take your time."

We piled back into the LeSabre, and I backed out of the snowy drive. By now it was almost nine, and I was frantic. Calvin's face loomed before me; I felt the irresistible pull of his soft lips on my neck.

"I need to stop by the college for a minute," I said on impulse. "I have to drop something off to a friend."

Tommy didn't object. Instead, he sat stiffly in the passenger seat, staring out the window.

We drove the few blocks to Calvin's dorm. I left the engine running and my maxi coat flung across the back seat: a promise that I would return quickly.

Adrenaline swelled my pulses. Every joint in my body throbbed as if badly bruised. I scampered quickly in my thin-soled T-straps through the darkness, feeling the cold on my half-naked feet and in my bones. Calvin was a hot fire in my brain.

I took the stairs two at a time, coming up through the propped-open fire-exit door. I was Cinderella from the ball. I tapped at his door. No answer. I tapped again. Then again.

"Who're you looking for?" asked a boy poking his head out from the room next door.

"Calvin." My tone implied privilege.

"He's gone."

I should have left it at that and headed for the dance with Tommy. I should have realized that the fever and chills alternately coursing through me signaled danger. But I couldn't resist one more knock, and then the knob was in my hand, turning much too easily, and the sudden chill of my own body startled me in the wake of damp heat that poured toward the open door.

It was like entering a sauna. First the dimness, then the steam rising from Isaac Hayes's brooding *Hot Buttered Soul* album and mingling with the essence of jasmine incense. The air was thick and moody, the candlelit walls alive with ambiguous shadows.

A motion from the corner of the room caught my eye, and then it became two separate motions I saw: one was Calvin rising up from the sheets, with nothing but his medallion around his neck; the other was the silhouette of a long dark body with large tubular breasts and a huge halo of black hair unfolding itself with knowing insolence.

Someone exclaimed, "Oh, my God!" There was a sudden flurry of sheets and pillows and brown limbs, then a woman's voice cried out, "Calvin, what the hell is going on here?" and I realized it was me speaking, using the tone of voice I had imagined only a woman capable of.

"Marsha!"

I didn't recognize my own name. I yelled, "Bastard!" and ran out, twisting my ankle when one of my heels caught on the carpet.

I was too stunned to cry. My chest threatened to cave in on itself. As I ran back out the fire exit, I found I could not catch my breath. Panic set in. It took several minutes of standing in the outside stairwell below, pulling in the frosty air with lungs so tight I thought they would explode.

I had never suspected, because I lacked the experience to suspect.

I stuffed my fist in my mouth and bit down hard until I tasted salt. I shook my hand free and thrust it into a thin layer of snow to stop the pain. And then there was nothing to do except walk back around to the other side of the dorm and get into my father's car next to Tommy Pendleton as if nothing had happened. My voice had disappeared somewhere deep in my throat. As if mutually agreed upon, I said nothing and Tommy said nothing. We went grimly on to the dance at the school gym, my heart as hard as a rock.

The gym was decorated with Christmas tree boughs and ribbons. An inflatable Santa-and-reindeer set hung from the ceiling. A huge fir tree stood in the middle of the floor, lit up and covered with red balls and silver tinsel.

After we'd gotten ourselves settled and I'd managed to swallow some punch, Tommy asked me to dance. We moved stiffly around the floor, nodding to people we knew. "You look very nice," he told me. "You really do."

His touch left me cold inside. I kept my face turned.

We joined Tommy's red-haired friend Paul Malloy and his date, a pale white girl named Lisa from Firelands. Tommy and Paul immediately began whispering together. I made a point of ignoring them all, including Lisa, who was feeling ignored by Paul. She kept trying to show off her corsage that seemed to have taken root right there on her wrist.

"So are you and Tommy going together?" she asked.

"No," I told her and turned my head. Monica and Camille appeared then in jovial moods with dates they'd gotten from a Catholic school in Cleveland. They were both dressed and perfumed and oiled, looking like Cheshire cats.

"How's your health?" asked Monica boldly, with a meaningful look at the clock.

Camille flashed a wicked smile. "Feeling a little sick, Marsha?"

Sitting there with them all, my surroundings melted away and I realized how alone I was, nursing my grief in this empty space. I was seized with panic, afraid I could never dare desire again. Cold terror set in like rigor mortis. In my mind, the door to Calvin's room kept shutting sharply behind me as if forced by a fast wind.

Monica whispered to me that she had a fifth of Wild Turkey in her Rambler. I rose up and followed like a sleepwalker, leaving Lisa and Paul and Tommy sitting there. Outside in the wintry air I shivered in my thin dress. We sat on chilly vinyl car seats, me on one end, Camille on the other. Monica opened the bottle deftly, trying to prove she was practiced. Before us, our lighted school blazed like an alien spaceship that had just landed next to the expanse of football field.

I took several long swallows of fiery liquid.

Monica poked me with her elbow. "Come on, girl, what's bugging you? It's Christmas. Tommy looks go-o-o-d." She urged the bottle on me again.

I swallowed my agony and enough Wild Turkey to fuse my

nerves back together. The slow burn rounded off the razor-edge of suffering. Camille took the bottle and shoved it under the front seat. The three of us climbed out and bent, shivering and coatless, into the fury of white.

The fiery pain that seared me comes only once in one's life: it is that first scorch of real grief. It is like losing a limb; surprise and horror join forces at the junction of what should be the impossible. At that moment I would have traded my sight to erase what I had seen in Calvin's room.

When Camille and Monica got up to dance with their dates, I informed Tommy flatly that we had to leave. No explanation. He seemed only mildly surprised. As I gathered my coat and purse, I saw him pause and say something to Paul. When we walked out, Camille and Monica cast knowing glances at me over their dates' shoulders.

In the car, when I put the key in the ignition, I burst into tears and cried for several minutes into the collar of my maxi coat, without explanation. I lowered my head onto the steering wheel while Tommy sat dutifully by.

Finally he said, "Is there anything I can do, Marsha?"

"No," I sobbed.

"It was probably hard for you to see Phil Willis there with someone else."

Phil! I hadn't even noticed.

"I know," said Tommy, "it's always hard to be with the wrong person." Consumed with my grief, I took this as an apology, Tommy's acknowledgment of his failure.

"I'm not ready to go home yet," I told him. I eased the car onto the highway, away from town, and turned directly into the snow. I had no destination, only found satisfaction in the motion of the car. We ended up driving eight miles in the wrong direction, to the edge of Lake Erie, where we sat in my father's car, listening to CKLW from Detroit and staring out at the black frozen space ahead.

As for what happened next, I can't make any excuses for Tommy, except to say that perhaps he was just plain curious about himself and desperate to have an answer.

And as for me, I had grown sleepy from the Wild Turkey and my own grief, and when I closed my eyes I could almost imagine it was Calvin, gathering me against him, then brushing his lips against mine, pressing against my chest, then bearing down on me, lifting my dress, tugging at my orange fishnets.

"Do you really want to do this?" I asked the boy hovering over me, my eyes still tightly closed against the black void. There was no answer, just a purposeful sigh into the hollows of my right ear.

That was all the encouragement I needed to move over the edge. How simple it was to plunge downward when the bottom was no longer in sight! All that foolish, dutiful teetering I had done, adding to the ever-spiraling tension between me and Calvin—the tortured refusals, the last-minute "I can'ts" whispered breathlessly through our tangled bodies—now gone flat as a bicycle tire. What did it matter? The next thing I knew, strong hands were extended and someone waited below to catch me. Warmth melted my frozen body, and I fell into forgetfulness, floating gently alongside the two joined bodies in the front seat of my father's car. I dropped off to sleep then, and upon opening my eyes later I was surprised, even shocked, to find myself crushed against Tommy Pendleton inside the cold damp car. The side windows had steamed over, the windshield wore a thick coat of snow. Tommy was sitting up straight again, staring out where the lake should have been. He was wearing his black-framed glasses. With one hand, he reached out and gently caressed my hair as if I were a small animal he had just rescued.

After that night, Tommy Pendleton and I still didn't speak much at school. Sometimes in class I'd catch myself looking at the back of his head, trying to connect it with an old longing that never surfaced. As for Calvin, I kept taking him back, a sucker for his inexhaustible excuses, so we were together off and on for the next year or so. He finally admitted he was engaged to a tall black girl named Charmaine from New Jersey. By the time we actually broke things off, it seemed easy. I was already packed for college, a new life ahead.

Over the years I have often compared myself to that anonymous girl, the one in Calvin's bed that night: her sweat-glistening face, her swollen mouth, her big brown legs unwinding themselves from Calvin's back, her breasts rising and falling obscenely, her eyes like flames.

Tommy and I performed nothing like that in the front seat of my father's car. It was something much simpler, much less eventful, and, under the circumstances, quite forgivable. So much so that I maintained I was a virgin until my freshman year of college when I met Nicholas Rush from Chapel Hill, North Carolina.

Now, as I headed back down the green slope toward where Tommy's casket was being lowered into the ground, I was startled to hear my own name. "Marsha! Marsha Hendrickson!" A tall brown woman in dark red, with a black hat, moved from the group of mourners toward me. "Is it really you, Marsha?"

"Mrs. Pendleton!" She saw my tears and approved of them. This was that same woman who had coaxed Tommy and me closer together in her living room some twenty years before, to record a lie that would give her comfort later on.

"Oh, I'm so glad you could come!" she said. "This means ever so much to me. You remember Tommy's brother Joseph? This is his wife Margaret." They were a handsome couple who studied me solemnly. I'd forgotten how much alike Joseph and Tommy looked; it was like seeing double. "This is Marsha Hendrickson, Tommy's high school girlfriend." I let the exaggeration pass.

Joseph and Margaret nodded with mild interest. Mrs. Pendleton clutched my arm. "Betty said you'd be here. She's already back at Tommy's now getting things ready for the potluck. You *will* join us, won't you?"

Before I could respond, she went on, "Praise the Lord, he didn't have to suffer long. The pneumonia came on so quick. He lost his hearing, then his eyesight. In the end, he couldn't remember even simple things. But he wasn't one to complain, not my Tommy. Always kept things to himself."

"That was Tommy," I agreed.

"Yes, Lord love him," she said. She turned to Joseph. "Tommy and Marsha shared an apartment for a while."

She let the innuendo sink in. Then she pulled me against her hip, her hand gripping mine. That was when I knew she knew, that the word "AIDS" would never pass her lips, that she was still trying to make things right. As if we were all off to a party, and not a tear on her face.

"I'm afraid I have to get going," I said. "I have to see students at four." It was a lie, but one that just as carefully matched the conviction of her own sweet deceit.

"Isn't that too bad?" She seemed genuinely disappointed. "It would be so nice . . . so nice to talk again . . ."

Suddenly I was sixteen years old, sitting impatiently on the Pendletons' sofa, thoughts of Calvin having reduced everyone around me to the dispensable. Mrs. Pendleton was removing the corsage from the box, eager to pin me down like a butterfly in someone's collection.

"Oh, please come," she was now insisting, then caught herself. "I'm sorry." She squeezed my waist briefly, eyes lowered. "I'm so sorry it all turned out this way."

I couldn't tell if she was apologizing or blaming me, but in that moment she had come as close as she probably ever would to admitting the truth.

"You take good care, Marsha. It was so nice of you to make it today." She stepped away then, awkwardly, the heels of her dark red pumps catching in the thick green lawn. She clutched Joseph's arm for support. Together they paused at the edge of Tommy's grave and stared down into it. Her face was resigned, and if I hadn't known better I would have thought she was a stranger hesitating out of curiosity, not a mother whose heart was wrung with grief. I wondered then how many times, over the years, she'd studied those photos of Tommy and me, maybe even had one framed for the mantel where it sat like an accomplishment, giving silent testimony. It may have given her much comfort, which was all she was really asking of me now. I turned and walked away. It seemed the only right thing left to do.

OFF-SEASON TRAVEL

Afew weeks after Ellen won the contest that had something to do with peanut butter, the supermarket arranged to fly her and Glenn to the small resort town of Puerto Cobre, on the west coast of Mexico across from La Paz. Even as they bounced along in the dilapidated taxi on the dirt road from the airport into town, Ellen thought how impossible it seemed that they'd actually disentangled themselves from the multiple complications that shaped their collective life in San Francisco: the children, the fixer-upper house, the asthmatic dog, the stack of bills, the unfolded laundry, the undefrosted refrigerator, Glenn's job, her job, the firecracker-like gunshots at night from the projects over the hill, the surreptitious drug-dealing of hooded silhouettes on their corner, and their own mutual complaints swirling together and lost in the fog of what could never be fixed. Long ago, specifics were forgotten. All the two of them could remember was that at one time there had been something good, and that what was left was very, very wrong.

In the taxi Ellen was thinking how Glenn, so familiar he'd gone strange, seemed no longer to belong to her. She watched him stare out the window at the brown, barefoot children playing outside their tarpaper shacks alongside the road fifteen hundred miles south of San Francisco. He was murmuring, "They're so poor," while Ellen considered how she felt nothing, nothing at all.

The supermarket paid for all ground transportation and put

26

them up at La Gran Duquesa, a small, elegant hotel with a narrow stretch of private beach. The imported white sand was dotted with palm-frond cabañas. Inside the flagstone courtyard was an oblong swimming pool, complete with a full-service bar and submerged stools. A bartender in a red tuxedo jacket was briskly polishing glasses to the rhythm of piped-in Muzak. He barely glanced up as Ellen and Glenn made their way up the outside stairs to the third floor. Their room was small, with two double beds separated by a nightstand, but beyond the sliding glass door to the balcony was a wide view of the ocean.

While Glenn showered, Ellen pushed the door open and stepped out onto the balcony into the warm evening air. She wore cut-offs and her oldest son's Little League T-shirt, and carried a bottle of beer in her hand. At home she never drank, but now she took a long swig of beer and considered how, at forty, she still had time to try out a different sort of life.

That was when she noticed a woman to the right at the wrought-iron railing, her back to Ellen, studying the fiery halo of sinking sun that scorched the surface of the ocean. Ellen thought she should announce herself. "It's beautiful, isn't it?" The woman turned around, startled. "The sunset." Ellen gestured toward it.

The woman was tall, striking, and black. She wore a foundation a couple of shades too light so that her skin bore an eerie pallor. Her eyebrows had been plucked until there was only a thin arched line above each eye. Her full mouth was lipsticked pale orange, a color Ellen wouldn't have dared to wear at the risk of looking jaundiced. But on the woman it looked elegant. She wore white pedal pushers and orange sandals. Ellen couldn't help noting with a small pang of envy the long, elegant brown hands, neatly manicured, resting lightly, one on each slim hip.

"Looks like we're neighbors. We just got here."

The woman stared at her, like someone expecting an apology. After a moment she said, "I didn't realize they'd put anyone right next door. After all, it's off-season. The hotel's practically empty." She paused. "I'm Marjorie Pierce."

"Ellen Fitzgerald." Ellen held out her hand and Marjorie leaned forward perfunctorily to accept it. Her fingers were cool, her palm warm. She pulled away as soon as they'd clasped hands.

"Well then . . ." She straightened herself up, raising one slender hand to wave away a small insect. "I better go get dressed."

"Marjorie?" It was a man's voice, half-plaintive, half-annoyed, coming from the open door of her room. A white flash of curtain stirred in the breeze. "Marjorie?" There was a sense of urgency in his tone. "Where the hell . . .?"

He stepped onto the balcony, a tall brown man dressed in one of those awful flowered shirt-and-short sets American tourists wear when they travel to warm climates. When he saw Ellen, he looked as if he thought maybe she'd scaled the side of the hotel on a rope. "Oh, *buenos días,* or is it *noches* already?"

Marjorie introduced them. "Lafayette, this is Ellen. Ellen, my husband Lafayette."

They shook hands. His hand was huge and warm. He peered beyond her to the yellow rectangle of her open door. "We didn't expect neighbors," he said. "You here alone?"

"No, my husband's inside." The shower had stopped. She could hear Glenn moving around inside the room. "Glenn?"

The sunset behind Marjorie and Lafayette lit up their bodies like burning effigies. From behind the hotel the faraway evening sounds of the town, faint traffic and chatter, wafted up.

Glenn padded out on the balcony in bare feet and shorts. He was a tall man, instantly dwarfed by Lafayette. Ellen introduced him. More handshaking between Glenn and Lafayette.

Comments on the sunset, the warm night, the fragrant air.

Marjorie tried again to excuse herself.

"Hold on there!" Lafayette plunked one heavy arm down on her shoulders. His eyes were slightly slanted, his eyebrows thick, his forehead broad. He was handsome in a comical sort of way.

"We're having dinner at the El Toro. Why don't y'all join us?"

Ellen looked at Marjorie. She stood slightly behind Lafayette, her neck caught in the hook of his arm. Her orange mouth twisted, then tightened.

"Oh, I don't think so," Ellen was saying at the same time Glenn was accepting.

"Sure, sure, it'll take us a few minutes to get cleaned up . . ." Glenn looked smugly over at Ellen.

Lafayette's big face lit up like a jack-o'-lantern. He released Marjorie and clapped his hands together.

"Okay then! Half an hour? Downstairs in the lobby?"

Marjorie, without a word, pushed past him and went back inside. Ellen had the grim sense she wasn't interested in having dinner with a strange white couple.

"See you soon," grinned Lafayette, backing toward the door. "Glen and Ellen, right?" He clicked his fingers as if fixing their names in his mind.

"Like the wine," said Glenn. It was one of his favorite jokes. Ellen had heard it a hundred times, exactly ninety-nine more than she cared to.

"Hey, now, *there* you go!" said Lafayette, catching on. He jabbed his finger at Glenn. "That's funny, man. Very funny." And he kept the grin on his face as he backed through the door to his room.

Glenn whistled as he lathered his face. Ellen spoke from the shower. With water coursing over her, she generally found it easier to say what was on her mind. "I think it's weird to go off and eat dinner with total strangers."

The whistling stopped. "What the hell are you talking about?" Ellen knew from the tightness in his voice that he'd pulled one cheek taut to accommodate the razor. "They're nice people." He said this enthusiastically, in the hopeful voice he used to disguise disappointment.

"*Nice?* How can you tell?"

Glenn poked his head up against the shower curtain. Half of his jaw was coated with white shaving foam. "I think it's important to find opportunities to mix with people of other races."

Ellen opened the shower curtain. "Are you kidding? That's how you think of them? *People of other races?*"

"You know what I mean," he said. "We don't have any black friends and now's a chance to mingle. It's a good opportunity."

"Oh God, Glenn."

He turned around and picked up his razor. "Now you're going to tell me I'm a racist. Well, I think when people make an effort, you need to respond."

"I only wish you'd asked me if *I* wanted to go."

"What do you want me to do, go over there and tell them we're not coming?" He used his accusing voice, the "it's all your fault" voice.

"Yes, actually, I do." The shower water rained down on her. Ellen felt the familiar tightening of contrariness inside her, her final defense against anger.

Glenn shook his razor at her. "Why the fuck do you do this? We're on *vacation*, for Christ's sake."

"Not for *Christ's* sake." Ellen plunged her face into the powerful stream of water. "We won a supermarket contest because after I get off work I spend half my life at the supermarket. That's why we're here, Glenn."

Glenn's voice vibrated through the shower curtain. "You really expect me to go say we're not meeting them for dinner?"

"You mean these nice *black* people, don't you?" Ellen said. "You know we're not doing them any favors, don't you? You accepted. Now you can un-accept."

"You're out of your mind. They'll think we're . . ."

Ellen popped her head through the curtain again. "If you'd paid any attention, you'd realize that the wife, what's her name, Marjorie, didn't want to go out with us either."

Glenn was trimming carefully around his mustache. "Ellen, shut up. Can't we just go out and have a good time for once?"

They never fought with conviction anymore. They lacked the energy for it. As usual, Ellen thought, Glenn had missed her point and continued on, confident in his.

The El Toro was a big pink mission-style stucco five blocks down from the hotel. Glenn, dressed in a white shirt and black linen pants, fell into step with Lafayette. He and Ellen had not spoken the whole time they were getting ready. Ellen, in her loose cotton dress, watched his back with a mixture of annoyance and lost affection. The familiar hunch of his shoulders. The awkward launch of one slightly bowed leg stepping in front of the other. These things had once inspired tenderness. Now they conjured up, at best, indifference and, at worst, irritation. Over the last few years her heart had hardened and shrunk into a tight kernel of ill will. Ellen no longer loved Glenn. He knew it too, but they hadn't spoken about it. Now he was pointing toward the sea and Lafayette nodded furiously. Ellen's eyes followed the direction of Glenn's finger. In the twilight a surfer was cresting a wave.

Lafayette's voice drifted back to her. "I'll take you out there tomorrow, buddy. We can rent boards."

Ellen turned to Marjorie, who had been silent. "Is your husband having a midlife crisis too?" She meant it as a joke, an offhand way of connecting with Marjorie and trying to stave off her own rising despair.

But Marjorie kept her head averted, showing no sign of having heard. Ellen thought how beautiful Marjorie looked in her red linen shift and black T-strap sandals. Beside her, she felt matronly and clumsy, as if the extra ten pounds she carried had just announced themselves in some audible way.

Ellen fought the urge to turn around and head back to the hotel when Marjorie said, with precise enunciation, "What do you mean, a *midlife crisis?*"

Ellen tried to capture levity in her straining voice. "They're talking about surfing tomorrow. Two grown men. Isn't that *crazy?*"

Marjorie seemed not to comprehend. They were now passing three cabbies lounging around a taxi stop. Marjorie ignored the "*Ssssst, morena!*" from the shortest of the group, a man with his shirt unbuttoned and a gold cross on his chest, who had fixed his liquid-eyes on her legs. "Surfing?" she said vaguely, and looked out at the dark water without further comment.

They were given a table on the patio, just a few feet from where the band was setting up. Ellen listened to the rhythm of the incoming tide wash over Glenn's and Lafayette's voices, smoothing them out until they were indistinguishable from each other. In San Francisco it was usually much too cold to ever really enjoy the beach. Only crazy people went into the water there, and then not for long. Now Ellen had a sudden desire to abandon her dress and go fling herself into the water. It had been a long time since she'd been swimming and the thought of gliding through water appealed to her.

"Nice night for a swim," she murmured to Marjorie, who was busy studying the pink, portfolio-sized menu.

"I never learned to. I've always been afraid of water."

"We're in the minority in our neighborhood," Glenn was saying congenially, as if testing this fact out for Lafayette's approval. "Mostly Mexican and Asian, I'd say. A few blacks."

"Yeah, well, tell me about being in the minority," Lafayette said. "We're over in the Oakland Hills. We lived in San Francisco when we were first married, but the weather didn't suit us. Don't you know about the radio towers on the top of Twin Peaks, the ones that send out subliminal messages that say, 'Black people, move to Oakland'?"

Glenn looked startled. Lafayette burst out laughing. "It's a joke, man, though not far from the truth. For a major city, San Francisco's got a tiny black population, you know." The waiter interrupted for their orders, and Lafayette ordered two bottles of wine. "This your first time here?" he asked after everyone's wine glass had been filled.

Glenn was eager to tell exactly how their trip had come about. He had told their neighbors and relatives, and even now, as the words spilled from his mouth, his syntax never varied. It was as if he were reciting a speech. Ellen couldn't get over how small he looked across from Lafayette. Glenn, who at times had loomed larger than life, whose presence had taken up all the space in her life, now seemed to all but disappear in the candlelight, and if she squinted her eyes ever so slightly she could cause everything about him except for the white shirt to fade into shadow.

"We came here years ago for our honeymoon," Lafayette said. "Just after I got out of med school."

Glenn leaped on this. "Med school," he said. "So you practice medicine." He was obviously impressed. And pleased. A

33

black doctor. Ellen could read his mind. She downed her glass of wine and poured herself a second. The wine went right to her head, bringing up a roar of unrecognizable voices, all clamoring to be heard.

"A cardiologist." Lafayette grinned and reached out to squeeze one of Marjorie's hands. "I take care of other people's hearts and she takes care of mine."

It was obvious, from the weary expression on Marjorie's face, that this was an old joke. "No I don't," she said flatly. "You're quite capable of caring for your own heart."

Touché! the voices in Ellen's head cried in unison. The woman has got some spark! Before she realized it, she was giggling aloud. Marjorie glanced up sharply. Ellen imagined what Marjorie was thinking: giddy white woman, no common sense. She recovered herself just as Glenn kicked her under the table. He quickly launched into one of his favorite stories about a client of his who was suing a drugstore over a folding lawn chair that unfolded and fell on her head. He had moved to rescue mode, diverting the attention from Ellen.

"Ellen doesn't usually drink so much," he remarked as Lafayette poured her a third glass. He had shifted into paternal mode, the one which guided him to apologize for her behavior.

"Yes, I do," Ellen lied and smiled broadly. She raised her glass and perversely proposed a toast. "To four days of rest and relaxation, to travel." She looked deliberately at Marjorie. "To new friends." It was the voices in her head talking. Strained, self-conscious. Ellen had never said anything so foolish in her life. She was sure Marjorie winced.

Everyone obediently raised a glass, then self-consciously clinked rims and stems together in the center of the table over a bowl of pink flowers floating in water.

Ellen leaned across to Marjorie. Maybe the woman was shy. "Do you two have children?"

There was a quick flicker in Marjorie's dark eyes. "No." She shook her head. "You?"

Ellen held up three fingers. "Three. Three boys. Bad, terrible boys. Three, six, and ten." She clicked them off on her fingers. "I haven't had a vacation since the little one was born. Between working and raising three boys . . ." Ellen stopped. She realized she was "going on," as Glenn would say.

Marjorie's eyes rested on her unwaveringly from across the table. In the candlelight Marjorie's skin glowed like bronze. "Boys can be a handful," she said carefully.

"Mine are monsters. They keep me in a constant state of uproar. I needed this break, let me tell you. Just the other day they had me so frazzled I wore two different colored shoes to work. I didn't even notice until one of the secretaries pointed it out in the afternoon."

Marjorie never changed expression. Ellen was sorry she'd made the effort. It's not shyness, she decided. Probably if I were black, I wouldn't want to feel obligated to sit and entertain some white woman.

Marjorie readjusted herself in her seat, then unexpectedly she leaned forward. "I can beat that, girl," she said. She spoke under the voices of the two men. "Last week I mailed our bills in a public trash can."

"You what?"

There was the merest hint of a smile on Marjorie's mouth. Lafayette glanced over at her. Marjorie, unaware, went on. "That's right, girlfriend. Walked right past the mailbox up to a public trash can and tossed my letters in. Bills mostly, if you can believe that. They just kind of floated around down at the bottom in a sea of Coca-Cola."

Lafayette laid a heavy hand on Marjorie's arm. "You don't need to be telling everyone about that."

Marjorie ignored him. "I had to reach down inside that can,

just like a bag lady, and fish out my stuff." Her mouth twisted ever so slightly. Ellen couldn't tell if she was smiling or getting ready to cry.

Lafayette frowned, removed his hand, and turned back to Glenn. He went back to explaining the difference between good and bad cholesterol.

Marjorie continued. "Sometimes," she said, her voice barely audible, "I think I'm losing my mind."

She pierced a prawn with the tines of her fork. And then, as if she had been asked, she leaned over and offered Ellen a taste of the broiled scampi. Very delicately, her bracelet jangling on her thin wrist, she lifted her fork to Ellen's lips and deposited one large prawn in her mouth. "They make outrageous garlic sauce," she said. "You'll love it."

Lafayette had launched into a repertoire of uneasy racial jokes. Ellen heard him say, "And then the rabbi said to the black guy . . ." He finished up one with the punch line "But the doctor told me I was impo'tant!"

She thought Glenn laughed too hard. He told a "There was a black guy and an Italian guy" joke, which came out badly for the Italian guy (though if told to an Italian, the black guy got the raw deal), and then launched into his "special pig" joke which could be adapted from the old black man to the "red-neck farmer" version. Lafayette tipped way back in his chair and hooted.

Marjorie and Ellen managed to insert small bits of polite talk into the conversation. Marjorie was a registered nurse. She worked in pediatrics, but had taken a leave of absence from the clinic. She didn't say why. Ellen managed to find out she was originally from North Carolina, and that she and Lafayette had bought their house in Oakland almost ten years before.

Later, when the band, a group of four young men, struck up

a Spanish rendition of "Feelings," Lafayette dragged Marjorie up from the table to dance, and Glenn followed suit with Ellen.

For the next song, a fast salsa number, Ellen danced with Lafayette. She stepped all over his toes while he chuckled and skillfully maneuvered himself around and beside her. Marjorie danced distractedly by herself, with Glenn next to her rocking back and forth on his heels and clicking his fingers. Ellen thought how much of what Marjorie did seemed like a duty. The couples traded back and forth for several more numbers. Ellen felt embarrassed by Glenn, his awkward, jerky motions and the earnest working of his mouth in concentration. Then she felt ashamed of herself for her lack of charity. She saw herself and Glenn as she was sure Marjorie saw them: strangers straining too hard toward friendship.

When the wine wore off, Ellen pleaded weariness. She was surprised when Marjorie suggested that the two of them walk back to the hotel so the men could stay longer.

"Absolutely not!" protested Lafayette, though Ellen could tell Glenn thought it was an excellent idea.

Glenn asked for the bill, and it turned out Lafayette had already slipped the waiter his credit card. Glenn began objecting—Ellen thought, ah, methinks he protests too much!—and yanked out his own wallet, displaying an array of credit cards, most of which should have been buried in their back yard and put out of their misery.

"Put your money away, man," said Lafayette, "this is *my* treat. You can get it next time."

Ellen thought she understood what was happening, as she and Marjorie picked their way silently, even gratefully, over the darkened sidewalks—that Glenn and Lafayette, just a few feet behind, were taking odd solace in each other's anonymity. In the darkness she was filled with longing, but it had nothing to do with Glenn. Ellen knew she was mostly at fault with Glenn, that what she'd known for a long time he was now only beginning to realize. Cowards that they were, neither of them had the guts to bring it up. What Ellen couldn't figure out was why Marjorie didn't love Lafayette and which one of them, Marjorie or Lafayette, was at fault.

Before she fell asleep that night, she rolled over in the dark, confused by and drawn to the heat of Glenn's body. She began to kiss his chest, pretending he was a stranger, imagining a different face, maybe even Lafayette, dancing inches from her. Glenn exhaled sharply into the air, then pushed himself suddenly inside her. Afterwards, Ellen felt ashamed of herself. Glenn held on to her tightly and whispered, "I told you all we needed was some time away." Ellen closed her eyes and imagined she had dived into the ocean and was riding the crest of a wave just before it crashed and spilled her onto sand with the consistency of angel hair. She pushed away from Glenn and turned over on her side. She lay there for a long time pretending to be asleep. She knew from the way Glenn shifted around behind her that he knew it too.

The next morning, just as Ellen was rousting herself out of bed, Lafayette knocked on the door to invite Glenn to play golf, something Glenn had never done in his life, but which he eagerly agreed to without consulting her. Apparently the surfing idea had been abandoned. Ellen sagged back against the pillows and realized she was paying for last night's wine. Glenn brought her two aspirin and a glass of water before he left. She rested another half hour or so, with the drapes drawn, then got up and went downstairs, forcing herself to eat some of the continental breakfast offered in the hotel lounge. The lounge was empty, except for a small Mexican woman in white who was reading a magazine and sipping coffee.

A few minutes later, Marjorie appeared. She was wearing white shorts and a red halter top. She looked rested. Ellen felt self-conscious about the whiteness of her own legs compared to Marjorie's smooth brown calves. She tucked her legs under her, tried to make herself seem smaller.

"Good morning," said Marjorie coolly. "I see Lafayette talked Glenn into golf." She studied the tray of breakfast rolls a moment, examined a piece of fruit which she rejected, then poured herself half a cup of coffee.

"Glenn's thrilled. I woke up with a hangover."

"They're kind of two peas in a pod," Marjorie observed. "I don't play golf."

Ellen had finished her second pastry and stood up. "I think I'm going down to the beach to get some sun," she said, by way of invitation. "What are you planning to do?"

"I have a massage appointment," said Marjorie. Before Ellen could ask her more about this, she had turned, coffee cup in hand, and headed back upstairs. Ellen watched her go, started to call out, then thought better of it.

Ellen strolled out on the empty beach and took a short swim. The water was warm. It was like taking a bath. She found herself staring occasionally up at the hotel for some sign of Marjorie on the balcony. No one else was on the beach. She tried pretending she missed Glenn, but she didn't. She floated on her back in the water and let the sunlight burn through her eyelids. She imagined herself being carried out to sea. She imagined washing up on shore on the other side of the world, dressed only in her swimsuit, without wallet or money, and no way to prove who she was.

On her way back to the room, she stopped at the desk and asked if there had been any phone calls. Nothing. She asked about going into town and the desk clerk told her to walk out front when she was ready and take a taxi.

Aside from the open-air market, downtown Puerto Cobre was mostly made up of stores with overpriced souvenirs. She stopped in front of a window displaying an orchestra of stuffed frogs dressed to look like mariachis. She bought postcards for the boys, though she'd see them before the postcards got to them, and she bought her mother-in-law a shawl that was exactly like something she could buy at home in the Mission District. Then she strolled out along the seawall and watched a group of teenage boys and girls flirt and tease one another.

The heat was overpowering. This time of year in San Francisco the fog was clearing late, if at all, and Ellen imagined the general dreariness of gray skies. She bought an *horchata* from a street vendor and drank it slowly, savoring the sweetness. Then she climbed in a taxi and headed back to the hotel. It was still early.

Glenn wasn't back yet, and the air in their closed-up room was suffocating. The maid had come and straightened, and left a card on the pillow which said, "Your room was cleaned by Rosa." Ellen opened the sliding glass door to let in the air, found a *People* magazine, and went down into the courtyard of the hotel. She longed for a breeze, but the air around her was still. The wind chimes overhead hung silent. An American couple sat waist deep in water at the pool bar, laughing and drinking, and getting drunker by the minute. Ellen guessed they were in their sixties. The woman was dressed in an awful, ruffly, skirted pink one-piece, her fat white thighs floating in the water. The man wore turquoise swimming trunks that came up to his armpits, and wrap-around sunglasses. Ellen heard the man say to the bartender in badly accented Spanish, "*Una otra bebida par la mujer!*" and then he yelled over to Ellen, "How do you say 'bride' in Spanish?" Ellen shrugged. Newlyweds.

She tried to imagine what it would be like to get married at their age. Twelve years she had been married to Glenn, plus the three years that they lived together while he finished law school. Her mother had warned her. "If you live together first, chances are it won't work out." Ellen had laughed, called her provincial, myopic, old-fashioned. Last year her mother died very quickly of cancer. She had been married exactly fifty-three years, something which she saw as a triumph.

The woman in the pink bathing suit began to sing "Well, I'm always true to you darlin' in my fashion . . ." The man leaned over and kissed her on the forehead. The top of his bald head was freckled from the sun. They both looked as if the reddened skin on their shoulders were made of leather.

Feeling weak from the sun, Ellen got up and went back upstairs. She was halfway curious to see if Glenn had returned, knowing he wouldn't have, and he hadn't. She rinsed out her bathing suit in the bathroom sink and hung it on the balcony railing to dry. The sliding glass door to Marjorie's room was closed, the curtain drawn.

Ellen wandered down the hall. It was dead silent. She paused in front of Marjorie's door and listened. She wondered if Marjorie were in there and if she would mind if Ellen knocked. Ellen raised her hand and tapped lightly on the door with three fingers. She waited. The hallway carpet smelled faintly of insecticide. She tapped again.

Just as she was about to give up and turn away, the door was cracked open just a couple of inches. Ellen could make out only the tips of Marjorie's fingers, and a crescent of light from one of her eyes.

41

"Yes?" she said coldly, as if they were strangers.

"Oh, sorry, did I wake you?"

"Do you need something?"

"Just wondered if you'd heard from Glenn and Lafayette."

"No, and I don't expect to."

"They've been gone a long time. How long does golf take?" Marjorie shrugged.

Ellen couldn't make herself leave. "How was your massage?" she persisted. "I was thinking of getting one myself." This was a lie. Ellen disliked massages.

Marjorie widened the door slightly. She was wearing a robe that she held together with one hand. Ellen could see the white lace of a brassiere through her fingers. "Massage is relaxing," said Marjorie. Ellen couldn't decide whether Marjorie was making fun of her or not.

"Did you go to a man or a woman?"

"It's a woman, but she leaves at noon," Marjorie said. "You have to check with the desk clerk for her schedule." For a moment Ellen thought she was going to shut the door. Instead, she said, "Come on in," and stepped back to let Ellen by.

The room was dark and claustrophobic, the curtains pulled shut. There was a stale, tight odor Ellen associated with sleep. A man's wet swimsuit dried over the bathroom doorknob. There were two open suitcases overflowing with clothes. Right off the bat, Ellen noticed the twin beds, like out of a fifties movie. Both had been slept in. Otherwise, the room was like Ellen and Glenn's room, just turned around.

"Lafayette thrashes," Marjorie remarked, though Ellen hadn't asked. Her robe fell open partially and Ellen saw the flatness of her brown stomach. Marjorie's hair stood stiffly off her head.

The twin bed nearest the door was rumpled.

"What time is it?" Marjorie yawned.

"Three. Four. It's really hot outside. I'm bored to death. I guess I don't know what to do if there aren't kids jumping all over me."

Marjorie sat on the edge of the unmade bed and scratched her scalp.

"Look," Ellen said, "Maybe I should go . . ."

Marjorie looked up. In the semidarkness the blue-white globes of her eyes stood out against her dark face. "It's up to you."

But Ellen didn't go. Instead she took a chance. "You want to go down in the courtyard and sit in the pool and have a drink? They have a bar right in the pool. I never drink at home, but you're supposed to drink on vacation." She meant this as a joke, but Marjorie didn't respond. She looked at Ellen as if expecting her to make the decision for her. "Of course if you don't want to . . ."

"Okay," said Marjorie. She got up and went into the bathroom to shower. Ellen took a seat in the vinyl chair in the corner. It took Marjorie almost half an hour to get ready. Ellen stared at the chaos of the darkened room and thought about what it might be that makes people fall out of love with each other.

They waded waist-deep to the bar and sat on the submerged stools.

"This is nice," said Marjorie. She looked down at her legs floating weightlessly. "I don't usually like the water."

Ellen smiled. She felt she had accomplished something, that Marjorie was beginning to trust her. "These places always seem so artificial to me," she remarked.

"How do you mean?"

"You know, fake sand, a pool, when you could swim in the ocean . . ."

Marjorie shrugged. "I like it. It's not meant to be like real life. That's the whole point."

Ellen's piña colada was too sweet, almost syrupy, but she sipped at it anyway.

Marjorie surveyed the courtyard with its large pots of colorful flowers. "I'm leaving Lafayette," she said matter-of-factly and toyed with the umbrella in her drink.

Ellen wondered if she'd heard right.

"We don't even live together anymore as it is. I've been staying with a girlfriend in East Oakland. And I've just rented an apartment down by the lake. When we get back, I'm moving there."

Ellen curled her toes over the rungs of the underwater bar stool. "I don't understand."

"Lafayette begged me to take this trip with him. I told him there was no point, but you can see how Lafayette doesn't take no for an answer. It's what makes him a good doctor, I guess. That drive he's got. The man never gives up. Nothing's ever finished. Not even us." She took a sudden interest in the gold cross she wore on a chain around her neck.

Marjorie was perfect, thought Ellen, from her earrings to her nails to her long legs shimmering in the water. "You both seem like such nice people." As soon as the words were out of her mouth, she knew she'd said something foolish.

"Oh, we are. You know, responsible, respectable, nice people. Lots of friends. Church-going. Very nice. No one nicer than Marjorie and Lafayette." There was an edge to her voice.

"You can't work things out?"

Marjorie shook her head. "Out of the question."

"You're sure?"

Marjorie trailed one of her manicured hands through the water. Without looking up she said, "Three months ago our son died. It was a Saturday. I was at home painting the trim of our new sunroom."

Ellen didn't say anything. She looked up at the brilliant blue sky and tried to imagine infinity. She couldn't make sense of what Marjorie was saying. She hadn't even known Marjorie had a son.

Marjorie began to recite. "It was an accident. You know how accidents are. Nobody's fault. Lafayette took Michael—that was our son's name, named for my father—ten years old—for a bicycle trip. An overnighter. Up to the Napa Valley. You know, sleeping bags, the whole bit. They were crossing the highway. I don't even know where exactly. Lafayette said the road was clear. No cars. Michael was right behind on a new mountain bike we'd just bought him. There was a rise to the right. A car was coming fast, but Lafayette didn't see it. Lafayette got to the other side." She paused. "Michael didn't."

Marjorie ordered another drink. "I hate to drink," she said. "I work out too much to handle alcohol."

"When?" Ellen asked softly. "When did you say your son died?"

"Three months ago. Three months ago yesterday actually. He's buried in that cemetery in Piedmont. But you didn't ask me that, did you?"

"How terrible," said Ellen. Her mind jumped to her own sons, fifteen hundred miles away. "Lafayette must feel terrible."

"Lafayette feel terrible? Jolly old good-time, good-natured Lafayette?" Marjorie laughed. "Yeah, he's heartbroken, but you'd never know it, girl. No, he's too busy being the big strong black man, just like he wanted our son to be. Tough. Better than everyone else. Faster, smarter, sharper, tougher. Better than the white boys is what Lafayette always said you had to be."

Tears appeared from under Marjorie's sunglasses and ran down her cheeks. The bartender looked away. Ellen wanted to reach over and touch Marjorie's hand, but she didn't.

"The thing is," said Marjorie, "I can't stand to look at him. I can't tell you just how much I can't stand to look at him."

Ellen ordered them each another piña colada. She took several long sips. The combination of the alcohol and the sun made her feel fuzzy, forgetful, almost relieved. Ellen imagined losing her boys. She imagined losing Glenn. In the crossfire from the gun battles in their neighborhood, to a falling tree, to a reckless car, to one of those rare lightning bolts that could mean the demise of an entire family. It was a terrible thought and Ellen knew it, but she had run it sometimes like a dare through her mind. And now here was Marjorie, a lightning rod for Ellen's own fears. It had actually happened. The worst had actually happened.

Ellen said to Marjorie. "What a terrible loss for you."

"You have no idea," said Marjorie and she took a long sip through her straw.

"No," said Ellen. "You're right, I don't." Her legs were suddenly chilled in the water. "Is there anything I can do?"

Marjorie turned and looked at Ellen as if she were a crazy woman. "Anything you can do? Don't you think if there was, I'd ask?"

Glenn was exhausted and sunburned when he returned at seven from scuba diving. Ellen had fallen asleep on their bed and awakened to the sound of the key turning in the lock.

"Scuba diving?" she said drowsily, wondering if she'd somehow gotten the day wrong. "Scuba diving?"

Glenn scratched his head sheepishly. "Golf didn't exactly work out." He explained that he and Lafayette had decided instead to rent equipment from someone named Hector who took them out in a leaky boat. "Lafayette's a maniac," he told her proudly, as if this signaled some accomplishment of his own. "The guy is fearless, utterly fearless. Doesn't let anything stop him."

"And you?" Ellen said. "You've never scuba-dived in your life, so tell me who's the maniac?"

"It was incredible, Ellen. You should see the stuff that's down there."

"I think it was a very dangerous thing you two did."

"The man's a barracuda," said Glenn. "You know where he grew up?" He paused for emphasis. "South side of Chicago. You know, poor. Serious poor. Typical story. No dad. Just a grandmother. He told me it was sheer stubbornness that got him to college and into med school. I believe it. The man is a barracuda."

"I thought you had to have a license or something for scuba diving."

"This is *Mexico*," said Glenn. "I wish I'd had the boys with me."

Ellen's mouth felt dry and thick. "I hope you don't really mean you wished you'd had the boys with you. It's bad enough you'd risk your own neck."

Glenn peeled his clothes off. His skin had a sheen, as if it were still coated with water. "What did *you* do, sleep the day away?" He meant this as a joke, but Ellen sensed he might have also considered it a possibility.

"No. I sat in the pool bar and got drunk with Marjorie."

She flung herself back on the bed and let the ceiling whirl. Four piña coladas and a bowl of pretzels for dinner. Ellen was in love with Marjorie, the mystery of Marjorie, all the pain inside her. That Marjorie had made her her secret sharer, something that Glenn had no idea about, gave Ellen a sense of sudden purpose.

"Marjorie's some woman," Glenn said, standing naked before Ellen. "Lafayette's a lucky man. He's so in love with her. Just like me with you." He bent down and rubbed his face against hers. Ellen pulled away from the sandpaper roughness of his cheek. He kept on. "You were so sweet last night!"

Ellen sat up and pulled even farther away. "They're getting divorced," she said fiercely.

Glenn laughed. "Yeah, right." He poked her playfully in the crotch.

"I'm serious. They're getting divorced. Marjorie told me this afternoon."

Glenn didn't buy it. "Nah, she's just pissed we went off today."

"I don't think so," Ellen said. "I think that's Lafayette's version." She wanted to hurt Glenn. "You know he's just using you to avoid being around Marjorie. You're a distraction."

She was saving the best for last.

"JE-sus," said Glenn. "Am I in the right room?" He looked around with an exaggerated gesture.

Ellen pulled on her cutoffs and the Little League T-shirt. "I want to do something interesting tomorrow, Glenn. I want to rent a car and go see some sights. We only have a couple days here and I'm bored out of my mind."

Glenn looked uncomfortable. "Well, maybe in the afternoon. I promised Lafayette I'd do this fishing thing with him tomorrow."

"Fishing thing?"

"Yeah, fishing thing. You know, a couple of hours out in a

boat. I'll be back before you know it."

"But you hate boats. You get seasick."

"Lafayette does too. But he's got these patches . . ."

Ellen managed to stand up. "I don't fucking believe you!" she said and went into the bathroom and started the shower full blast. "You don't know the first thing about your friend Lafayette!"

When she came out, Glenn was gone. She went downstairs and ate a bowl of lousy American soup by herself in the empty hotel snack bar. Disgusted, she went out for a walk on the beach to clear her head. The sun was setting. She left the pristine strip of white sand and wandered down a beach littered with beer bottles and scraps of paper. Several Mexican families were grouped along the sand staring out at the glowing horizon. A woman with a baby squatted by the edge of the water. As Ellen passed, the woman smiled up at her. Ellen smiled back, enjoying the thought that what had just passed between them, two strangers in a lightning-quick exchange, went deeper. She considered then how easy it would be to keep walking, never looking back until La Gran Duquesa was a speck in the background. She wondered where she might spend the night and what Glenn would do if she didn't return. She tried to imagine what he would tell the children when he returned home without her.

On her way back, the wet sand cooled the soles of her feet. A half dozen young men sat on a rock in the shallows drinking beer. One of them waved and Ellen waved back. She could hear Glenn telling her she was too careless, but she was beyond caring. La Gran Duquesa loomed ahead, turned a rosy pink in the sun's last light. Ellen ducked under the rope that separated the two beaches. She considered her return a defeat. She glanced up toward the shared balcony. It was empty. Her own door appeared to be shut, but the door to Marjorie and Lafayette's room was wide open. From where she stood, Ellen could see the sail of white drapes luffing in the breeze. She stopped and listened. Drifting downward was the muted sound of crying. Immediately she thought of Marjorie, so tightly contained, finally giving in to grief. Then she got a pang thinking it might be Glenn, but she was sure it wasn't. A moment later she caught sight of Marjorie exiting the hotel and briskly retreating down the beach. The thin, disturbing sobs continued from above. Ellen tried to imagine the person who could make such sounds; she was both fascinated and saddened.

Lafayette and Glenn left mid-morning. They'd invited her, but she'd said no. It was just as well, Ellen thought, she would go to the beach and read. She had no idea what kind of fishing they could do at that time of day, but she put on a cheerful front as the two of them trooped off together toward Lafayette's rental car, Glenn with his long pale legs in a pair of shorts and Lafayette sauntering in his flowered shirt and shorts.

Ellen stopped by the desk and picked up a beach chair. She spent the next few hours on the sand, with a book she'd brought along. The sun burned into her flesh, and she imagined all the dangers away as she watched her thighs darken. Mexican peddlers appeared now and then on the opposite side of the rope and called out to sell their wares. This time of year there weren't many, but occasionally she was interrupted by an insistent "Psst, señorita!" and someone holding up a scarf, a shawl, a dress, a hat and motioning for her to come take a closer look. She shook her head no, then discovered that any acknowledgment was interpreted as encouragement. She turned her chair and pretended not to hear them.

An older Mexican man in a white shirt and loose dark pants

came along the beach sweeping the sand smooth with a broom. He passed close by, and Ellen observed him peripherally, but he never looked her way. Besides her, there was only a middle-aged gay couple in matching blue briefs, each with a pair of blue eyecups, spread-eagled on mats. Shortly after, the elderly newlyweds she had seen the day before in the pool spread out an oversized Mickey Mouse towel and played cards. They got redder and redder in the sun.

So this is vacation? Ellen thought. To hell with vacation. Vacations are for people who have good lives they can return to. She closed her book and gave in to the dizzying heat.

It was mid-afternoon when Ellen woke up, hungry and dazed. The sand was too hot to walk on. She slipped on her sandals, wrapped a towel around her waist, and went inside to order a sandwich and a soda from the hotel snack bar. As she passed through the lounge area, she caught sight of Marjorie sitting by the window overlooking the pool bar. She was holding an ashtray in one hand and smoking a cigarette.

Ellen started to walk the other way, but Marjorie glanced up calmly. "Hey." She blew out a stream of smoke.

Ellen tightened her towel around her self-consciously. Now that she was inside, she became aware that her oiled skin was not browning, but reddening. She made a joke about how vacations encouraged unhealthy lifestyles: drinking, smoking, tanning. "I'm out working on a case of skin cancer. Want to come out and sit in the shade with me? We could grab a cabaña."

Marjorie stubbed out the cigarette. Her expression was blank. "Okay," she said. She seemed relieved, as if she were being rescued. "I have to get my suit."

A few minutes later Marjorie joined Ellen in the cabaña. She was wearing a black two-piece bathing suit and a pair of sunglasses. She tied a red scarf over her hair and draped a white towel over her legs. Neither of the two women spoke. Though she had hoped Marjorie would talk, Ellen said nothing. Instead, she read her book and Marjorie slept. Or at least Ellen thought she slept. It was hard to tell whether her eyes were closed behind the dark glasses. Her body remained perfectly still.

At last, when Ellen reached for a bottle of water, Marjorie said, "I could lie here forever. This is almost as good as massage."

Ellen took a long swallow of water. The sun blazed against her exposed feet in the sand. "I have no desire to go back to San Francisco," she remarked. She wanted Marjorie to ask why, to recognize their common bond.

What Marjorie said was "You have good reason to go back. Your children are there." She was reminding Ellen of the gulf between them.

Ellen carved a little hole in the sand with her big toe. She watched it fill itself, grain by grain, in a miniature avalanche. "If I didn't have them, I wouldn't go back."

"But you do," Marjorie said. "You're blessed."

"I don't believe in God," said Ellen. "Not the way you do."

"I don't believe anymore," said Marjorie from behind the dark glasses. "It's easy to believe in God when you have everything you want." She placed one hand on her forehead, as if checking her temperature. "Lafayette says what happened is God's will. I say any God who would want my son to be dead isn't the God I want to worship."

She said nothing else after that, but lay absolutely still. Ellen studied her periodically from over the top of her book: the narrow waist, the slight pucker of her navel, the muscled brown legs, and the gold cross glinting on the chain between her breasts. She felt a deep protectiveness toward Marjorie, infused with a longing and envy that extended beyond the boundaries of the roped-off beach.

When Glenn returned, Ellen resigned herself to temporary forgiveness and agreed to wander with him through the streets. They bought tacos at a small stand several blocks away and sat on the brown sand of the Mexican side of the beach. Glenn chatted about inconsequential things: his plan for cementing over the garage floor, which flooded during the rainy season; his thought that he would circulate a neighborhood petition to get rid of the bus shelter on the corner where kids dealt drugs. Because she thought it was deceptive of her to talk about their life together, Ellen changed the subject and ended up telling him about Marjorie and Lafayette's son.

It came as no surprise that Glenn knew nothing about it. He was silent for some time afterwards, staring out over the water, holding his half-eaten taco as if it were something he'd just found on the beach.

"Are you sure?"

"That's what Marjorie told me."

Glenn looked as if Ellen had somehow betrayed him. "He never mentioned it."

"He probably won't."

"I don't get it. He said nothing!"

"He's putting on an act."

"Jesus," said Glenn. "Marjorie really told you this?"

Ellen almost felt sorry for him.

"Yes."

"I didn't realize you and Marjorie covered so much territory."

She could tell by his expression that his mind was working quickly, running over the events of the last two days, trying to put the pieces into place.

"We haven't really," Ellen tried to explain. "Marjorie keeps a lot to herself."

"And you?" asked Glenn, turning to her sharply. "What do you keep to yourself?"

"Oh, Glenn . . ." She scrunched her napkin into a tight ball in her fist.

"I'm going to go call the boys."

"You don't need to . . ."

Glenn got up and began walking swiftly back toward the hotel. He never looked behind. Ellen followed, but didn't catch up. When she got back to the room, Glenn was already on the phone.

Ellen went out on the balcony. She stood against the railing and looked out at the ocean, now dark and turbulent. She could hear Glenn's voice, full of fake cheer. "Hey, *amigo,* this is your old *padre* calling you from Mexico!" From the tone of his voice she knew he was talking to their oldest, Mark. He was telling him about the scuba trip, the fish, the plants, the coral. "Let me speak to John for a minute . . . Well, get him and tell him to hurry . . . Hey, Ben . . ." His voice rose. Ellen imagined Little Ben at the other end with his funny, crooked smile. "I went fishing, Ben, and scuba diving . . . your mom's fine, want to talk to her?" At the reference to herself, she stood poised to go back inside. But Glenn rattled on, excited. He talked on, faster and faster, as if time were getting away from him. "We'll be home day after tomorrow. You boys behaving? Let me speak to Grandma . . . Hi, Mom . . . yeah, yeah, I know I said that, but I thought we should just check in . . . they haven't burned the house down? . . . oh, she's fine . . . we're having a blast. Couldn't be more beautiful."

What? thought Ellen. This place isn't beautiful, it's hideous. There's not one pretty thing here, except the sunsets. There was a chill to the air. She wrapped her arms around herself and stood shivering against the railing. In a moment she would have her turn with the boys. But for now she was content to stand at a distance and simply imagine their voices.

It didn't bother Ellen one bit that Glenn and Lafayette set off to rent horses the next day. She had made it clear, hadn't she, that she preferred to be left alone? Yet as soon as Glenn was gone, she had regrets for the way she was going about all this. Marjorie had left for her masseuse and then was scheduled over at another hotel to have her nails manicured. Ellen learned this from Lafayette, who let it be known that he had arranged in advance for all sorts of appointments for Marjorie and that so far she'd had her hair done and her legs waxed. "I promised her the works!" he said cheerfully. He winked at Glenn. "You know how women are, they love to be pampered." For the first time Ellen noticed the thick gold band with a row of diamonds on Lafayette's ring finger. It was an ugly ring, expensive and gaudy.

"Not all women like to be pampered," she said.

Glenn shot her a warning look, but she pretended not to see and gathered up a string bag with her suit and towel, and fastened her money belt around her waist under her T-shirt.

Outside the hotel she caught a cab into the center of town again and bought serapes for the boys. She bought more post-cards and sat in a cafe and addressed them to a long list of people, some of whom she only vaguely knew. "What heaven!

Puerto Cobre sunsets are the most beautiful in the world," she wrote. It took her over two hours to finish all the postcards. Then she went for stamps and mailed them. Duty accomplished. She'd told everyone what they would want to hear. Then she counted her traveler's checks, wondering how far they would get her.

She imagined herself traveling around the world. She would write to the boys every day. She thought of Ben's small hard body in her arms and his sour baby breath on her face. Ellen began to cry. She left the cafe and walked along the seawall. She wept loudly, knowing that it was safe because she was anonymous, and because no one would really care about an unhappy *gringa*.

"Our last night!" said Glenn, with intended irony, when they'd both gotten back to the room. He was making an effort to keep things light. "Are we speaking? You want to go out to dinner, or are we still mad?"

Ellen started to say "Mad?" but didn't. Instead she said, "No Lafayette?" as a joke, to ease the tension.

"No Lafayette," he said. There was a rueful edge to his voice. "We're stuck with each other tonight." He added with hope, "Lafayette and I've got plans to get together back home. Know what he wants to learn to do? Hang gliding. Over there south of the Cliff House. Is this guy a nut, or what?"

"He's a nut all right," Ellen said. "A real nut with a death wish." She added, "Dinner sounds fine, your choice," because she didn't have the courage to disappoint him. She felt almost friendly toward him, but that was only because she knew that soon she would have to tell him. "I'm going down on the beach for an hour or so, before all the sun is gone."

"Take your sun protection," Glenn warned. "You're starting

to burn." He reached out and caught her in his arms. "Ellen, do you even love me anymore?"

She stared into the face she knew so well it struck her as comical. His anxiety pulled on her like a weight. "Of course I do," she lied, wresting herself free. "Don't be silly."

"I tried to give you time to miss me over the last couple days . . ." He slowly released her. There was no anger when he turned away, only a tired sadness. "I think I'll call the boys while you're gone," he said. "Make sure they're okay."

"They're okay." Ellen started out the door. She paused and said with emphasis, "They're *okay*, Glenn." She felt bad for them both. "Tell the boys I love them. Tell them I've got presents. Tell them I'll see them very soon."

It was sunset. The sky was lit up as if it were on fire. Along the horizon the light was so blinding Ellen was forced to avert her eyes and focus on the dark waves lapping at the edge of the beach. Tomorrow they would go home. Tomorrow she would tell Glenn.

She found a spot on the sand and sat down. Instantly her chest expanded and she filled her lungs with air. She stretched her arms up over her head and let the last warm rays of sun play over her face. When she turned to lie down, she caught sight of a figure running down the beach toward her. She made out pink shorts and the flash of white T-shirt. As the figure got closer, Ellen recognized Marjorie, barefoot, pounding along the shore. She was coming fast and hard, her arms pumping at her sides.

Ellen put on her sunglasses to block out the glare of the setting sun and watched as Marjorie picked up speed. She was pounding harder and harder on the packed sand. Her head was thrown back, she was gulping in air. Ellen had no idea Marjorie was a runner. But then she thought how little she really knew about Marjorie at all. As she got closer, Ellen could hear the faint smack, smack of her bare feet striking the wet sand. She ran past Ellen, never noticing her. Ellen had a sudden urge to leap up and try to follow. There was an intensity in Marjorie's stride that dissuaded her. Without warning, Marjorie made a ninety-degree turn and plunged headlong into the surf. She completely disappeared. For a moment Ellen thought she was witnessing a suicide. Marjorie, who had made such a point of telling her she couldn't swim. But Ellen found herself rooted to the spot, unable to make a move to stop her. Her eyes focused on the spot in the water where Marjorie had disappeared, now streaked by orange light. Ellen had a vague thought that if she had to go for help she needed to know exactly where it was Marjorie had gone in. The waves rolled in and curled onto the beach. Ellen sat transfixed.

A moment later Marjorie resurfaced, and Ellen saw her dark arms pulling water and the flash of pink shorts above the waves. Now she swam as hard as she had run, her arms punching at the water. White foam followed in her wake. Her body bobbed up and down on the waves. Behind her, a large wave broke and rolled in. Marjorie came with it. She landed on the beach, coughing, her legs spread out behind her. When she stood, her hair hung ruined, dripping wet and sparkling with sand. She let the water run off her legs and onto the sand. She was out of breath, and her chest heaved. She placed her hands on her hips and sucked in air.

Ellen got up and moved cautiously toward her, beach towel in hand. When Marjorie saw her, she turned her head fast and looked back out over the ocean, her chest still heaving.

"Take the towel," said Ellen.

"I want to stay wet," Marjorie said. Droplets of water glistened on her eyelashes. Without makeup, she was beautiful, young. Three Mexican boys in blue jeans stood on the other side of the rope, idly watching the water. Marjorie observed them. "You know, this place makes me really sick. They aren't even allowed on the hotel beach."

Ellen didn't say anything.

"I guess it's the same the world over," Marjorie remarked matter-of-factly. "Black and brown people are usually on the other side of the fence."

"I thought you said you don't swim," Ellen said.

"I don't, I almost drowned out there." She cleared her throat several times.

"That was stupid," Ellen said, but Marjorie didn't answer.

Ellen turned and walked toward the hotel. She glanced back twice. Marjorie stood motionless in the same spot, her back to Ellen. Dwarfed by the ocean and backlit by the lowering sun, hers was a childlike silhouette. A breeze came over the water. Ellen thought about how she would explain it all to Glenn. She'd try first getting an apartment. Just during the weekdays. She'd come back on the weekends, help out, take the boys places. She'd still be involved, she'd still be a mother, but she wouldn't be a wife. And during the week she'd work longer hours. She might even exchange numbers with Marjorie. They'd get together and have coffee in the afternoons. Or lunch. They'd get massages, have their nails done together. Ellen would buy better clothes.

She passed through the courtyard. The pool was empty. She took the stairs fast and easily. The door to their room was partially open. On her approach, she heard the sound of voices. Then falsetto male laughter, followed by a deep voice. Ellen paused just outside the door and peeked in. Glenn and Lafayette were sitting, one on either side of the double bed by the window, drinking beer. Glenn was in his boxer shorts and Lafayette had on the ridiculous flowered shirt and shorts. Glenn said something Ellen couldn't quite catch and Lafayette threw his head back and howled too hard, like a wolf. Then Glenn burst out laughing and rolled back on the bed, clutching the beer bottle to his chest. They were playing at being great big ignorant boys getting away with something.

Ellen backed away a couple of inches so they wouldn't see her. She stood shivering in the hallway and listened to her husband laugh in a voice that could have been Lafayette's. Then she realized it was Lafayette's voice, full of exaggerated heartiness. Why was it, she thought, she was no longer able to distinguish the joyful sounds her own husband was capable of?

A COLD WINTER LIGHT

The winter Olivia turned sixteen she discovered her father had taken up with a black woman, someone unknown to her, but someone possibly connected with her father's old high school counseling job in Elyria, eight miles north by the edge of Lake Erie.

Olivia came across the snapshot stuffed in the back of a dark drawer of her father's basement work table. It lay imprisoned under a screwdriver and a crushed nail box half full of old rubber bands. Olivia had been deliberately snooping again, as was her habit of late. She considered it her duty to periodically patrol the cabinets and closets and drawers of her house. On the days she got home from school before everyone else, she held unopened mail up to the light. It seemed to be the only way she found things out in this house, now that her parents no longer spoke to each other.

The snapshot, a Polaroid, was stuck to the bottom of the work table drawer. Olivia carefully pried it out with the tips of her fingernails and held it up to the rectangle of winter sunlight framed by the high basement windows: a tall, dark black woman stared back coyly, the way subjects do when the photographer knows them intimately. Along the bent edges of the snapshot, spots of color and paper were missing. But the woman herself was intact.

Olivia stared hard. The woman was beautiful. She was what her father's mother would call "*too* black" in that half-deprecating, half-sympathetic way some light-skinned people had, even though her own husband, Olivia's grandfather, was the color of black walnut shells.

The woman wore a medium-sized natural; her features were broad, perfect, her eyes shaped like almonds. She was long and leggy, about the same age as Olivia's mother. She wore a short red leather skirt that hugged her hips and a see-through black blouse with lace on the wide collar. From her earlobes dangled large silver hoops that reflected light from a source Olivia couldn't see. The woman had posed herself familiarly in the doorway of a kitchen Olivia didn't recognize. The bottom right-hand corner of the photo was feathered by the decorated lower branches of someone else's Christmas tree.

Down to the last detail, this woman was the exact opposite of Olivia's small, white, red-haired mother.

Olivia turned the photo over. On the back in lazy, loopy handwriting was written: "Merry Christmas to my Chocolate Santa. Love, Wilma."

Olivia suddenly understood what she'd suspected all along. Christmas Eve, two months earlier, she and her mother and Pam and the boys lounged around the living room idly stuffing themselves on tangerines and nuts and chocolate while the open boxes of Christmas tree ornaments sat untouched. A space had been cleared over by the picture window for the Christmas tree. Hours before, Olivia's father had slammed off in a huff to search for one, irritated that her mother had waited until the last minute. No one else had wanted to ride along with him, preferring the warmth of the house to the freezing night. The red and green metal tree stand stood empty under the mantel.

Waiting for him, they'd all pretended not to, as Olivia's mother played a Nat King Cole recording of "Winter Wonderland" over and over, and flipped through magazines. Around ten or so she brought out eggnog from the fridge. She seemed about to burst from some unnamed emotion, and turned giggly and reckless, mischievously pouring a shot of rum in everyone's eggnog glasses. She could be capricious, a bad child, when Olivia's father wasn't around. In his absence, she often resorted to small, harmless indulgences, treating her children as if they were all just friends.

Then, much to Olivia's annoyance, her younger sister Pam had started acting drunk and talking crazy. Leave it to Pam to spoil things! Olivia's mother sighed and put the rum away and told Pam she'd better straighten up fast before her father returned.

The hour had grown late. The fire in the fireplace burned down to embers, and a chill spread inward from the walls. Olivia glanced at the ticking clock with growing agitation. Her mother fell asleep curled up on the sofa and the boys sprawled in the middle of the floor and played with their Lego set. Pam slipped off to the kitchen and whispered to someone on the phone behind the closed door.

Chilled, Olivia pulled on her robe and sat in the overstuffed chair, staring out the broad picture window at the snow falling, cold and white. She pretended to be watching her brothers, but she was waiting. Each time a car passed on the snowy road, she felt herself stiffen. When at last the headlights of the red station wagon turned into their driveway, Olivia leaned over and poked her mother awake. Just in time, too. Her father crossed the threshold, irritable and flustered, dragging in a short-needled, scrawny tree. "Well," he said, "what do you expect when we wait until Christmas Eve? All the lots were empty and I wasn't about to go tromping off through the woods at one of those cut-your-own places." He fussed on and on and stamped his snowy boots in the front hallway. Then he argued with the boys about the mess of Legos on the floor while the tree lay on its side, forgotten.

That was when Olivia first noticed that her father had skipped several shaves and his hair was lengthening into a natural. It had been a while since she'd looked directly at him, but while he and the boys screwed the tree upright into the stand she sat in the overstuffed chair, warm inside her robe, studying his gestures and expressions, and drawing her own conclusions.

Olivia considered stealing the snapshot, but then decided against it. She pushed the picture to the back of the drawer and placed the screwdriver on top. She kept thinking of the woman's wide, pouty smile, intended (and this was the unthinkable part!) for Olivia's father.

Bastard, Olivia thought. She thought of her mother upstairs in the den, obliviously glued to the Merv Griffin show and waiting for the children to get home from school. It was like a quadruple deception somehow: her father's infidelity, the woman's beauty, the woman's blackness, and now, Olivia's discovery.

Olivia stood a moment longer under the bare beams, her sock feet soaking up the cold from the cement floor. Her father had promised last year to finish off the basement and turn it into a family room, but he'd gotten busy with his new job at the college and never found time. The room remained rough and approximate, the ceiling pipes exposed.

Olivia turned and walked back up the basement steps to the kitchen, closed the door softly behind her, and took the wide-mouthed jar of cold water out of the refrigerator. She poured a drink. Outside the kitchen window the yard lay blanketed in snow, and the pond beyond was frozen solid. Grim February, what Olivia's mother jokingly called "the longest short month."

The front door banged shut, and Olivia knew Pam had finally dragged herself in from school, a good hour late. Pam was only thirteen, but she tried to act grown, wearing her skirts so short there wasn't much left to the imagination. Now she was going with a twenty-year-old hoodlum named Reggie who wore a dew rag and washed dishes for a living over at the college cafeteria. Reggie drove a beat-up Ford around town and called Pam "sweet thang."

Imagine, in the eighth grade, with a grown-up boyfriend! Old fast yellow Pam, calling herself slick, walking downtown and swinging her hips with her big chest poked out.

Sometimes, at night when everyone was asleep, Pam would go out. Last summer Olivia had caught her at it. She awakened to muffled clunks and bangs in the next room, Pam's room. There were voices whispering. She sat up in bed and looked out the window. Once her eyes adjusted, she made out two silhouettes of neighborhood boys over by the pond. A moment later the soft swift shadow of Pam in her bathrobe and bare feet made its way across the grass in the moonlight. Olivia watched Pam and one of the boys disappear across the field and past the line of trees that marked the edge of their property. The second boy paced along the edge of the pond, staring into the dark water.

Olivia crept quietly out of her room to Pam's. The high aluminum-framed window had been pulled to one side. She had a clear view of the pond straight ahead. She knelt on Pam's bed and leaned her elbows on the windowsill. The air smelled of moist, freshly cut grass. Olivia thought of closing the window and locking Pam out, but she didn't have the courage to hurt her mother. Instead, she did nothing, just watched with a mixture of envy and disgust. Sometime later Pam traipsed back across the damp lawn, her hair askew. She wore a smug, elfish grin. Olivia ducked down and scurried back to her own room. She heard Pam's feet scrape heavily over the windowsill, then the thunk! of her body hitting the bed. A few moments later a car engine revved from the road.

The next morning Olivia eyed Pam hard until Pam put her hand on her hip and said, "What are *you* looking at?"

Olivia hissed, "You better not get pregnant, girl," and Pam rolled her eyes.

"I'm *serious!*" Olivia warned.

Pam snaked her neck several times and glared. "You don't even know what you're talking about, Miss Whitegirl."

Now, Pam strolled into the kitchen with the one book she'd bothered to carry home from school. She was lighter than Olivia, with skin the color of shredded wheat, but her features were broader and her hair was naturally nappier though, like Olivia, she had a perm and wore her hair in a shoulder-length page-boy. She clunked across the floor in her black snow boots.

"Anybody call for me?" she asked in her deep raspy voice.

"I don't know, stupid, I just got here myself." Olivia sipped her water. She considered telling Pam about the snapshot, just to shock her into getting all big-eyed. But the timing was wrong.

Pam leaned back against the kitchen counter. "Reggie said he saw you today."

"Big deal," said Olivia. "I wouldn't know him if I saw him." She walked out of the kitchen.

"That you, Olivia?" her mother called out from the den.

Olivia poked her head in. The drapes were drawn and the room was dark and overcrowded. Over in the corner her mother's sewing machine was set up with a long piece of brown wool fabric spread out under the needle. Olivia's mother made almost all of the girls' clothes. She saw to it they were two of the best-dressed girls at school. New clothes every week when she could. She spent a lot of time poring through catalogs and choosing patterns and calling the girls into the den to be measured.

"Have a seat." Olivia's mother patted the empty space on the sofa next to her. She'd pulled her bathrobe on over her nurse's uniform and propped up her small white feet on the coffee table.

"You sub at the hospital today?" Olivia asked. She sat gingerly on the edge of the sofa.

"Just this morning. Pam home yet?"

Olivia nodded. The den struck her as depressing. Her mother spent too much time there. Beyond the heavy drapes spread the cloudless blue sky, and in the over-bright, frozen air the winter sun sparkled on the snow banked along the sidewalks.

"Can you pick up the boys from Boy Scouts at five? Gina and Jerry are coming by tonight for ribs and I've got to make potato salad."

"I thought Daddy picked up the boys on Wednesdays."

Olivia's mother never took her eyes from the TV screen. "Well, he can't tonight," she said sharply.

Olivia pulled herself up off the sofa. She towered over her mother. "Is he going to be here when Gina and Jerry come?"

Her mother shrugged. "I don't know and I really don't care. You know how he is." She reached up and ran one small white hand over Olivia's brown arm. "You look so pretty today. I'm glad the new skirt fit."

"I don't understand why Daddy can't pick up the boys." It was the closest Olivia had gotten to outright accusing her father of what she now knew to be true.

Her mother sighed. "Don't pay any attention to your father these days. What matters to me now is you and the other kids."

Gina and Jerry Woods were Olivia's parents' longtime best friends. They lived on the other side of town by the golf course with their six teenage children. Gina wasn't American, she was actually from some war-torn Eastern European country, and she had an unpronounceable name, so everyone just called her Gina. She was heavyset, blonde, and pale, and spoke rapidly in a heavy accent, a mixture of black and Eastern Europe. She did hair for a living. Jerry was quiet, a mail carrier with light skin the color of wheat and eyes with a greenish cast. All the Woods kids had the same wheat-colored skin and green eyes and sandy hair. They were notoriously wild kids, rowdy and undisciplined, and the boys were as handsome as the devil himself. You could spot a Woods boy a mile away. It irritated Olivia when people mixed her up with them and asked her if she was a Woods.

Gina and Olivia's mother were drinking beers together in the kitchen while Gina stuffed herself on barbecue. "Earl don't know what he's missin'," she said of Olivia's father.

Olivia's mother shrugged and said, "Maybe he does."

Over ribs and potato salad Olivia listened to her mother and Gina Woods talk, as they had for years. Their words were familiar, even predictable, but the meanings shifted with kaleidoscopic quickness into new patterns Olivia could now comprehend. She knew that by listening, without appearing to, she would find out the things no one told her directly. Jerry Woods and Olivia's brothers were huddled on the sofa in the den watching the game on TV, and Pam was in her bedroom, tying up the phone. The two women seemed to have forgotten that Olivia was even in the same room.

Olivia's mother's voice was tired, uncertain. "I don't know what I'm going to do with Pam. She acts just like her father. Doesn't tell me a thing." And Gina, through a mouthful of barbecue, spat back advice and gestured emphatically. "Don't let her throw you off balance. I've got *two* of 'em at home don't act right. Just last week I caught Rita and Lizzie smoking, and then turns out they been cutting school together. Jerry don't know. He'd kill 'em."

Olivia picked a piece of white bread apart and rolled the sections into little hard balls between her thumb and index finger. Her mother let out a sigh of sympathy. "It's hard nowadays," she said. "I try to give both my girls a certain amount of freedom. I don't want them to feel . . . you know, any more different than they already do."

Gina licked barbecue from her fingers. "Thaz why I let my girls do like they want. I can't keep 'em under lock and key. I hear the talk. But you got to go easy with mixed kids. They got it rough."

Olivia pushed herself forcefully away from the table. "Excuse me," she said stiffly, "I have homework."

Her mother and Gina smiled up at her in unison. Their faces were bright and approving. "You're a good girl," said Gina, patting Olivia's behind. "And getting so grown-up too!"

Olivia was halfway down the hall when she heard her mother say with conviction, "Olivia's my dependable one. I don't know what I'd do without her."

By Saturday another big snowstorm was predicted, and Olivia's mother left early with Pam for Fisher-Fazio to stock up on groceries. The boys played whiffle ball in the cold basement with their jackets and gloves on. Olivia could hear the smack-smack of the bat hitting the plastic ball. She turned on the vacuum in the living room and cranked up Aretha Franklin as high as she could on the stereo console. "Ain't no way / for me to lo-o-ove you-ou / if you won't-a let me . . ." Sister Caroline's background vocals soared on top at ear-splitting levels. Olivia sang along, squatting down to get under the sofa with the vacuum wand.

Out of the corner of her eye, she caught a movement in the doorway. She glanced over to see her father opening the front hall closet door. He pulled on his heavy winter coat and pressed onto his rising natural the Russian hat with ear flaps that so embarrassed her. At Christmas she had given him a black beret and he rejected it, saying he'd look like a Black Nationalist. He had treated the hat as an insult from her, uncomfortable with the implications.

"They wear berets in *France*," Olivia had said sarcastically, and her father snapped back, "I'm not French." What she felt like saying now was "And you aren't Russian either," but she didn't.

Her father gestured impatiently for her to turn down the music. She pretended at first not to understand, then shut off the vacuum and stood up stiffly, arms folded across her chest. "What?" she mouthed.

"You're going to blow my damn speakers!" He'd taken to referring to their collective family belongings in the first-person possessive: my sofa, my refrigerator, my car.

Olivia leaned over and lowered the volume to a whisper.

"Where's your mother?"

"Grocery."

Olivia stabbed at the living room carpet with the long wand of the vacuum.

"I have a committee meeting this afternoon. I'll be home late."

"On a Saturday, Daddy?" She had the snapshot on her side. She could afford to be impulsive.

"I have no idea what you mean." He took up his briefcase in one hand and an umbrella in the other.

"When will you be home?" Olivia pushed, hand on her hip.

He frowned. "Did she take your car or mine?"

"I thought it was her car too."

"Don't be smart-assed, girl, and you know what I mean." He cleared his throat several times. "I'm asking you in a nice way, am I stuck with the Corvair?"

"No, she took the Corvair. She wouldn't think of taking *your* precious station wagon."

Olivia's father pulled open the front door. A blast of cold wind gusted through. He paused. "By the way, I read in the paper that your boyfriend what's-his-name Michael Blakely got a speeding ticket. I don't want you driving around with him anymore."

Olivia laughed. "If you paid attention to what goes on around here, you'd know that Michael and I broke up over two months ago."

Her father slammed out the door. Through the picture window she watched him scuttle like a beetle down the icy driveway to the station wagon. Big white flakes floated down and settled on the shoulders of his heavy dark coat and on the crown of his Russian hat.

Olivia held up the vacuum wand and shook it at his receding back, as though marking him with a curse. He climbed into the station wagon and sat behind the frosty windshield, warming the engine. "You know how I hate your lyin' ass," she yelled after him. "It's a little late to try to get black on us now!" She switched the vacuum back on, and cranked the stereo volume up so loud the walls vibrated. "This is the house that Jack built, y'all!" Olivia sang. "Remember this house. This is the land that he worked by hand / This is the dream of an upright man . . ."

All that Olivia told Tonya when she drove over through the thickening snow in the Corvair was that they were going for a drive. Tonya's mother was perturbed about the weather. "I'd like to know where you two are off to, just in case," she said in her polite white way. "The roads could get really bad."

Olivia smiled broadly. "I'm running an errand for my mother at the mall."

"Just the two of you?" Tonya's mother had never come right out and said it, but Olivia knew she was growing more and more worried about "certain influences."

Tonya got busy with her mittens and boots.

"Just the two of us," Olivia confirmed.

"This doesn't involve boys?"

Olivia knew exactly what kind of boys Tonya's mother meant. Black boys. She felt irritation rising in her chest. Her friendship with Tonya had been so much simpler when they were younger. Now sometimes Olivia wondered why she bothered with it at all.

"No boys," said Tonya. "I told you, Olivia and I are going alone!"

"When can I expect you home?"

"How about six?" said Olivia. She had learned that by phrasing her responses as questions she got a lot further with Tonya's mother.

Tonya's mother was not pleased. "Tonya will miss dinner." Olivia knew dinner was not the issue at all.

"Tonya can eat at my house."

"Well-l-l . . ." Tonya's mother couldn't look Olivia straight in the face anymore.

"My mom's making spaghetti, Tonya's favorite."

"I wish you'd asked in advance."

This was how it always was with Tonya's mother—Olivia negotiating and reassuring, Tonya remaining silent and depressed.

"We'll call you from my house, okay?" said Olivia brightly.

Tonya's mother looked at Tonya. "Seven o'clock," she said sharply. "I want a call from you by seven o'clock."

Inside the Corvair, Tonya let out several groans. "I *really* want to run away. I can't stand it anymore." She said this at least three times a week. "Let me come live with you, Olivia."

"Why? You think I have it any easier?"

Tonya smiled ruefully. "At least your father's gone all the time. My mother is *always* there."

Olivia started up the clanking car heater.

"Quick, get out of here before she changes her mind." Tonya sank low into her seat. "She's in there thinking up some excuse to call me back in."

There was a slight movement of the curtain at the living room window.

"Your mother's changed" was all Olivia said bitterly as she backed the Corvair down the drive.

Snow fell steadily in big, wet flakes. The houses and bushes looked like pieces of furniture covered in protective white sheets. Olivia made a left at the corner and drove slowly over sludge and ice to the edge of the college campus. She peered out the fogged-up window. "Look and see if my dad's station wagon is in that parking lot over there."

Both girls craned their necks. The lot was empty.

"I knew he was lying," Olivia muttered to herself.

"What are you talking about?"

"You'll see." Olivia stopped at the red light marking the main intersection downtown. She turned on the radio and sang along to "Ooh, Ooh, Child" by the Five Stairsteps. She felt bored by Tonya, irritated with her presence. She was sorry now she'd brought her along, but she had, and now she was stuck.

Turning onto Route 58, they found themselves on the tail of a large truck. The snow was so thick now that all they could make out were red taillights and an occasional glimpse of revolving rubber tires spitting snow. Oncoming traffic was dense and slow, a succession of blurred headlights on the two-lane highway.

"Maybe we shouldn't go," said Tonya, nervously wiping at the windshield with a mittened hand.

Olivia boosted the volume on the car radio. When she didn't know the words to songs, she substituted nonsense syllables. It didn't really matter, you could sing whatever you wanted, it was all the same.

"What are we doing, Olivia?"

Olivia clicked her fingers and hummed. The song ended. "What are we doing? Looking for my father, that's what we're doing." She dug down in her coat pocket and pulled out the snapshot of the black woman. She handed it to Tonya, without explanation.

Tonya held the snapshot in her mittened hands and stared. "I don't get it." Recognition slowly dawned. "Your father? Does your mother know?" Olivia could see that Tonya was intrigued.

Olivia shrugged. "My mother needs to dump his ass. She sacrificed everything to marry him and now look at how he's acting." She said it as if the events signaled some fault of Tonya's.

Tonya was poring over the snapshot carefully. "She sure is pretty. God, what I'd give to have skin like that. I get so white in the winter."

Olivia snatched the snapshot back and stuffed it in her coat pocket. "She's not that pretty. My father's rebelling, that's all," she said sarcastically. "My father's decided to try being black after years of being an Uncle Tom."

"Why do you hate him so much?" asked Tonya.

"You don't know him." Olivia felt the car tires spin briefly on a slick patch in the road. "You don't have a clue."

Tonya asked Olivia to stop at Lawson's. She returned with bubble gum, a sack of chives and sour cream chips, two blisteringly cold red cream sodas, and two sticks of beef jerky.

"Why do you wanna buy that old nasty stuff?" remarked

Olivia grouchily, but she ate anyway, sitting there in the Lawson's lot, staring out at the bleak intersection and watching the snow pile up on the sidewalks, the bushes, even the telephone wires overhead.

A low-slung black Olds pulled into the lot and honked. One of the windows was covered over with a piece of tattered plastic attached by long strips of masking tape. There were three boys inside, two up front, one in back. The driver pulled up next to the Corvair and motioned for Olivia to roll down her window.

"Say, mama," he called cheerfully, leaning out of the car so that his thick hair caught the falling white snow like a net. "I couldn't help noticing you and your friend over here by yourselves."

"I'm not your mama," Olivia responded, but she kept her window down just the same.

"And just where might you two lovely young ladies be going on a cold, wintry afternoon like this?" the boy asked. He was brown-skinned with wide eyes and long lashes. Pam's type, thought Olivia. Fast. Nothing but trouble.

"We're visiting a friend," she said, keeping her jaw tight. She felt the pressure of his eyes. Let him look all he wants, she thought.

"We'd sure like to hook up with you two and your *friend*," said the boy. "I'm Freddie and this here's my partner Bobby and that's my play cousin Louis. Where y'all from?"

Tonya was trying to peer past Olivia. "The driver's so cute," she squealed. Olivia silenced her with a look.

"I'm Rhonda, and this is my friend Regina," said Olivia. "We're stewardesses from Cleveland."

"Stewardesses!" the boy guffawed. "Stewardesses! You two?" He consulted with the two passengers in the Olds and turned back to Olivia. "Where y'all from in Cleveland?" he asked, amused.

"East 98th," Olivia said coolly. It was the first thing that came to mind.

"Both y'all?" Freddie began to laugh. He gestured toward Tonya. "Her too? You're pulling my leg. I know *she* ain't from there."

Olivia poked out her lip and raised her eyebrows. "She's my cousin," she said meaningfully.

"I don't mean no disrespect," Freddie chuckled, "but I'd like to catch *her* down on East 98th." He turned back to his companions and said something. The sound of laughter spilled from their open window. He looked back over at Olivia. "Y'all like to skate? We're going to the roller rink."

Olivia let out a world-weary sigh. "I told you, we're on our way to our friend's house."

She rolled up her window and started the engine. The boy tooted his horn in a fast staccato, but Olivia concentrated on shifting the Corvair in reverse.

"Why can't we go to the skating rink?" asked Tonya. "Just for a half hour. Come on, they were *cute*."

Olivia resisted the urge to slap her. "You sound just like Pam," she said. "Besides, your mother would kill me."

"My mother's not here. Why do you always have to be such a goody-goody, Olivia?"

"Why do you want to go off with some hoodlums?" said Olivia. "That driver was a white-girl lover, couldn't you tell? He figured you'd be easy. Don't you know anything, girl? I was just saving you a lot of trouble."

"I really hate it when you play me off," Tonya sulked.

"I *said* you were my cousin." Olivia's patience had worn thin.

"You played me off," Tonya insisted. "Why don't you make up your mind whether you're my best friend or not?"

Olivia clicked on the wipers to clear the windshield. She kept her voice steady, purposeful. "I can't get you in with black kids, Tonya. I have my own troubles. You're on your own."

They both fell silent as Olivia made a right turn toward the lake and the north end of town where the high school was. She didn't care that she'd hurt Tonya, her words had come as a relief. She was worn out trying to keep people around her happy.

They sat in the empty high school parking lot and watched the snow fall. Every few minutes Olivia started up the engine and ran the heater. Snow covered the hood of the Corvair.

"This school looks like a prison," remarked Tonya.

"This is where my father used to work."

Olivia's father had counseled dropouts and taught driver's ed in the red brick building for almost fifteen years before he was hired last year to teach sociology at the college. He had been asked as a response to increasing pressure from black students who demanded more black faculty. Olivia had been present at several of the student demonstrations. She remembered the night her father had gotten the phone call.

"They never wanted me before," he told Olivia's mother bitterly. "Suddenly I'm in high demand when it's convenient for them."

"It's only right," she said. "You deserve this."

"They don't believe that. I'm just a quick fix. And these young black students . . ." He'd paused. "They think I can work miracles."

"Maybe you can," Olivia's mother had said. Because, Olivia thought bitterly, it would take a miracle.

It was only weeks later that D.T., one of the campus radicals, stood in the band shell of the square and announced through a bullhorn to a crowd of college and high school students that

Olivia's father was "an Uncle Tom, the white administration's puppet, married to the oppressor, hired to appease, and an enemy to the struggle." Olivia had been standing right there, after school, on the edges of the swelling crowd with three black schoolmates, and she'd heard it with her own ears, the truth that she had never dared put into words. She found herself caught up in the words themselves, felt the crowd's anger and frustration, and found resonating deep within her the chant that grew with the crowd's increasing enthusiasm, "Power to the people!" She never mentioned it to her mother, but when she looked at her father from then on, she felt wave after wave of pity and contempt.

Inside the idling Corvair, Tonya began to complain. "I'm so sick of cold and snow. When I go to college, I'm going to move some place warm. I want to have a tan and feel warm all the time."

"I like the snow," said Olivia, feeling ornery, "even if it is white."

She was considering the one lone car parked in a far corner of the lot. It was a blue Buick LeSabre with a solid layer of snow on the hood and roof. Ice covered the windows.

"How long do we have to sit here?" Tonya asked.

"You didn't have to come," Olivia reminded her. She put the car in gear and, as a concession, slowly circled the lot. She drove past the LeSabre. There were no tire tracks anywhere near it, just a smooth layer of snow.

"What are we doing here?" Tonya asked.

Olivia didn't answer.

"Let's go to the mall. I never get out of the house."

"Just cool your jets," said Olivia in her mother's voice.

Tonya slumped in the seat and pulled her coat more closely around her.

78

"Okay, Miss Impatient, we'll go to the mall."

Olivia turned the Corvair in the direction of the street. Out of the corner of her eye she saw the flash of headlights. Through the falling snow a car approached, turning slowly into the wide white parking lot from the other side. The shape of the front of the car registered as vaguely familiar, though Olivia's thoughts didn't acknowledge this. The car plowed through the curtain of white, a slow, heavy creature, headlights glowing, windshield wipers slapping against the glass. And then, without warning, Olivia was seized by recognition.

"Oh, my God!" she exclaimed. "Oh, my God!" She hadn't really believed, had she? She hadn't bargained for the sudden wave of panic that swept over her. She slammed on the brakes and ducked her head below the windshield. Her right foot trembled on the brake.

Tonya was a second behind her, sliding out of the seat onto the floor. "Did he see us?" she whispered from under the dashboard.

"Shshshsh!" Olivia raised her head slowly. She heard the rumble of the other engine beside them, and the smack of wheels on wet snow.

"Oh, my God, he's seen us."

"What should we do?" asked Tonya, still crouched on the floor. She was furiously twisting the ends of her scarf.

Olivia gave a backwards glance, but the rear window was a blur of white. She cracked her window and peered over the top into the frosty air. The red station wagon had pulled up next to the blue LeSabre, where it sat, exhaust smoking in the air. Now the passenger door was opening. Out of the car stepped a tall dark-skinned woman in a long navy-blue maxi coat and black boots. She was drawing up the hood of the coat over her head with red-gloved hands. She leaned down into the car, and at that moment Olivia felt every muscle in her body constrict. Then the driver got out. He came around to the passenger side, and the two figures stood there in the snow, apart and talking. Gone was the mystery of the woman in a red leather skirt posed in the kitchen doorway. The very ordinariness of the two figures, man and woman, struck Olivia with a note of sadness. They were trapped like figures in a paperweight, snow whirling around and containing them.

Tonya dragged herself halfway up to the passenger seat. "Are you going to talk to him?"

"Hell no, I'm not going to talk to him!" said Olivia fiercely. She watched her father lean forward and plant a kiss on the side of the woman's face. She realized then that he was wearing, not the Russian hat he'd left the house with that morning, but the black beret she'd given him on Christmas. Flat like a saucer, it caught the snow, turning the top of his head white.

Olivia's foot slipped off the clutch. The car jerked forward, then died.

The woman turned ever so briefly in their direction, but her face was hidden by the wide hood of her coat. She looked back at Olivia's father for a moment before walking quickly toward the LeSabre, her shoulders drawn up in the cold. Olivia's father, head down, trudged back around to the driver's side of the station wagon and climbed inside. Olivia heard the dull thud of his car door closing.

"Here he comes," warned Tonya, her face stricken.

Olivia turned the key several times in the ignition and pressed the accelerator. The engine wouldn't turn over. She began to curse, her exhalations making soft, smoky circles in the air.

The red station wagon backed up slowly, exhaust curling up over it like smoke from a chimney. It turned and crossed the lot. The LeSabre's headlights flashed several times. The station wagon honked twice. Now headlights flooded Olivia's rear mirror. The station wagon was behind them, then swerving, and now the red hood of the car was abreast. It slid past, slowly, and made a sharp turn back into the snowy street.

"He looked right at you," said Tonya. "I saw him."

Olivia rammed the accelerator again with her foot. The engine roared, and the car lurched forward.

Now the LeSabre was alongside. Tonya twisted around in her seat. "Can you see her?" she asked.

"Shut up" was all Olivia could say. The LeSabre passed and turned in the same direction the station wagon had.

Olivia braked softly on the ice, felt the slight skid of tires, and then because the LeSabre had turned right, made a left. She roared up to the stoplight and made another fast left.

"That light was red!"

"I don't care." Olivia sped up and shot over the icy railroad tracks that separated one side of town from the other.

"Slow down!" said Tonya.

The Corvair's wheels spun on a hidden patch of icy railroad tie, the back end of the car swung unexpectedly halfway around to where the front had been, and Olivia found herself completely turned around on the snowy road staring into oncoming headlights from the other side of the tracks.

"You're going to kill us!" Tonya slapped the dashboard with her mittened hand. "Olivia, stop it!"

Olivia backed up against the curb and turned the steering wheel. Two cars swerved around them with a blare of horns. Between the falling snow and the tears she couldn't be sure which way the road went, but she made no apologies to Tonya, just buried her chin in her coat collar and counted in her mind the number of times the sticky wipers clicked across the windshield.

Tonya ate at Olivia's. She phoned her mother to weasel permission to spend the night, citing bad weather and snowy roads as good reason. Olivia, the only one still at the dinner table, heard the painful struggle on Tonya's end. No, she didn't need to come back home and pick up her nightgown, she could wear one of Olivia's. Her voice was feeble and discouraged. Yes, Olivia's mother was home, and no, there wouldn't be boys there. Finally, Olivia's mother intervened.

Olivia busied herself with twirling strands of overcooked spaghetti onto her fork with the help of a soup spoon.

"Hi, it's Lois," her mother said reassuringly into the phone. "How are you, Sue? Can you believe this weather? I didn't think the girls should try to go back out in it."

Olivia chewed, and concentrated on her mother's negotiations. She wished Tonya would go home.

When Olivia's mother hung up, she winked and said triumphantly to Tonya, "It's all set."

"I hate my mother," said Tonya.

Olivia's mother squeezed herself back down at the table between the two girls. There was a weariness about her that made Olivia feel protective. "Your mother means well."

"But you don't track down Olivia every step she makes," Tonya said. In the harsh kitchen light her features seemed all squeezed together and pasty. "You let your kids have *freedom*."

Olivia's mother sighed. "I don't know if it's so much freedom . . ." She paused. "I guess I just try to take into consideration that my children are, well, half black, and these are difficult times." Dead silence followed.

Olivia thought how those were Gina's words coming out of

her mother's mouth. *Half black. Difficult times.* She hated her mother's small, thin mouth, so smugly set in the shape of those words. Olivia began to imagine the snow falling on them there in the kitchen, forcing its way through the roof and the ceiling and piling up on the table. She saw her mother and Tonya, two strangers suddenly lit up in the cold winter light. Slowly they disappeared into the whiteness, indistinguishable from all the other white people she knew.

"If my children were white," Olivia's mother went on matter-of-factly in this new voice of betrayal, "I would probably be inclined to be more like your mother—stricter . . ." She glanced over at Olivia. "I believe in speaking frankly about these things. It's so much better when things are out in the open, don't you agree, honey?"

The front door opened, then slammed shut. Heavy footsteps announced Olivia's father's return. Olivia heard him bang the hall closet door and bark something at the boys.

Olivia's mother sighed. "Oh, well, just when we were having a *real* conversation." She got up with her plate in hand.

Footsteps thudded toward them in the hallway. A moment later Olivia's father filled up the frame of the kitchen doorway. He was only a medium-sized man, unremarkable in most respects, but he suddenly seemed bigger. His hair, Olivia noticed, was mashed flat on his head from the beret.

"What's for dinner?" he asked without looking at any of them. He took the lid off a pot on the stove and stared down inside.

"I didn't realize you'd be home for dinner," said Olivia's mother. "It's all gone."

His expression tightened, but he made no comment. Instead, he went to the refrigerator and caused a big commotion going through its contents.

While he searched, Olivia's mother brushed past him on her way out of the kitchen. Olivia heard the den door close and, a moment later, the muted sounds of canned television laughter.

Without looking at the girls, Olivia's father began to speak. His face was as blank and remote as the empty parking lot earlier. "I'm going to need to use the Corvair tomorrow morning." He cleared his throat and leveled the words in a careful monotone just above Olivia's head. "So don't plan anything. I'm taking your grandmother to church."

He seemed to notice Tonya for the first time. "Well, hello there, Tonya. How are you?" Without waiting for her answer, he turned and walked out of the room.

Olivia let herself collapse back in her chair. "God, I hate him," she muttered. She slouched lower, kicking her legs out. "And I can't believe what my mother just said to you. I can't believe either of them anymore."

Tonya sat wordlessly. She poked indifferently at the food on her plate.

Olivia straightened herself. "Hey, you want my family so bad? You want my mother? You can have her. But, remember, then you get *him* too." She stood up and pushed her chair in hard under the table. "You can have them both!"

She strode down the hall to the coat closet where she found her winter coat and boots. The Corvair keys jingled in her pocket. The snapshot was still stuffed deep inside her coat pocket. She fished around and pulled it out. On a whim she held it up, exposed, where anyone could walk in and see her with it. Excitement surged through her as she waited to see who might happen in. Pam? Her father? The boys? Her mother? She could imagine the expressions of shock on their faces.

It was Tonya, though, who appeared in the doorway. Her cheeks were streaked with red. "Your father went down to the basement," she whispered. "He looked mad." Then she saw the snapshot. "What are you doing, Olivia?"

Olivia smiled and gently waved the snapshot to the empty living room.

"I think I should go home," said Tonya. "I better call my mother."

"Do what you want." Olivia walked around Tonya and headed back into the kitchen. A cold draft blew up from the basement through the open door. Below, she could hear her father pacing and the sound of his radio being tuned. A few seconds of station-searching, then the radio was snapped off. It got very still. Olivia inched herself to the top of the basement stairs. A pool of yellow light marked the center of the basement where her father's work table stood. She was certain he was going through the drawers.

Behind her, Tonya waited pale and uncertain in the kitchen door.

"Watch this," Olivia said, holding up the snapshot by just a corner, between her thumb and forefinger. The black woman twisted back and forth in her fingers. A flash of red leather skirt, the sparkle of silver earrings. It was as if she had come alive.

"Dare me?" said Olivia. She didn't wait for the answer.

She released the snapshot. It hovered for a moment, caught on a current of air, and then the black woman began her looping descent. Slowly, slowly, she fell over the basement stairs, graceful as a falling leaf. Olivia looked down. The picture had landed face up on the bottom step.

With great calm, Olivia carefully closed the basement door, taking comfort in the soft click of the latch.

Her mind leaped forward to the tremendous changes that lay ahead. They began with her descent into the wintry night, leaving Tonya in her place. From now on, regardless of the lateness of the hour, the changing months, the shift of seasons, the occasions that would mark her growing up, she, Olivia, would come and go in the Corvair as she pleased, unhurried and unquestioned. Now it was just a matter of saying, "Excuse me," as she slipped past Tonya and down the hallway to the coat closet. She pretended she didn't hear her mother's voice calling from the den, "That you, Olivia?"

THE NATURE OF
LONGING

When Cousin Pearl was young she was the most beautiful of the Farrell girls, or so everyone said. I hoped to be just like her when I grew up, but folks cautioned me how a boy shouldn't want such things.

Cousin Pearl sewed for white women. Sometimes, when Mother and I visited the house, Pearl let me sit among those perfumed and powdered ladies, testing the very boundaries of my small boy's desires as I devoured with my eyes and mind the lay of silk, the up- or downsweep of a poignant line, the fluid contours of the female body, so unlike my own poor boy's shape, celebrated in the tease of texture and color. I began to suspect quickly the impossibility of my desires, distilled in Pearl, but denied to me as a man.

Everyone knew about Miss Pearl's abilities as a seamstress. By the time I knew Pearl she was famous in our county. Well-to-do women rustled up to her doorstep in their long skirts with requests for custom-made clothing. "Our Pearl," they cooed over her proprietarily, sipping tea in Grandmother Blanche's parlor.

That was around 1909, the year the National Association for the Advancement of Colored People was founded. How things change! Why, just this last year our Mr. Edward Brooke in Massachusetts became the first black U.S. senator in eighty-five years. (They do say "black" now. Everybody does.) And our poor Mr. Adam Clayton Powell enmeshed in some tedious scandal that makes me cringe just thinking about it. Thank goodness Pearl isn't alive to see all the trouble.

Pearl, for whom the world was a petal-perfect flower! My beautiful Pearl. Exquisite she was, like a fragile beach shell. Her father's Irish blood had bleached her skin to beige. A Mohawk ancestor can lay claim to the indigo blue in her irises. How I loved that haughty twist of her head when she concentrated, and the confidence with which she pulled against her enviable frame the yards of uncut crepe and messaline, measuring and honing, articulating the endless possibilities of form.

Sometimes she'd use me as a mannikin. "Now hold this over your shoulder. Let me see, no a little more here." My skin fairly jumped at the soft brush of her fingertips working to protect me from the stick of the pins she inserted with lightning speed.

Those white women, young and old, may have loved her, but I adored her. Pearl. Pearl at the piano on hot summer evenings, playing Strauss waltzes, Chopin preludes, Debussy. Pearl with her what-they-used-to-call "good hair" twisted back from her face in a braid or a bun, little ringlets spilling onto her smooth forehead.

She and Grandmother Blanche and Minnie and Inez all lived in the old Victorian house on Pine Street I now inhabit and maintain with the same fastidiousness they once did: the rosy twilight parlor, the cool, darkened pantry where I once sneaked jam, the English garden still full of misty spires and lacy foliage where sometimes, as a boy, I lay on my back among the foxgloves and columbine, concealed and ecstatic.

In the evenings now, when I have repaired to the living room, I close my eyes and conjure up the melodies of Pearl's crepuscular serenades drifting over the decades like ground fog.

Minnie, mostly silent, sits in the parlor sewing by hand, dreaming of unspoken things. Grandmother Blanche and her niece Inez, corsets loosened, rest in their chaises on the screened-in porch, murmuring. Outside, the summer breeze stirs, never violating the stillness within.

There were moments when the music stopped being music and became an intimate outpouring of Pearl's soul. None of us dared even to tremble.

Pearl went to finishing school and then to college. For several years after, she taught part-time in a nearby academy for young "colored" women, but it closed, and after that, there were no such jobs for "colored" women. She had always wanted to be a poet, but instead turned to sewing, richly textured materials, satins, silks, and lace.

"Always be nice," Grandmother Blanche inculcated. "A real lady never shows her true feelings."

How obedient was my dear Pearl. So obedient that she gave up what she loved best and came home to spend her entire life in this very house.

Shortly before I was born, Cousin Pearl took up with a light-skinned man named Trevor something. How long this went on I can judge only by the letters they exchanged, almost six months' worth. But Trevor was only a porter on a train that ran North to South, and soon his tales of travel bored Pearl, who strove for real experiences (experiences of the soul, as she put it). She needed an educated man, everyone could see that, someone who understood her finely tuned sensibilities. "Pearl's so high-strung," they used to say, "so nervous." Pearl kept Trevor's letters in her gilded memory box, letters that Minnie sneaked and read on the sly. She divulged their contents years later just before she died. Those letters, Minnie wept to my mother, were so unworthy of Pearl, oh that poor, poor Pearl! They were so *physical,* Minnie whispered, her voice raw with emotion, so *low.*

I was almost fifty before I got my hands on those letters; Minnie had not destroyed them after all but stored them among her own things, even relished them, after Pearl died. I came across them when I packed up the last of Pearl's things for safekeeping.

Even now, sitting on Pearl's love seat, which I reupholstered last year in red velvet, I read those rough-hewn words with unexplainable pangs of jealousy and the slightest churning of my own fleetingly satisfied desires. Trevor's letters were the outpourings of a man's deepest passions. I have often found myself yearning for Pearl's poor Trevor, now dead in his grave, whose explicit tendernesses dedicated themselves so genuinely to Pearl. For I myself have certainly never known such love; *a real lady never shows her true feelings.*

And so it was one afternoon in the garden, where Pearl's old-fashioned roses still climb untamed around the arbor and over the walls, that Pearl did what she believed to be right and extended her hand in farewell to Trevor. They parted as friends. There were no more proper colored men around.

Minnie and Inez were much plainer and simpler than Pearl, and a little older, and they jokingly referred to themselves as unclaimed treasures, even when they were well into their eighties and white-haired. Frail women with the foreshortened vision of those who have not been out in the world. Women whose limited knowledge of men kept them sequestered in their own tight company. Women whose tomorrows promised little more than repetitions of yesterday.

They were the warning I didn't heed. Though it roared through my blood, so did the generations. We are, I have discovered through these bitter years, stitched together with the same constrained stuff, but different only in this way: a man alone has so much more to hide beyond drawn blinds, for companionship comes more naturally to women. My own fraternity has been limited mostly to books. I am of the generation that keeps its own secrets and its own shames.

I am, after all, the town librarian here. Such a man may live alone, keep a maid, cook for himself, and no one raises an eyebrow except in greeting.

Over the years nephews have come and gone, unobtrusively, innocently, quickly; my own light complexion has made mention of blood ties conceivable. These boys were the troubled sons of women who could never love them enough. Two hours out of New York City, these boys walked the cobblestones of my garden paths, shimmering and muscular in my dressing gown, their necks white in the sunlight. They were quick for my hospitality, just as quick for my generosities, and even quicker with good-bye. That was when I was much younger, when the full torture of my desire moved me to haunt the very same train station where Pearl met her porter. I often roamed that platform unobserved, bird-watching binoculars around my neck, discreet to the point of extinction.

Or so I thought, until today. But I will never visit that platform again. A good citizen I have always been in a town that tolerates nothing else. I am, after all, the keeper of books, in the stone library built in 1805, fifty years from the day my paternal grandfather found himself a free man above the Mason-Dixon line. My father's people were slaves. My mother's people on Pearl's side had always been free. My father never learned to read, but Pearl and my mother saw to it that I had books as a child.

And I, in reciprocation, see to it that the town's children and grandchildren are nourished by the books I carefully stamp and date for them. Winter, summer, fall, and spring, scores of them climb the stone steps and push open the heavy doors to browse my shelves. Nine to five, Mondays through Fridays, Saturdays noon to four. I have come to know them all by what they read. They bring hearty literary appetites it is my duty to satisfy. I direct the young ones to the Young Adult section and introduce them to such literary children as Gritli's and the Peppers and the young March women. "Thank you, Mr. Farrell," they chorus, using the surname I inherited with the house. Their faces are fresh as new paper. They clutch my worn books in their hands. I roam the aisles, among my bound companions, occasionally sampling aloud the familiarity of a paragraph, something to recommend to a young friend. My own joy builds under the tight cork of expectation as I observe the freshness of their imaginations, the certainty of their trust. I have tended the minds of our town as carefully as I tend my garden.

Which is why the unthinkable occurrence of today has brought me up short, like a fist to my stomach. Quite by accident this afternoon, I came across the scribbling on the wall in the 800 section. The dreaded words I'd hoped never to see, etched in an almost illiterate hand, flashed at me next to the second shelf. White chalk on the green wall. The last rays of afternoon sun tinged them ever so slightly with pink. I never doubted for a moment that they were intended for me. I glanced around for my accuser, quickly combing my mind for the names of those who had come and gone today. I swatted at the green wall with my open palm, oblivious to the sting. I furiously erased. The filthy words clung to my fingers, their fetid odor filling my nostrils. I went directly to the washbasin and soaped my hands over and over until the white dust dissolved and I could catch my breath. When I returned to the desk, two women and a small boy awaited me with expectation and a stack of books an arm long. I broke with policy and allowed them all, adding an extra week besides.

"Thank you so much, Mr. Farrell," the two women said, the one prodding the little boy to do the same. I watched them leave before I went over and locked the door behind them.

Now I am alone. I begin to stack stray books on the reshelving cart for my assistant. I check the wall once again just to be sure. It appears clean, like new, but the memory has left me weak with agony. Back at my desk I open a drawer and pull out one of Pearl's old hand mirrors. In it, peering back at me, is my light brown face, the small pouches of flesh forming under my eyes, the thinning hair, the full, wasted mouth. The words fill my throat with phlegm. I speak them slowly, for the first time in my life, to that passive, old man's face searching mine for answers, in the hushed boundaries of the closed library, when the rest of the world is safely on its way home to the supper table.

It is true, I think, *I'm nothing but an old black faggot.* Except that my accuser spelled it *fagut.* And I consider the poignancy of such ignorance and wonder if it might not have aroused a certain perverse amusement in old Pearl herself.

Mirror away, I collect my briefcase and pull on my sweater. Outside, the air is warm, the streets benign. My organs are gripped by agitation. I choose the shortcut to the deli, where I pick up a little creamed herring and a loaf of bread for dinner. The ugly incident replays itself in my mind. I keep hoping it isn't the boy I gave *Oliver Twist* to earlier. And then I hope desperately it isn't any of them.

All the way home I am on guard, expecting the words to ambush me again. Where are they? I wonder. Are they lurking behind each row of neatly trimmed hedges, or a passerby's spectacles, or in the window of that house?

The security of all the years I have lived here, respected and considered, now teeters like a pane of glass on the edge of a cliff. What will tomorrow bring? And what, after all, is my defense?

My German woman Hannah, who lives downstairs and keeps house for me, is off tonight. Every Wednesday she goes two towns over to visit her sister. Normally I relish the time alone, but tonight I feel an urgent need for the comfortable routines associated with Hannah's presence in the house. To hear her greet me with "Gut even'ning, Mr. Farrell" and offer me a taste of whatever she is preparing for us both. To give things the shape of habit. Though we seldom eat together, at my request she has joined me occasionally on the porch for a light supper. Tonight would surely have been one of those nights. We would have sat together, Hannah and I. She is a genteel, quiet creature, one who understands my need for solitude, who has never questioned the things she does not understand.

She is priceless, in sharp contrast to the servant Grandmother Blanche kept here in the old days. Willie, the young, fast dark-skinned black girl who used to sneak me cookies and twist up her face to make me laugh. I quicken my pace, briefcase heavy in my hand. Even Willie, I think, would be a welcome sight tonight.

Cousin Pearl called her Wily Willie. Willie had worked for my grandmother for years, and was probably forty when I first knew her, but she looked and dressed like a child. She giggled through household tasks, swiped butter from the pantry, and hid my grandmother's little trinkets in her room until she was caught and slapped. There would be tears all around, a firm reprimand from my grandmother, and all would be forgiven, the two embracing in mutual adoration.

Cousin Pearl considered Willie "uppity" and ill-mannered.

She went so far as to blame Willie's complexion. To be born so black is a terrible burden, she told me once. Darker races lack breeding. They simply can't help themselves. But Willie worshipped Pearl. It was Pearl to whom Willie came for counsel when she crept into the house at dawn after a weekend in a Harlem dance club, where she'd picked up a man and a swollen eye. Pearl briskly set about preparing Willie an ice pack and ordering her to rest all day in the overstuffed chair next to the fan in the parlor. Minnie and Inez discreetly looked the other way as they poured their own breakfast tea and commented on the weather (which was going to be unquestionably hot, but always made a good topic). "Willie fell down the basement steps," they told me soberly when I asked. "You mustn't go down in the basement. It's no place for a boy."

As I turn up my walk, I have an unexpected pang for Willie. I miss her, and for a moment I imagine her small figure in the garden, like a haunting. The day lilies have done surprisingly well this year, peach and tangerine blooms bursting from their beds holding the last glow of twilight. This time of day the light plays tricks.

By the porch I pause to check the mailbox, just as Pearl always did. I pull out a handful of routine bills, bank notices, and an advertisement. In their midst is, however, one light blue card-sized envelope addressed to me in a mysterious hand, with no return address. My heart quickens. The words from the wall are in my throat again. I imagine them written across the blue stationery, and then across the hedge dividing my property from the next. My neighbor's wife is filling the bird feeder suspended from a low branch of their flowering plum. Her back is to me. I set down my deli sack and briefcase and raise one hand in greeting. How badly I want her to turn around right now and wave back, to call out, "How are you this evening, Mr. Farrell, don't you wish it would rain?" But her back remains to me, intent as she is on filling the feeder.

My hands shake. I break the seal on the envelope with my finger. It is a personal letter, written in dark ink on thin blue paper in lovely scalloped penmanship.

It reads:

Dear Mr. Farrell, This is regarding the note you sent me some time ago in response to an advertisement I ran last winter for a pen pal. I am sorry to have delayed so long, but I was ill and am just now recovered. I, too, am a book lover. I live just outside New York City in Piermont, and am a retired schoolteacher. You mentioned that you are a librarian. If you haven't already selected a pen pal, perhaps you would like to exchange some correspondence with me, as I suspect we have much in common. At your suggestion, I am currently re-reading all of Trollope. I agree that "there are worse things than a lie . . . it may be well to choose one sin in order that another may be shunned." Sincerely yours, William Tunning

I reread the letter twice, repeating the words aloud. Then I carefully fold the blue stationery and replace it inside the envelope. My note! I'd forgotten all about it, sent months ago during that long, dark crawl through February when the snow seemed to never want to stop. But now, with the scales tipped in favor of anonymous cruelty, an unknown friend has restored the balance.

A faint pulse of excitement stirs inside me. Trollope, I think, with small delight, another old queen who likes to read. And as I gather up my things and mount the front steps, I begin to consider exactly how I might open my letter to this Mr. William

Tunning and what all I will convey to him. My breath stops. I pause to catch it. Words!

My neighbor's wife has gone back inside. Briefly I look out over their empty yard where an occasional firefly flickers gold. My house is silent. It is only of late that I no longer think of it as Pearl's house. The night is warm. I pour a glass of red zinfandel from a corked bottle and take my meal to the front porch where I watch the shadows deepen. I wait for someone to walk by, someone who will see me sitting here, and who will call out.

This is the same porch on which my Grandmother Blanche sat on similar summer evenings next to a kerosene lantern, reading bowdlerized Shakespeare with an eyeglass held stiffly in one hand. Her favorite play was *Othello*, but I am confident her version bore no reference to "the beast with two backs." I often sat next to her, waiting patiently for Pearl to emerge from her room where she took a "ten-minute lie-down" before the evening meal.

How I loved the women of this house! How I looked forward to their familiar routines and shared in their simple pleasures. And how courageously they suppressed the unwitting desires that beat on soft wings at the backs of their hearts. They satisfied themselves with mouse-sized portions of well-cooked food on the Haviland china I still keep carefully laid out behind glass (it comes out only on those rare occasions I have a visitor). They took their pleasure in reading nightly to one another from the Bible, and maintained a decorum in their lives that allowed for no disruptions of routine, no nasty intrusions by those who might not understand.

A manless world, forged by their feminine imaginations, inward bound by the peculiar laws of that time.

I learned early not to inquire about Mr. Farrell, Pearl's father, who had long ago deserted the family after periods of unemployment. Grandmother Blanche kept tucked away inside her bureau drawer an old daguerreotype of him, which she impulsively thrust at me one day. I looked only briefly before she caught it up in her hand and buried it once again beneath her cotton underthings.

He was handsome, brown-skinned, wore sideburns and a confident smile. From my grandmother's few references to him, I learned he'd gone to Alaska to fish, where his party was either set upon by wolves or froze to death. But Pearl and Minnie and Inez pieced together, sotto voce, a scandalous portrait of the young dancer from New Orleans who lured him to the flashy nightlife of that southern port.

Pearl wrote numerous poems about Mr. Farrell. She kept her little couplets in a lacquered box which she gave me shortly before she died. The poems were shockingly candid, often written from the point of view of the dancer. As a young boy, I had so learned to treasure words, and my innocent Pearl tested hers aloud on me in a throbbing voice, assuming, I suppose, I was too young to understand. But unbeknownst to me and thanks to Pearl, I became in those secret moments the wicked dancer in red, bangled and sequined, swirling through shadow and smoke in pulsing rhythms for strangers below the edge of a stage, just out of reach of the hands reaching for me, stroking the air beside me, and always, always, and infinitely desiring.

Shortly after my mother and I arrived for our Sunday visits, Pearl summoned me upstairs. Her bedroom was my sanctuary. She'd remove my shoes, then hoist me up on the middle of her four-poster bed, covered by the hand-stitched silver quilt intended for her trousseau. I lay back, feigning weariness, but it was only an excuse to scrutinize the framed Degas print overhead. It was a study of dancers, young girls bent over to lace their ballet slippers, their net skirts standing off from their buttocks as vain as peacock feathers. If I looked closely enough, I could make out their hard, taut naked bodies beneath. I knew better than to ask about the painting, fearful she might put it away. I dreamed of myself among the dancers, absorbing and being absorbed, until we were one long feminine body, swirling under the canopy of Pearl's silver quilt.

Sometimes Pearl sewed and we listened to arias from her favorite Italian operas. Passion, love, jealousy, murder, revenge: Lucia's mad scene, Adelina Patti singing "Casta diva." Pearl sang along in undecipherable syllables that elicited dangerous visions of rapture, and lifted the veils of gloom from my young soul.

Occasionally she explained the stories to me with euphemistic precision full of "berefts" and "forsakens" and "unrequiteds." She hinted at unmentionable explosions of emotion under a harmless surface of pageantry and music. I lay contentedly on her bed, shoes off, toes free, staring at the dancers overhead, running bits of Pearl's filmy leftover material between my fingers. Pearl's voice wove itself in and out of my thoughts.

Now the air has thickened with the scent of jasmine crawling over the porch trellis. It is a heady fragrance, one which makes me light-headed, almost fearful. There is a movement in the neighbors' yard, a young girl walking down the drive to the street. I believe she is visiting the family, though we have not been formally introduced. She wears a light-colored dress that shines in the darkness above the hedge. I stand up in hopes that she will notice me, but she is looking toward the corner where a car has eased to a stop. The girl stands at the edge of the drive and stares. It is a young man in the car, and he peers out the open window. A woman's voice calls from out of the darkness, "Elaine!" Or is it "Ellen"? I am suddenly saddened that I don't know who the girl is. She turns quickly, furtively. She says something to the boy that I can't catch. The boy says something back. He drives halfway down the street and waits while she hurries back to the house. I hear a screen door squeak open, then slam. The street is quiet. The boy has turned his motor off. I wait, but the girl does not return. The boy finally drives off. I find my wine glass is empty and so go inside to fill it.

I am haunted by the silence of my own house and the loneliness welling up inside. Today's episode is a fearful presence, a ghost pursuing me, shaking its wispy finger at me, warning that books will never be enough. Not so, I murmur as the crickets stir outside. I feel the weight of the day pressing down on me. Panic builds to dizziness. I inhale and lean against the kitchen counter. Not so, I repeat.

Pearl was in her fifties when she began to have fainting spells, especially in the summer. Minnie and Inez would administer smelling salts and bring her to, whereupon her eyelids fluttered and her expression turned morose. She would accept a little cordial, which the women called medicine, and sit quietly, fanning herself and staring steadfastly into the yard. Sometimes she would turn to her piano and play. Everyone would remark with relief how good it was to "have our Pearl back."

When Grandmother Blanche died at ninety-five, it was just Pearl and Minnie and Inez living alone in the house with Willie. They quickly closed the gap my grandmother had left, tending to the house and garden with characteristic resignation. Mother and I continued to visit on alternate Sundays for what Cousin Pearl referred to as "supper." My mother saw it as her duty. "They're all alone," she explained to my father. He couldn't have been dragged here by wild horses. He died never having set foot in Pearl's house.

I recall that one Sunday evening we arrived for a late supper at the house. I was eight or nine, dressed in a white linen suit and straw hat I had begged Mother for. The women fussed over me tremendously. "Isn't he precious?" And Pearl filled my pockets with hard candy root-beer barrels. My mother herself wore a filmy, flowery summer dress and a matching hat. My mouth full of sweets, I observed the outline of her loose, warm limbs through that dress, catching the scent of perfume that rose off her biscuit-colored skin.

Pearl insisted this evening I was to sit at the table next to her, and not eat with Willie in the kitchen. "He needs to learn proper table manners," she explained as she sat me down beside her.

Minnie said grace and carved a plump, parsley-covered chicken. Inez passed around homemade apricot jelly and stuffing. We ate from the good china carefully arranged on my grandmother's monogrammed linen tablecloth.

Pearl spoke longingly of Paris, as she often did, but this was the first time I understood she had traveled there for three weeks with a white family whose children she once baby-sat. Though the trip had taken place years before, she talked as if it had been yesterday. The subject of Pearl's travels disturbed the others. "Shshsh!" said Minnie. "You'll give *ideas*," and she nodded in my direction.

Pearl sighed. "*Bon appetit, ma famille!*" she said and began to eat. When my plate was filled, I remarked, "*Merci beaucoup!*" for Pearl's benefit and everyone laughed. "Listen to him!" cried Mother. "Listen to how he talks!" She grinned down at me. But Pearl reached over and touched my hand gently. "You, my dear, are a most elegant little boy, and you mustn't let others tell you otherwise."

After dinner we clamored for Pearl to play the piano. Willie was in the kitchen scrubbing dishes. Minnie and Inez and my mother and I sandwiched ourselves together on the love seat. We waited for Pearl to strike her first chord.

In the twilight Pearl could have been twenty. Her noble face glowed from the falling shadows. I watched in fascination as her fingers strode over the ivory keys, then trickled lightly downward, her head in soft sway at the end of that long, smooth neck. Pearl played for an hour: Chopin waltzes, Bach preludes, a little Schumann.

"Oh, do play on," said Minnie, as she always did. She used the time to doze softly and think. We all urged Pearl on, and as the evening came, a soft sort of languor overcame us, a sense of overwhelming peace and contentment. My mother pressed my hand, grateful for what she perceived as my patience.

Pearl announced each piece she played. She moved to a transcription of the Flower Duet from *Madame Butterfly*. It was pleasant and light, and I found myself matching the beat with a happy rhythm in my own head. Then she paused and the house fell silent. Mother squeezed me to her. Pearl's hands were poised over the keys. She stared straight ahead at the gathering gray. Then, without warning, she began a disturbing piece in a minor key. To this day I don't know what it was, but suspect it may have been Tchaikovsky, or something equally inflammatory, the vibrations of which penetrated the deepest recesses of my soul and drew out passion like a sickness. I saw Pearl's face grow more and more darkly animated, her eyes taking on a hellish brightness. Her fingers flew over the keys, her breath came in gasps. I felt a wild explosion of expectation. Then Pearl stopped. Her hands crashed down on the keys in a violent, rebellious discord. A shudder ran through her slender body. With ferocity, she struck randomly at the keys again and again until the music became a jangle of frayed nerves and anger. To everyone's horror, she swept the music onto the floor. The women all leaped toward her.

Pearl reared up, tall and formidable, clutching at her throat with her hands. I don't know if that gesture was meant to stifle or wrench forth the silent scream that seemed to grow from deep within, emerging ever so slowly, but with fluidity, from that small, delicate throat. It was a noise I will never forget, like the sound of water trying to escape the tiny aperture of a broken pipe. She staggered as Minnie and my mother caught her on either side. Mother plucked up Pearl's fan from the piano bench and waved it at Pearl's constricted face.

"I—I," began Pearl.

"Not in front of the boy," hissed Minnie. "Oh, thank God Mother isn't alive."

"I can't take any more!" cried Pearl before she wilted against the piano. At least I believe that is what she said.

Minnie waved salts under her nose, Mother knelt helplessly at Cousin Pearl's side, and Inez wrung her hands. A trio of mercy and despair. But Pearl hadn't fainted, she was crying. I had never seen a grown-up cry, and I remember even now the weight of my astonishment. Minnie quickly escorted me to the back of the house, where she advised me to sit quietly. I didn't move, but sat obediently, measuring the soft quickening in the very center of my heart against the murmurs from the front rooms. I paged through Pearl's postcard album, studying castles and cathedrals and colorfully dressed white people dotting green hillsides, places I have since visited many times over, going beyond where Pearl ever went. But then it was not the pictures I was thinking of. My boyish eye moved feverishly beyond. At its sharpest point of vision, it witnessed over and over the spectacle of Pearl's wanting to give in to the floor below.

While Pearl rested, Minnie drew me to her and proclaimed in a firm voice, "You needn't worry, my little lamb. She only had a little spell. Your Cousin Pearl is just fine now."

At that moment a faint connection worked itself between Pearl and me like an insistent cat: recognition began uncurling from its sleep. In the years that followed and never separated us, understanding grew. I visited and wrote her faithfully. We spent hours in each other's company without a word. Since her death, it is Pearl's posthumous consent I have counted on. It is that which forms my company. She protects me even now from the dark lies of others as I glide easily through these unchanged rooms, stacked on top of one another, the walled mazes of her celibate will offering up the startling evidence of our very likeness. It is from her own desires that I must draw my courage.

In the fading twilight of my curtained living room I remove my clothes, abandoning the constraint of stiff seam and tyrannical stitch. Pants folded, shirt off, I go to the hall closet and pull from the hanger my silk dressing gown, pure fluidity, the one Pearl made for herself and wore, oh, those many evenings in her room while she sewed.

I pour a second glass of wine, urgency summoning me as Pearl once did. What appears to be the ease of my next decision is exigency in disguise. At my secretary, I pry open several boxes of stationery, choose the plain, and select two pens in case one runs dry. I arrange them on the butterfly table beside the love seat. I lean over and turn on the Venetian lamp, pausing to observe both pens and paper in the expectant way one might consider a silent phone. Words! My greatest fear is just how wrong they can be.

The pens, the paper, the rising imperative of my own longing fill me with agitation. I roam along the edge of the wall of books, counting off the book spines with the tips of my fingers until I find what I am looking for. There, among the hardbound Trollopes, is a well-worn volume of *Barchester Towers,* left unfinished from last winter, page marked by a thin scrap of red velvet. It is here, I tell myself, I will make my start. It is here I must take my comfort. There is no trick to warding off tomorrow. For the moment Trollope is my sin. Mr. William Tunning is another.

COLOR STRUCK

They'd always gathered at Mother's for Thanksgiving. That was before Daddy died and the house on East 23rd was sold to a Chinese man, Lee Wong. Think of it! Ten of those Wongs crammed into the old stucco house that used to feel crowded with just five: Mother, Daddy, Caldonia, Vesta, and Clayton. It made Caldonia shake her head in disbelief. At the phone company she worked with several Chinese women who could barely get their mouths around English words. The words, when they spoke them, stuck like peanut butter in their throats.

Caldonia's latest obstetrician was Chinese, or was it Japanese? She never could keep it straight. A Chinese girl at work had recently corrected her and said, "I'm Filipina." Then she reached out and laid her narrow hand on Caldonia's rounded stomach, so unexpectedly that Caldonia felt she'd been intruded on. The girl, seeing her surprise, smiled and said, "For luck. For me. I want a baby too." Caldonia was troubled by the warmth of the girl's hand long after it had been withdrawn.

Up until a month ago, Caldonia's Chinese or Japanese or whatever-she-was obstetrician had been seeing her once a week for the last month of pregnancy. The doctor was a small, friendly woman with bright eyes who dressed in elegant suits, as if she were running off to business meetings instead of squatting on a chair to peer up between her patients' legs. She spoke proper English without any accent. "Everything looks good," she told Caldonia. "Everything looks just as it should."

This was Caldonia's third child, the conception so unexpected that at first she had not told Fred about the pregnancy. She waited over a week. Not that she would have ever considered not having the child, but she needed time alone to absorb the fact that, even with Iris and Nadia both in school, she was going to be the mother of a baby again, faced with diapers and sleepless nights.

Now, as she busied herself in the kitchen, she longed for the past Thanksgivings at the East 23rd Street house, when Mother had festooned the doorways with crepe paper and Daddy, in his matching slacks and sweater, carried out the holiday routine of washing and polishing every inch of his two black Cadillacs. Standing in that immaculate driveway, chamois in hand, he always greeted and chided them all as they arrived, his children, then his grandchildren, encouraging everyone to pause and admire the shine of fenders and hoods, and listen to him brag for the hundredth time, "Look at that, a hundred thousand miles and not a scratch, not a bump . . ."

Thanksgivings with Mother and Daddy had always been so perfect. There was plenty of room and more than enough food for anyone who happened along: neighbors, friends, extra relatives, dropping in for some of Mother's famous sweet potato pie. "Oh, and while you're at it, honey, try a little taste of turkey and a bit of oyster dressing, and just go on ahead and get you some of my bread pudding too."

But the last year had brought many changes. Daddy was dead and Mother had squeezed herself and her possessions into one of the cement-block Harriet Tubman Senior high rises in West Oakland. Her cramped fourth-floor apartment with its tiny kitchenette overlooking the freeway no longer accommodated the swell of family. She now boiled tea water on a two-burner stove and heated up frozen dinners in a microwave.

And Mother, gone stoop-shouldered and irritable, complained that the grandchildren made her nervous when they came to visit. She reproached them for being too loud in the elevators, always threatening to pull on the emergency buzzer, and she worried they'd tear up her furniture, so she'd covered everything in plastic, including runners along the beige pile carpet. She spoke more sharply to Caldonia, Vesta, and Clayton, her three grown children, as if they were still children themselves, wearing on her last good nerve.

Everyone agreed Mother wasn't herself these days, dependent on a cane after her hip operation in the spring, forgetful, eyes blurring from encroaching cataracts, balance uncertain. As Vesta took to saying, "Mother's just an old crab. I can't stand to listen to her."

What Mother announced to Caldonia about Thanksgiving this year was "I've retired from cooking and now it's somebody else's turn."

What she meant was "It's up to you, Caldonia. Clayton and Vesta are useless."

So Caldonia and Fred won by default, even though Caldonia was just a month past giving birth and still feeling sore and irritable. This child had come cesarian, a fact that dulled Caldonia's sense of accomplishment. It seemed the child had not really come out of her own body. Now here she was, barely recuperated, roasting the turkey and browning homemade bread crumbs, all because she knew better than to count on Vesta and Clayton.

"Y'all gonna have to pitch in, I'm not the Lone Ranger, you know," she told them by phone, with special emphasis in her voice just to make the point. She wondered if God was growing weary with her impatience. After all, He'd seen to it that Caldonia and Fred were blessed with so much.

That's how friends and family saw it too. She and Fred seemed to make good choices, beginning with each other. Fred was always getting promotions and raises on the police force. Caldonia had just made supervisor down at the phone company. They paid their bills on time, they attended church, and they'd saved enough money to put Nadia and Iris in a private Christian school.

Their good fortune wasn't lost on Vesta. "Y'all got all my luck," she was fond of saying. "I can't seem to win for losing."

But luck always has a limit. It started with the cesarian birth of this third child. Caldonia suspected Fred was a little disappointed the baby wouldn't be a boy, though he'd never say such a thing.

In her hospital bed, breathing hard and pushing, she recalled the Filipina woman's hand touching her. At the time, she had felt too startled to be annoyed, and then she realized the woman meant no harm. But it felt like a curse. And her labor was long and hard.

When the pains got worse, the doctor ordered a cesarian. It was a disappointment, but after a short sleep and the drowsy aftermath Caldonia found herself coming to in the bright light of her own excitement. She made out the shape and length of a perfect form—eyes, ears, fingers, and toes all there and accounted for. She cried out in happiness, a miracle even the third time, grasping the wrinkled little thing in her arms. But later, after her mind cleared, Caldonia got a good look. She began to suspect a blunder, a genetic contretemps. During her sleep something had happened. The child, made up of parts of her and Fred, did not seem to belong to either of them, and she wasn't sure where to lay the blame: on God (whom she fiercely loved) or Nature (whom she tried to respect) or the very chromosomes in the cells of her own body which had bleached the child the color of milk, tinted her eyes pink, stained the thin spread of hair an off-shade of lemon.

If Fred hadn't reassured her that the baby emerged from her body, she would have been certain there was a hospital mix-up and some white couple was going home with her child. Later she recalled an article she had seen once years before in *National Enquirer:* White Couple Gives Birth to Black Baby. The article went on to say that the woman, unbeknown to her, carried black genes. The husband accused his wife of infidelity and divorced her immediately. Caldonia thought about the situation in reverse: Black Woman Gives Birth to White Baby. But it wouldn't work because a black woman's baby, no matter how light, would always be black.

Fred had to remind her that this was a gift from God, and that whatever God had in His plan they must accept with humility. Caldonia cried bitterly anyway. "It's our child," he kept telling her. "What is wrong with you?" But Caldonia prayed secretly and fervently that the child would darken.

From upstairs there came a soft cry. Caldonia set down the wooden spoon she'd been stirring the cranberry sauce with and turned down the flame under the pot. She was quicker to attend to the needs of this child than she'd been with Iris and Nadia. By the time she'd gotten upstairs and was peering into the crib, the baby was sleeping soundly again in her nest of quilts. Caldonia had taken to dressing her in blue; pink was so unflattering, causing her features to all but disappear in that little white face.

Often, while the baby slept, she sat close by and watched her. She wanted to understand exactly who this child was. She couldn't help comparing the luscious dark silk of her two older daughters' baby skins, how warm they were to the touch. This child seemed cold and foreign, a baby from some northern clime—Scandinavia, perhaps, a place inhabited by people with white skins and canary yellow hair, with eyes like frost. And yet Nature had played a trick, for the baby's small lips were full, her cheekbones high, and her nose broad like Fred's. And her hair, which was plentiful, was a thick cap of tight nappy curls. Daily, Caldonia checked the little crescents just below the child's tiny fingernails, but she found no indication that the skin there intended to darken.

Caldonia lingered by the sleeping baby, reassured by her soft breathing. From a certain angle, with the blinds drawn, the child might almost be considered pretty. There was a loud knock, followed by several more, at the front door. Caldonia pulled herself away from the child and hurried down the stairs, fastening her apron strings as she went. It was baby sister Vesta, the first to arrive. And barely noon, but since Vesta's tenth or so separation from Harold Sr. she was in the habit of showing up places early.

"You're going to take all the skin off your knuckles pounding on my door like that," Caldonia scolded. Vesta was holding a large green salad in a wooden bowl, covered with Saran Wrap. Behind her, Rosie and Li'l Harold were still piling out of their dented and badly rusted red Toyota with the bad starter and moody brakes and the cockeyed windshield wipers. As usual, they were already fussing with each other.

Caldonia stepped back and let Vesta pass, bearing the salad bowl, which reminded her of a miniature terrarium.

"Now, why'd you go and dress the salad like that?" Caldonia was annoyed. "Dinner's not until two."

Vesta was unfazed. She was already peeping into the living room to inspect the new sectional furniture Caldonia and Fred had ordered from a catalog. "Oooooh, this musta costed y'all a fortune!" she exclaimed. "Mmmmmm, and light colored too.

I'd never dare have something light colored with Rosie and L'il Harold around."

Vesta had never been considered pretty (certainly not the way Caldonia was—high school homecoming queen and so on!), what with her lumpy potato shape, funny lopsided smile, and eyes set too close together like a moth's. She was the lightest of Mother's children, honey butterscotch, but her complexion was uneven in places, scarred dark by childhood acne. And Vesta had never learned to dress. "*Really,* Vesta!" Caldonia would exclaim as Vesta arrived in skin-tight pants displaying all her bulges, teetering along in shoes so high she'd break her neck if she fell off. Today she was wearing yellow and black striped tights two sizes too small and an oversized yellow turtle-neck with black pockets. Caldonia thought her sister looked like a misshapen bumblebee. And those red shoes, like Minnie Mouse! She had never seen anything so ugly and cheap-looking.

Rosie and Li'l Harold burst through the door and flung themselves on her. These wild children were the opposite of Iris and Nadia—careful, precise children who rarely made messes, and whom Vesta had referred to disparagingly one infamous Christmas as "those little prisses." It took two whole weeks for Caldonia to get over that slight.

"Where's the baby?" cried Rosie, and Harold echoed "Where's the baby?" They'd come clutching armloads of complicated toys with small and multiple loose parts that would soon be scattered. They continued to press themselves against Caldonia with wet kisses and sticky hands.

"Yes, where *is* the baby?" Vesta wanted to know, bending over to see if the plastic flowers in the vase were real.

"She's 'sleep, upstairs," said Caldonia gently.

"Y'all named her yet? Mother's fit to be tied about that poor child."

Caldonia made her voice firm. "*No,* we haven't decided on a name yet."

Vesta clucked her tongue like an old woman. "Scandalous," she said cheerfully. "You can't have a no-name child."

Before Caldonia could snap back, Vesta went on, eyeing Caldonia's new beige curtains at the window, "I can't wait to have me my own place. I'll tell you, girl, Clayton is driving me nuts. He's so damn picky, picky this, picky that. He blew up at the kids the other morning, I mean really lost it, because he said they'd eaten all his cold cereal. Can you believe that? Yelling at my kids. Over cold cereal!"

"Brother's doing you a favor," Caldonia reminded her. "What you need to do is get things straight with Harold."

Vesta blew big air from her mouth. "That man works my final nerve!" She turned so quickly on her red shoes that her heel left a scuff mark across Caldonia's polished hardwood floor.

"Harold *is* your husband . . ." said Caldonia.

Rosie and L'il Harold started on a mess in the hallway.

Caldonia jumped in. "You kids set your toys over there and then you can go swing out back. Take turns. No fussing. I don't want to have to come out there."

When she turned around, Vesta was poking her face into the oven for a peek at the turkey. "This thing's big as a elephant!" she exclaimed, swallowed up in steam.

"Girl, get outa my oven. You're gonna make it cook uneven."

"I could baste it."

"It's self-basting," sighed Caldonia. "Close the door."

"Where *is* everybody?" Vesta asked.

"Fred's in the family room watching the game, but don't bother him, and the girls are down the street."

Vesta was wearing that awful wig again, the straight hair page-boy three shades too light for her complexion. It reminded

Caldonia of one of the old Supremes. So what if Vesta's real hair was thinning, it was all that worry over Harold. If she'd just ditch him once and for all, her hair would thicken, her skin would clear, and her whole life would improve. She'd lose some weight, could afford decent clothes, and she'd get another man if that's what she wanted.

Caldonia didn't believe in divorce, but in this case she thought it was high time Vesta and Harold Sr. split up for good. How those two had managed to last all these years was a mystery! Everybody'd warned her from the start, that very first day Vesta dragged Harold home from high school. They'd succeeded in putting a stop to their eternal fussing long enough to produce two unruly children, but otherwise it was always hurricane weather at Vesta's.

Daddy'd had a fit. He had forbidden her to marry Harold, told her the boy was all flash and foolishness, barely one step up from a hoodlum. But Vesta was so hardheaded and downright silly (Caldonia frequently thought, a little simpleminded, if you wanted to know the truth), she just thumbed her nose at Daddy and forged ahead with a huge wedding, marrying Harold in an expensive ceremony at the Methodist church Mother attended. Daddy ended up bankrolling the whole business, including the expensive lace dress with train, though everyone knew Vesta had about as much business wearing white as the devil himself.

So it was that Vesta had spent these last fourteen years paying the piper. Over and over she'd packed up the children and left Big Harold lock, stock, and barrel. This time it was Clayton who relented and let her move in with him in his two-bedroom apartment down on Lake Merritt. It was supposed to be temporary, just until Vesta made other arrangements, but now six months had passed and Clayton had confided to Caldonia his patience was wearing thin.

Foolish Clayton! It wasn't as if Caldonia hadn't cautioned

him. He was always getting suckered into things like this, and now he was whining to her. Said he was tired of coming home from the college where he taught accounting to find the living room floor littered with Rosie's black Barbie and her accessories, and the horse doll with the eyelashes and purple hair and all *her* accessories, and pieces of Little Harold's Lego set strewn around, and an oblivious Vesta curled up on the sofa with Clayton's plaid bathrobe over her legs watching *Jeopardy* and eating Cheez-Its out of a crumpled bag.

At first Caldonia tried to listen patiently, the way the Lord would want her to. But she finally had to tell Clayton straight out that he needed to "put the girl out." She spoke from experience. Just a year ago she and Fred had hosted Vesta and the kids, and now here they were having to spend good money replacing their sectional furniture that Rosie and L'il Harold had crayoned on.

Vesta leaned across the countertop to steal an olive from the cut-glass dish. "You know, Clayton's bringing a woman over today," she announced coyly.

Caldonia launched into making biscuits. "A woman? He didn't mention it to me."

"That's because he's afraid you won't approve." Vesta let that sink in. "Let's see, Jean or Jane. Shoot! I never can remember her name." Vesta headed over to the fridge for a diet soda. She found a can, popped the tab, and brushed a loose strand of wig hair from her face. "You ain't heard about her yet?"

Caldonia shook her head. "I can't keep up with Clayton's women. It's enough to keep up with three children."

"This one's *different*," said Vesta knowingly. "And he's crazy about her too." She paused, watching for Caldonia's reaction. "Now I don't want to say something I shouldn't . . . Mother said don't upset you . . ."

"Then don't," said Caldonia and rinsed her fingers off at the sink. From the basement family room came a whoop and a shout from Fred.

"Well," Vesta went on, "I haven't seen him like this with anybody for a while. She spends the night four, five times a week."

"What? With you and the kids there?"

Vesta nodded and swiped another olive.

"She's pretty and polite. Mother thinks so too."

"Pretty and polite!" murmured Caldonia. "You and Mother."

Vesta seemed especially pleased with herself. "There's something you won't like about her, but I'll let you find out on your own." And she let out a ladylike belch and squished the diet soda can in her right fist.

To herself, Caldonia murmured, "Lord, Lord, Lord," and then, mercifully, the baby cried and she excused herself and went upstairs in search of her third child.

Clayton arrived shortly after one-thirty, sporting a new trim haircut and supporting Mother's stout crooked body against his skeletal frame. He reminded Caldonia of a marionette, arms and legs dangling off the sides of his body as if held on by wires. Nervous energy seemed to eat up any pounds that might have settled onto his frail frame.

Once Caldonia had asked Mother about Clayton's puniness and his high voice, worried that Clayton was being denied entry to manhood, but Mother cut her short and asked her what on earth had gotten into her? What could she possibly mean bringing up something like that, was she trying to say her baby brother was *gay?* Mother's eyes had hardened like marbles. No, that wasn't what Caldonia had meant at all, she'd only said he was "frail," but by then it was too late because Mother'd already interpreted, in the narrowest terms available, what Caldonia meant about Mother's favorite child. "He's a good son.

He finished college. He's done well for himself and he does well by me. Don't you talk about your brother that way."

Clayton kissed Caldonia on the cheek, and now he was kissing Vesta too. "Let's see, it's been an hour since I've seen *you*," he teased.

"Ha ha ha," murmured Vesta, unaware her wig had slid an inch off her forehead and a portion of her mashed-down real hair was exposed. "You're still pissed off at the kids about that cold cereal, I know you."

Mother shot them both a look and said she needed to sit down right away, she wasn't feeling right. They found her a comfortable spot on the new sectional sofa in front of the living room television where she announced, "Now, I don't want to look at no football." Clayton crouched on the floor and began to search the channels. A quick perusal through the networks produced mostly oversized men tumbling around in helmets.

"How about a parade?" Clayton suggested.

"Don't want to see a parade either. Just find something pleasant for me to look at and turn down the sound."

Clayton settled on a PBS travelogue of pubs in Ireland and got Mother adjusted. Caldonia brought out glasses of juice for them both.

"Oh, goodness, you know I can't digest all that acid," said Mother.

Caldonia took the glass back to the sink and added water. There was just the slightest edge to her voice as she said, "Vesta, take this back out to Mother, please, and tell her it's good for her. Just a little cranberry juice and some mineral water."

Clayton hovered in the kitchen doorway, glass in hand. His eyes burst like raisins from his light-brown face.

"Jill call yet?" he asked in a voice meant to sound matter-of-fact, but which came out overeager and tinged with plaintiveness. He had a nervous habit of rocking on his heels, then rising onto his toes as if in preparation for ascension.

"No, nobody's called," said Caldonia primly, wiping her hands on a kitchen towel.

Vesta let out a shriek. "Ooooh, honey, and I called her Jane. Shoot, you know me, I'm just bad with names. Guess I been so nervous I'd call her Evelyn, I just don't call her by a name at all."

Clayton's complexion went gray for a moment. He leaned back hard onto his heels, suddenly grounded.

"Vesta, you are something else, bringing up Evelyn like that!" snapped Caldonia.

Evelyn had been Clayton's fiancée the year before. A beauty queen, Miss Black Something or Other, standing over six feet tall, with legs like a giraffe's, and eyes that had seen just a little too much of life for Caldonia's tastes. Evelyn Gilroy: the color of dark butterscotch, with flawless skin and a set of thick eyelashes that swept across her cheeks, blinking like a doll each time anyone asked her something. "I believe so," she'd say if something were true, or "I believe not," if it weren't. And she'd cold-shouldered Clayton's family, let them know they weren't really good enough.

But Clayton hadn't seen it coming, he never did. Evelyn kept him tied up in a knot so tight he wouldn't eat and he lost weight and took to having migraines. Like a fool he went ahead and spent all his money on the diamond ring he placed on her finger. He saw engagement, a lifetime of long, brown Evelyn, his forever; Evelyn saw only an expensive diamond. She had the gold melted down after the breakup and put the diamond in a pendant.

Caldonia had kept her mouth shut. "Six things the Lord hates . . . a false witness telling a pack of lies, and one who stirs up quarrels between brothers." She tried not to say anything bad about anybody.

Clayton looked at his watch. "Almost two o'clock. I better try calling Jill again."

"Turkey's about ready," said Caldonia. "And what did *you* bring for dinner, Mr. Clayton?"

Clayton's eyes shot over to Vesta. "Didn't Vesta bring my salad?"

Caldonia turned, hand on hip, eyebrows arched. "Well then, what did Miss Vesta bring?"

"Oh, shoot," Vesta moaned, without shame. "I thought the salad was from all of us. I mean, we live in one place, me and Clayton and the kids . . ."

"But there are four people living there," Caldonia pointed out, "and that means four big appetites."

"I'm sorry. I've got so much on my mind," sighed Vesta. "Harold called this morning wanting to know what me and the kids were doing today. He's wanting to come back . . ."

"I don't want to hear it," said Caldonia.

Fred was cheering again from the family room. Caldonia cast her eyes ceilingward. "Now watch, the baby'll start crying any second."

"I'll get her!" said Clayton. "You named her yet?"

As predicted, the thin high siren of Caldonia's newest addition scored the air. "Oh, shoot," said Caldonia. "I knew this would happen. Vesta, would you set the table, please?"

From the living room Mother's voice rasped out, "The baby's crying. Aren't we going to eat sometime today?"

Then the children surged through the back door, all four of them, Iris announcing that she and Nadia were back and that Rosie had yanked the barrettes from her braids, L'il Harold was spitting on ants, and what was Caldonia going to do about it?

Upstairs, Caldonia found relief from all of their demands, lifting the fussing child from the little crib. The blue watery eyes were squeezed into slits. The doctor had said sensitivity to light might lead to blindness. Keep her out of direct sunlight, protect her eyes and skin. He sounded like he was speaking of a household plant, to be tended in the dark. Caldonia held her until the cries turned to soft whimpers.

"There, there, sweetheart," she murmured. She carried the child down the back steps, avoiding the rest of the family, to where Fred sat on the edge of the family room sofa. She handed the baby to him. "There's my little girl," he said joyfully. His long-limbed dark body dwarfed the pale doll beside him. "There's my little sweetheart."

"Everyone's here," said Caldonia.

"Shoooooo, my little baby," he cooed into the child's ear and lay her against his thick, dark chest. "My little Angela, my little Monica, my little Bo-Peep."

Caldonia started out the door, then turned and paused a moment. She was trying to make sense out of Fred's long arms and the tiny wriggling shrimplike creature now being caressed, ever so gently, by his capable black hands.

I wonder, thought Caldonia, if I'll ever love her enough. It was an ugly secret thought, one that haunted her with all its awful possibilities.

Three o'clock, and Mother snored on the sofa. The turkey sat browned but untouched in its pan on top of the stove. The salad continued to wilt in the refrigerator.

The table, arrayed with Caldonia's wedding china, held an air of empty expectation. The kids were snacking on peanut butter and arguing over Chutes and Ladders on the dining room floor.

"I really think we should go ahead with dinner," Fred finally said, "meaning no offense to your lady friend, Clayton, but I don't want to hold things up any longer."

Caldonia saw her brother's face fall. "Maybe just a half hour more," she said sympathetically. "You sure she's got our number and the directions?"

Clayton nodded. He sat hunched on a hassock in the living room, clasping and unclasping his hands, looking himself like a scolded child. The phone rang. Both Vesta and Clayton practically leaped from their seats, but it was only a friend of Fred's from the police force.

The baby's tiny bright pink face nestled itself against Caldonia's bosom. She squeezed the nameless child to her. The funny little face called to mind a newborn kitten's. Caldonia knew the family was talking behind her back. Even Fred was running out of patience. She kept waiting for the name to announce itself, the way Iris's and Nadia's names had.

By four o'clock everyone was so bad-humored that Clayton finally gave in and agreed they should eat, but his voice was tight and hollow when he spoke. "Something must have happened to her," he said. "I really wanted us all to eat together."

Fred rounded up the kids. The girls danced their way to the table; the adults settled themselves around somewhat grimly. There was a scraping of chairs and the usual compliments about how good everything looked.

"I don't know *why* we had to wait so long," complained Mother. She surveyed the table with a critical eye. She focused in on Vesta, who was now holding the baby. "Oh, there's my sweet little grandbaby." She looked the child up and down. "When are they going to find you a name, hmmmmm? You've got to have a name. Such a shame, poor little thing!"

"I think my cousin's so pretty," said Rosie. "Pretty cousin!"

"My sister's going to be blonde!" Iris explained. "There's a girl at my school with really blonde hair." She added exploratorily, "The girl is white."

"Child needs a name," murmured Mother into her plate. "It's been a month now." She looked up hard at Fred. "I thought you were going to call her after your aunt."

"Iris, eat your food, Iris," said Fred warningly to his daughter. Mother maintained her sharp stare.

The doorbell rang. Almost a quarter to five. Clayton leaped up and disappeared into the hallway. Fred caught Caldonia's eye and winked as if to say everything was all right, she should ignore Mother, ignore them all. Caldonia could hear a woman's voice, hushed, then Clayton's, apologetic.

A moment later Clayton reentered the dining room with false cheer. "Hey, hey, hey!" he announced. "Everyone, can I have your attention? I'd like you all to meet someone. This is Jill."

At first Caldonia couldn't see much more than a pair of brown boots and a long black coat, but when the woman stepped from the shadows she was startled by the fine, straight hair the color of corn silk and skin the color of eggwhite.

Caldonia immediately looked at Mother for an explanation, but Mother was placidly spooning more oyster dressing into her mouth.

"You know Vesta and my mother," said Clayton, "and this is my sister Caldonia and her husband Fred."

"Hi, Jill," called Vesta cheerfully, then turned to Caldonia with a sly smile. She was enjoying this moment thoroughly. "Isn't she pretty? I *told* you she was so pretty," she observed for Jill's benefit.

Caldonia sat stunned. She felt betrayal, from Clayton, from Vesta, but most of all from Mother, who went right on eating. Vesta's ignorance could almost be excused; the girl was color struck, thought all white women were pretty, had been that way since she was a child. When she watched old black-and-white movies, she was always sighing over old pale-white, dead actresses.

Fred got up from the table and took Jill's coat. Clayton pulled out the empty chair at the end of the table for her, and Jill set about squeezing herself in between Nadia and Iris.

Still, Caldonia hadn't said a word.

"Let her see the baby!" cried Vesta. "Show Jill the baby!"

"Let her get settled first," Caldonia murmured. "She doesn't need to be bothered with the baby." She felt suddenly proprietary toward her child.

But Vesta was on a roll. "Ask Jill what she thinks about the baby."

Anger rose in Caldonia. "I don't need to ask Jill anything" was what came out of her mouth, and Mother's head shot up with the speed of a bullet.

Vesta didn't seem to care. "Now that I think about it," she grinned, "that could be Jill's baby."

Clayton was trying to change the subject, but Jill interrupted. Her voice, when she spoke, had the sharp bell-like sound of so many white women. "Clayton tells me you just had a baby. Congratulations."

"Thank you," said Caldonia, surprised by her own relief.

Vesta wouldn't let up. "Jill, look at this pretty child my sister has. She's got your coloring."

Clayton went to work fixing Jill a plate. "Turkey? Cranberry sauce? Gravy?" He went down the list with an eagerness that filled Caldonia with loathing. Jill murmured, "Clayton, not so much, you know I've already eaten."

Already eaten! Caldonia thought. Well, knock me over with

a feather. *Already eaten!* This, while everyone had waited so patiently, the kids getting fussier and hungrier. As if in sympathy, the baby on Caldonia's lap let out a long wail.

"Mama!" cried Iris and Nadia simultaneously. "The baby's crying." It felt like an accusation.

"Bring the poor little thing over to me," said Mother. "Let me hold her."

Caldonia snapped back, "Not now, she needs to be fed."

The baby began to howl full force. It was as if all the tension in the room had settled over her and drawn her little face up into tight red fury.

Jill asked Clayton to please sit down and not worry over her. Caldonia had a sudden, unexpected image of Jill emerging from her brother's bedroom and traipsing into the bathroom, dressed only in her panties and bra, in front of the children. Caldonia alternated between fury with Clayton and fury with the girl.

Fred turned to Caldonia. "Honey, want me to take the baby downstairs with me?"

"I'll keep her," said Caldonia. She got up from the table.

"Isn't she just the prettiest little thing?" Vesta prodded Jill. "I think she's so *cute*."

"She's sweet," Jill agreed, but she was staring hopelessly at the mounds of turkey and dressing Clayton had heaped on her plate.

"I told you the baby was cute, didn't I?" said Clayton, as if to leave no doubt as to what he might have said about the child. Then for Jill's benefit he launched into his version of how he'd been the one to get Caldonia to the hospital just in time.

"Don't be tellin' her that," said Mother, biting into a turkey wing. "Your sister was in labor for almost eighteen hours before that Chinese lady did something about it."

"MO-ther," warned Caldonia.

Jill tentatively reached out one pale hand and touched the baby's blanched skin. "I don't get to see newborns very often," she said.

"Let her hold the baby," insisted Vesta. Her eyes had gone round and bright. Without explanation, the baby stopped crying.

"Jill's eating," said Caldonia, pulling the baby back against her body. "The baby's too fussy."

"No, it's okay," said Jill. She was working hard at being polite.

Now Clayton was urging. "Come on, Caldonia, let Jill hold the baby."

Caldonia could see she had no choice without offending everyone. She leaned down and handed the baby to Jill. Jill gathered the child against her and rocked gently from side to side. "Mmmmm, she's so little."

Caldonia arranged the loose-knit blanket under the baby's body.

"Look at Jill holding the baby," commented Mother, her turkey leg held up in one hand. "Isn't that something?"

"The baby could be hers," said Vesta.

Caldonia caught Fred's eye and she saw a warning there.

"They sure look a lot alike," Mother went on, hope in her voice. She leaned across the table and studied first the baby's face, then Jill's. "They got that same pretty complexion, don't you think so, Clayton? What do you think, Jill? Is that a pretty baby to you?"

Jill was trying to be polite for them all. "What's her name?" she asked. A moment of silence followed.

"She doesn't have one," Mother said bitterly. "It's been a month now and Caldonia can't decide what to call her."

The heat rose in Caldonia's face. She snapped back, "The baby's albino," as if that answered anything. She meant the word to sound bold, even cruel, despite the fact the Lord would be shaking His head at her.

Clayton jumped in. "What Sis means is that she's not sure if the baby's eyes will have sensitivity to light . . ."

"That's not what I meant at all," Caldonia said matter-of-factly. "I mean what I said, I'm upset my baby is white."

It was the first time she'd actually said it. Not to Fred, not even to herself. But now it seemed necessary. And truthful.

The room grew very still. Fred cleared his throat. Mother murmured, "Hmmmmm mmmmmm!" disapprovingly under her breath. The children eyeballed one another with keen interest. But Jill didn't seem to mind. She looked straight back in Caldonia's face. "Isn't the albino trait inherited?" she asked.

Caldonia nodded. "It's from Fred's side."

"I still think she's pretty," defended Vesta. "Maybe she'll grow up and look like Jill."

"Being albino," said Caldonia, "is different from being . . ." She paused. She saw no point in offending Jill further. "A blonde nappy head just isn't pretty," Caldonia heard herself saying. "That's called funny looking."

Everyone laughed uneasily except Mother, who pursed her lips and murmured, "Y'all some wrong folks!"

Caldonia bent down and retrieved the baby from Jill. "I'm afraid she'll spit up all over you," she said with false concern.

"Maybe everybody'll think the baby's mulatto," said Vesta, her mouth full of stuffing. "That's what they call a white and black mix. You know, like you and Clayton." She used her fork to gesture toward Jill, as if joining her with Clayton in midair.

"Clayton and Jill are not mulatto," Caldonia said stonily. She felt her anger giving her direction. "Clayton is black and

Jill is white. Mulatto would be what they'd have if they had a child, Vesta. It's not the same thing."

"Hold on there, don't rush us now," said Clayton, but he said it only for Jill's sake. His smile had broadened, his eyes brightened. Caldonia could see he rather liked the idea of having a child with Jill. And she could see by Jill's tense but civil expression that this would never happen.

"I don't mean nothin'," said Vesta cheerfully. She grinned at Jill. "You know me, I'm just over here runnin' my mouth like I usually do. My best friend in grade school was white. 'Member her, Caldonia? Patty What's-her-face, that big old fat girl, pretty face though."

The baby began to fuss in Caldonia's arms. Quickly her bad humor escalated to rage and her face turned the color of Pepto-Bismol.

Caldonia excused herself.

"Feed the baby here," Clayton called after her.

But the truth was, Caldonia didn't want to nurse her baby near a stranger. She pulled shut the louvered doors that separated the kitchen and dining room. She sat down in one of the vinyl-backed kitchen chairs and arranged the baby's pink mouth at her brown breast.

The louvered doors opened ever so slightly and Fred squeezed through. If he was annoyed with Caldonia, he didn't show it. Instead, he bent down and kissed the nursing baby. "You know I love you," he whispered in her tiny shell-pink ear, "even if your mama's actin' crazy."

Caldonia had to smile in spite of herself. She hummed softly to the pink and yellow child. When Fred went out again, she caught a glimpse of Clayton's slender brown fingers caressing Jill's pale arm, and then the stiffening of that arm as Jill carefully and surreptitiously moved just out of reach. It was a simple gesture, designed not to embarrass Clayton in front of his family.

Caldonia looked down at her youngest daughter. She didn't know which was worse, going through life toward blindness or going through life white. In a way, it was kind of the same thing. How was her daughter going to feel, this little pale stalk in a dark field?

Iris and Nadia let themselves through the louvered door into the kitchen.

"Close the door!" Caldonia hissed.

"Mama, we love our sister," said Iris pointedly.

"Well, of course you do!" Caldonia hadn't meant to give the girls a wrong impression.

"We could put her in the sun," suggested Nadia helpfully. "She could get a tan and be like us."

The two girls ran their hands over the baby's little pink ones and cooed at her.

"She is like us," Caldonia corrected. "She *is* 'us.' "

"Excuse me . . ."

Caldonia's head shot up. The voice was clear and precise. It was Jill, first poking her head through the kitchen door and now standing in the doorway, small and white, not much taller than Nadia and Iris. Caldonia quickly covered her breast.

"I want to thank you for having me," Jill said softly. "And I'm sorry about all the inconvenience and the mix-up."

For a moment, before she was able to line up her thoughts, Caldonia actually thought the girl was apologizing for the absence of the baby's color. "The mix-up?" she said vaguely. She reached for the right words. "Clayton's friends are always welcome," she said. "Come back any time."

"I will." The girl smiled, and Caldonia knew they both were thinking how this would not happen. "Thank you," said the girl, relieved and forgiven, as if Caldonia had it in her power to do that.

That night, when the dishes had been washed and the kitchen swept, and the children put to bed, Caldonia asked Fred tentatively, "I've been thinking, do you think it would be foolish to name the baby Ebony?"

Fred burst out laughing. "Girl, what are you talking about?"

"I want to give my child a *real* name," said Caldonia.

"That's real all right," he chuckled. "What is wrong with you, Caldonia? You can't *make* her black, you know. Naming her Ebony would be as bad as naming a dark child Pearl, or Magnolia. We should call her Angela, after my grandmother."

"I just want her to know . . ." Caldonia began. "I just want her to feel . . ."

Fred looked at her long and hard. "She *is,* Caldonia" was all he said before he went upstairs and turned on the news.

Caldonia stood next to the sink under the framed "God Bless This Mess" sampler Mother had made for her last Christmas. God, she thought wistfully, in His infinite wisdom has given me this child without a name. She wasn't blaming God; she wasn't blaming anyone but herself for the pinch in her heart that prevented her from running right upstairs and calling the child by her rightful name.

WHAT JASMINE
WOULD THINK

It was months before King was assassinated. It was the fall after the Detroit riots. Jasmine Bonner cornered me in the corridor at school. She came straight to the point. "You have study hall with Lamar Holiday, right?"

Lamar, Lamar, of course Lamar. Tree-tall, dark chocolate, with a three-inch natural and a wide, sloppy grin that could change your life. He wore black and green Ban-Lon shirts and a small gold medallion of Africa around his neck. He sat two chairs over from me and took copious notes from his civics book in small, curved handwriting.

"Everyone knows Lamar and I are 'talking,' but I think he's creepin' on me."

It felt like an accusation. "Lamar?" I was breathless, all legs and arms and curly unkempt hair.

Jasmine glanced behind herself briefly. "Yeah, with this little half-and-half Oreo, Jeanie somebody. She's been trying to beat my time. All I'm asking you to do is keep your eyes open. Let me know what they do in study hall. You know, anything *suspicious*."

I nodded vigorously. Talking to Jasmine in the hallway of our school was a promotion of sorts. Students passing by took notice, and I stood straighter.

"Cool," said Jasmine, closing the deal, and she smiled.

After that, I went on red alert. Lamar didn't know it, but

130

we were now connected. Jeanie Lyons, the girl in question, sat by the window. She was high-yellow, with curly sandy hair and sea-blue eyes, but a flat, broad nose that gave her away. Not that she was trying to pass; everyone knew her father, our postman, black as the ace of spades.

I watched. Lamar didn't even pass her en route to the back table next to me where he and his friends congregated. And Jeanie, too sallow and freckled to be pretty, sat engrossed in *Valley of the Dolls*, and licking her long slender thumb carefully before each turn of the page.

Then, early one Saturday morning, on my way to a piano lesson, I spotted Lamar's white '63 Chevy convertible whistling down Route 10. No question that it was Jeanie crunched against him shamelessly, her sandy curls pasted by the wind against his dark chin.

I ran myself into a sweat getting home, where I dug in my schoolbag for Jasmine's phone number. My heart was in my throat when I dialed.

Jasmine's mother answered, sharply. "Who's calling, please?"

"Tish . . . Tish from French class."

"Tish?" Pause. "Just a moment."

The receiver clanked against something Formica-hard.

Time inched along. Nervously I chewed my thumbnail. Finally Jasmine picked up the receiver and spoke while crunching potato chips. "Uh-huh?" Her voice sprawled long and lanky on the other end. I pictured her spread out on a sofa inside her house on the other side of Main Street, large silver hoops dangling from under her halo of hair. Jasmine was one of the first girls at school to wear an afro and risk suspension.

"It's me, Tish." Conspiratorial. Hard as nails.

"Mmmmmmmmmm."

I threw out the bait. "I saw Lamar today."

"Ummmm-huh? Where?"

A woman's voice snapped in the background, and Jasmine said, "All right, all right." Into the phone she whispered, "I'm on punishment, talk fast."

This forced me to the point. Did she remember what she'd asked? Mmmmmmm-hmmmmm. Well, I'd seen Lamar's car. Oh, yeah? Yeah, and Jeanie Lyons was in it. What did I mean in it? *In* it. You know, close to Lamar. How close? Close. Just close or very close? Very close. It got so quiet on the other end you could have heard a rat pee on cotton.

At last Jasmine said, "I knew his black ass was up to no good," and hung up.

That was it? I turned around and dialed my best friend Angela. Rarely did I have anything newsworthy to say; mostly it was Angela pasting together the meager details of her overlapping romances with the squarest boys in our freshman class. I acted casual, introducing Jasmine's name with the smoothest inflection. I repeated the whole conversation, word for word, without one interruption from Angela. A long silence followed on the other end.

"I didn't realize," she said cooly, "that you were currently friends with Jasmine Bonner. I know for a fact that she's two-faced and uses people."

"Maybe *some* people," I shot back.

"Sounds to me," said Angela sullenly, "like Jasmine isn't interested in you at all, she just wants information on Lamar. Besides, she doesn't like white girls, you better be careful."

"What do you mean, 'careful'?" I kept my cool.

"You'll find out," retorted Angela in that knowing way she had when she didn't know anything at all. "You don't understand you and Jasmine can never be *real* friends."

In our town, Angela and I both trod a thin line. Angela lived on the right side of town to be friends with Jasmine, but she still straightened her hair and worried about it napping up in the rain, and secretly thought the Revolution was just mumbo jumbo. Her mother wouldn't allow her to go dancing at the Boot Center where all the other black kids went. In all fairness to Angela, she'd been stuck with me as a best friend since grade school, old goody two-shoes Angela, who could least afford it.

Contrary to Angela's prediction (and much to her annoyance), Jasmine passed me a note, folded into a triangle, in French class the next day. "Just wanted to say HIGH," she wrote. Tuesday, another note followed. Jasmine Bonner had invited me to sleep over. As if it were the most natural thing in the world, Jasmine and me, matching the rhythms of our lives, as if she weren't two grades ahead, as if I were an equal. Jasmine of the rainbow fishnet hose and matching sweaters and pleated skirts, who sauntered the halls with queenly grace. She must have owned twenty pairs of pointed-toe shoes, purple, orange, lime, with fishing-line thin laces. Jasmine who with bold nonchalance popped a piece of Wrigley's Spearmint and calmly picked out her giant afro with a cheesecutter in the middle of French class while conjugating the present subjunctive of *etre*.

I couldn't stuff my pajamas into a paper bag fast enough. It was a cool autumn night. My mother dubiously drove me south across the tracks, down through the park on Spring Street, past Angela's ranch house. She asked me what I really knew about Jasmine's family. Were her parents responsible people? Did Jasmine have a boyfriend?

"Jasmine makes good grades," I said, as if that proved anything. "She's always on the honor roll."

"And what about Angela?" asked my mother. She seemed to imply I could only have one friend at a time. "I haven't seen her around the house much lately."

I didn't dare condemn cautious, fraidy-cat Angela, carefully mincing her words at our supper table, easing my father's troubled conscience by her very presence. Angela, the Good Negro, agreeable and self-effacing.

When we got to Jasmine's I jumped out of the car, but my mother didn't drive off right away. I saw her hesitate, taking in the unfamiliarity of this end of the street, peering into windows darkened by early twilight, as if searching for a clue as to where exactly I was going.

Just before Christmas, Jasmine and I stretched ourselves across her unmade mattress inside the Bonners' gray shingle house at the bottom of Washington Street. As usual, the house was a pungent medley of frying fatback and greens and her younger sister Camille's hot-combed hair. Overhead, fine Huey Newton, framed inside his wicker fan chair, observed us skeptically. Jasmine rolled over on her stomach and came up on her elbows. I was envious of her perfectly round buttocks, slim hips, and long dark legs.

She studied me carefully, plucking wrinkles in her top sheet with long, slender fingers.

"I think Lamar's messing around with this white girl, Tish." Her tone was sepulchral. My flesh crawled. "She lives out on Gore Orphanage Road—in a farmhouse in a cornfield. Cindy something—Pavelka."

"You mean the one who hangs around Wanda and them and acts black?"

Jasmine nodded. "Little no-nothing triflin' tramp. She's got legs like bowling pins, girl. And she's been with just about every brother in town. They say she had an abortion last year."

"Why do you go on with Lamar?" I asked.

Jasmine studied me almost pityingly. Her eyebrows arched with older-girl wisdom, and then it dawned on me what she would never admit: that she and Lamar were connected sexually in some mysterious way only hinted at in the Motown 45's I knew by heart. I loved those melodies, the innocent lyrics shaded lightly with innuendo. Pure poetry and simple rhythms inciting the ache of fantasy. Without a word, Jasmine handed me Miles Davis for the turntable. We both lay back on her bed and listened somberly until twilight fell. That's how I passed my winter that year, vicariously learning the sting of passion without trust, a ragged wound torn open by Miles's horn.

There were evenings we'd drive around town with a stop at Dairy Queen for ice cream, with Jasmine peering through sleet-filled twilights in search of Lamar's Chevy. "He said he'd be at work," she'd say, "and he better be." A quick trip past Fisher-Fazio's parking lot proved he was: the pristine Chevy sparkled there like a diamond on the frozen blacktop. Jasmine's face would relax.

And sometimes, as Jasmine fussed at Lamar on the phone, twisting the cord with her fingers, I'd patiently feign interest in magazines, trying to pretend I couldn't hear the soft inflections of her voice, or understand their implications.

Evenings she wasn't off with Lamar, we listened to Miles or Coltrane ("traditional," Jasmine called it—she got the albums from her older sister Bekka, a student at NYU) and sneaked drags off the Kool Longs she stashed in her earring box ("Blow it out the window!" she'd hiss, fanning at the air around my face).

Sometimes she'd read me Sonia Sanchez or Baraka. As twilight moved to darkness, neither of us made a move for the light switch. Instead, we sank into silhouettes of ourselves, dark and indistinguishable shapes, consumed by words. We'd talk about who really killed Malcolm, and the importance of black economic power for self-determination and why the terms "Negro" and "colored" were passé, until Mrs. Bonner hollered through the curtain that hung instead of a door that it was two in the morning and we better shut that damn music off and let reasonable people get some sleep.

After Jasmine dozed off, I would lie awake, made nervous by the touch of her foot against my calf, wondering what on earth she could have ever seen in me, and promising myself to never disappoint her.

One afternoon after school a bunch of us drove to a frozen Lake Erie in Jasmine's father's black Ninety-eight to smoke and talk smack and look for someone named Peppy from Lorain who never materialized. Every time I spoke up, two of the girls exchanged glances and snickered. One of them pointedly stated she was sick of looking at peckerwoods every which way she turned.

Jasmine relished controversy. She seemed amused. "You talkin' about Tish? You don't know Tish," she snapped. "I got cousins in New Orleans lighter than her. Least she's got some wave in her hair. She *could* pass, you know that?" She reached over the back seat and ran her hand through my curls as proof. "See what I mean? Look at her mouth. Now try to tell me those are typical white lips."

I felt proud then, as proud as if I'd been black as ink. In grade school, stuck-up white girls like Kimberly Hubbard and Marjorie Grosvenor had called my mouth "bacon fat." Now Jasmine praised it. A full mouth was beautiful, couldn't be pursed like Kimberly's and Marjorie's into thin lines of superiority.

I began to sense I was someone other than the person I'd always been told I was. Over and over, the girl Jasmine saw inside me was being revealed.

But it all started long before when I came to understand that our town was really two. In one of Angela's more generous moments she had assured me, as if to assure herself, that I was really meant to be black, and she'd stuck her arm through mine and marched staunchly through the football stadium bleachers with me in front of everyone. Later, behind those same bleachers, she and three other girls jokingly christened me an "Honorary Negro." They each touched me and spoke words over my head, and I responded with "I do," to unite us forever. We were earnest, treating my whiteness like some cosmic prank that could be easily corrected. Then there were wisecracks about a fly in the buttermilk, which left us doubled over laughing. But deep inside I believed, and when you believe, the world shapes itself accordingly. Like the baptized, I saw through the eyes of the reborn.

On our way back from the lake Jasmine remarked, "You know, I take a lot of flack for hanging out with you."

"Then why do you do it?" I asked.

"Because," she grinned, smacking my arm, "you're different."

So I told her about my Honorary Negrohood and she fell out laughing so hard I thought she'd rear-end the car in front.

My family didn't grasp the incongruity of my presence in their lives. Instead they seemed to be blaming me for being other than what they expected. Sometimes I stared back at their puzzled faces, as we were seated around the dinner table, and saw only winter-pale strangers wearing masks of disapproval. The way my mother would turn to me sometimes and say, "Letitia, what on earth are you trying to prove?" pained me so much that I prayed they'd admit a terrible mistake had been made and confess to me who I really was. I was coming apart like a seam at the other end of a loose thread. I studied myself in the mirror, turning sideways, backwards, then facing myself again, trying to discern who it was that stared back at me. Not a person who belonged to these strangers. Just a person who knew the Revolution was inevitable. *By any means possible.*

"I don't know what you think you're doing," said my father, furious with me for announcing at the dinner table one evening that all whites would be dead by the end of summer. "I suppose this is what you call being 'cool'?"

The word slipped off his tongue like a mistake, and I cringed, secretly glad Jasmine couldn't hear the ignorance in his precise two-syllable inflection.

Keeping my eyes on my plate, I quoted Don H. Lee: ". . . after detroit, newark, chicago &c., we had to hip cool-cool/super-cool/real cool that to be black is to be very-hot."

My father threw his hands up in disgust. "You see?" he said, appealing to my mother. "This is what happens when our liberal chickens come home to roost."

My mother shot me a baleful look. "I think it's Jasmine's influence," she said flatly. "I like Jasmine, but she's giving Tish wild ideas. We never heard this kind of talk when Angela was around."

My father muttered bitterly, "There hasn't been a white face in this house for over a year!"

Pain left me speechless. The countenances around me stared in silent accusation. What they couldn't know was that an unseen hand had reached inside and rearranged my whole genetic makeup, creating a freak of nature simply called Tish. Either side I chose I would lose myself. And living in the middle required becoming two people, split, like the baby Solomon threatened to cut in half. So I stared into my dinner plate until the Currier and Ives pattern of sleigh and horse melted into a swirl of icy blue and I was sucked into a storm of color so violent that I mistook it for redemption.

In June I, not Angela, was invited to Jasmine's seventeenth birthday party. My mother was dubious. Would adults be present? Would the lights be on? Would I leave a phone number?

It was a typical basement affair at Cintrilla Robinson's, with red and blue strobe lights blinking from the ceiling and a bowl of fruit juice punch spiked around eleven with Johnny Walker Red by some brothers from Lorain wearing three-quarter-length black leather coats and smelling of Old Spice. I slow-danced at least three times with Lamar's best friend Tyrone to seven scratchy minutes of the Dells' "Stay in My Corner." Tyrone sang into my ear in a precise, sweet falsetto and pressed me close against a hard place on his thigh.

He murmured approvingly, "Mmmm, you can keep a beat."

Jasmine and Lamar made out shamelessly in the corner by the record player. From time to time their two silhouettes, topped by halos of thick hair, seemed to merge into one. Someone teased: "Y'all need to take that stuff to the bedroom!"

Awkward, I walked outside into a warm, starry night, holding my paper cup of spiked punch. Cintrilla and some senior girls I recognized from school stood talking on the patio. Cautiously, I joined them under the paper lanterns.

Tyrone followed right behind, but kept his distance. I watched him from the corner of my eye, pacing in the shadows, his hands shoved into the pockets of his St. Joe's letter jacket. He kept looking at the sky as if he'd lost something, but neither of us said anything.

Cintrilla smiled at me with surprise. "Aren't you in my French class?"

I tried to look as grown-up as I could in my flowered culottes and lime green shell. My eyes were so deeply outlined in Jasmine's mascara they felt brown and ancient as the Nile. "Mmmmm hmmmmmm," I said.

"You come with Jasmine and Lamar tonight?" Ruby Mason

inquired in a friendly way. I nodded. It made an impression. The girls studied me with mild curiosity. When they asked questions, I found myself answering in a voice that could have been Jasmine's.

"Tyrone digs you," remarked Jasmine ever so coolly on the way back to her house. We rode in the back seat of her father's black Ninety-eight. She was trying to pull the collar of her blouse around her neck to hide the love bites.

I was so flattered I felt sick. "Yeah," I said, trying not to care.

"You know he's Lamar's ace boon coon. Lamar told Tyrone you're cool—for a white chick." She jabbed me with her elbow. I looked out the window at the small dark houses rolling by. "Lamar and I are back together for good this time," said Jasmine. "He gave me this opal ring." She thrust her left hand out to show me, and I saw a flash of milky white under the streetlight we'd just passed.

I understood then her sudden burst of generosity about Tyrone. Ring planted firmly on her finger, she gave me a conspiratorial wink. Tonight she could afford to share.

Call it guilt or mild yearning, the next day I made my way over to Angela's. She asked about the party in a deliberately offhand way. I described Tyrone. I made sure she understood this was a man with potential. For one thing, he was a senior, almost eighteen, and he attended *private* school. I described his hands moving over my back as we danced and the softness of his lips against my ear.

Angela dramatically threw her finger against her lips and hissed, "Shshshsh!" as if I had cursed in church. She rolled her eyes in the direction of her mother's bedroom.

"Your mother can't hear," I said, feeling myself rise tall above

Angela. I was becoming less and less grateful for the friendship she bestowed on me in stingy little segments.

"You're getting in with a rough crowd" was all Angela said. "Mama says Jasmine's fast."

What she really meant was that she hadn't been included, but I didn't see that then. Disgusted, I got up and left. Angela didn't bother to walk me to the end of her driveway as she always did. Outside, the heat worked its way up from the pavement and burned through the soles of my sandals. They were sandals Angela and I had found in the College Shoe Shoppe two years before. We'd each bought a pair, agreeing we wouldn't wear them without telling the other. Now mine were showing the effects of two summers' wear, and Angela had shoved hers to the back of the closet, forgotten.

Angela's house on East Jefferson was an easy mile and a half from mine. By making a right on Lincoln, I passed Mt. Zion Baptist and a horse farm, and then a number of square brick low-income units where children rode bicycles in the street and front yard clotheslines were always full of bed sheets.

Just beyond was Jasmine's block; the houses were even smaller and poorer. The narrow streets, like many of their residents, were named for U.S. presidents. On the sagging steps of a turquoise house, some older black girls from school hung out playing 45's on an old phonograph. The humidity was cut by the scratchy rhythm of one of the summer's hottest hits, "Express Yourself" by Charles Watts and the 103rd Street Rhythm Band. Maxine Watson, the homecoming queen, danced in denim cut-offs in the dirt yard. When she saw me, she raised one light brown hand in greeting, and I thrilled at the acknowledgment.

But it was short-lived as a bright-skinned girl named Chick snapped, "What'd you speak to *her* for?" Chick had sat sullenly across from me one semester in ninth-grade algebra class giving everyone the evil eye. If she didn't feel like answering the teacher's questions on a particular day, she'd stage-whisper, "Kiss my black ass, bitch," so that the whole class would snicker. Now Chick was expecting a baby by her college tutor. Evil old Chick who lived ruthlessly on a higher plane than the rest of us, above fear of reproach.

I crossed Main Street, which divided our town exactly in half. The air sweltered. On Professor Street I passed the statue of Horace Percival Huckleman, honored posthumously for leading a troop of black soldiers during the Civil War. My parents lived up on tree-lined Elm Street, our house nestled among all the other professors' families. The yards here were midwestern-ample and the old three-story homes sat back from the streets in comfortable superiority. The gray summer air was still, silent, oppressive. Here, people kept to themselves. No noisy barbecues, no lawn parties, no children running and shrieking through sprinklers.

Up ahead two shimmering figures made their way slowly toward me: Kimberly Hubbard and Marjorie Grosvenor, in culottes and poor-boy tees. They were my two mortal enemies on the other side of the dividing wall. In reality, they lived on my street, but I might as well have been invisible, living a parallel life, unnoticed.

Kimberly and Marjorie could walk by you as if you were a leaf on the sidewalk, flipping their long straight hair with a casual flick of the wrist. They had a secret language of gestures and words that I had never been able to master. It was a language of privilege and confidence, designed to exclude.

At the beginning of ninth grade they took it upon themselves to corner me briefly by my locker. "So, Tish," Marjorie said, her teeth a flash of white in her summer-brown face. "We were just wondering, are you still going to hang around with Angela Winters now that you're in high school?"

I didn't understand, and my ignorance tested their patience. Marjorie gave Kimberly a significant look. "Angela's nice," she explained to me, "but you need to think about what's best for you now. We think you ought to know, and this as a friendly warning, that a lot of people think you're spreading yourself too thin."

Now, passing me, Marjorie and Kimberly fused together into one girl. "Hello, Letitia," their shared voice said, forced. I felt no compulsion to answer. Instead, I squared my shoulders, taking my courage from Jasmine. I never glanced their way, never even gave the impression of having noticed them, blowing them from my mind as easily as if they were chalk dust.

Jasmine tried to get me hired at the College Restaurant where she worked, telling Bud Owens, the black owner, that I was sixteen. But when I showed up he shook his head and shooed me out, telling me I was a chance he couldn't afford to take. I waited outside, humiliated, until Jasmine went on break and we wandered over to the college art museum, finding relief in the cool interior.

We sauntered by Del Washington, the black security guard standing awkwardly over to one side, sweating inside his uniform. Del was in his late sixties; for years he had done odd jobs for families in my neighborhood, and adults and kids alike called him by his first name. Now I felt ashamed to know him.

Jasmine couldn't stand him and went on to prove it. "Don't you think it's weird," she asked me in a voluble tone, "that white people hire black people to guard white people's art that they copied from black people?"

She pulled me over to a small Picasso. "Now there's one white man made a whole career off of imitating Africans."

Del pretended not to hear Jasmine's words echoing off the cool walls. We strolled back past him into the next gallery. "Some people are so damn worried what white people think of them. You know, don't you, you can't be a healthy black person and please white folks at the same time. It's a sickness, it's what makes black people go crazy, and then white folks can't figure out why niggas act like fools."

Jasmine's shoulder brushed roughly against mine, her eyes focused into empty space ahead. "We've been trying to please y'all for a long time, but now enough is enough. You watch and see what happens in Hough and every other ghetto this summer when they burn again. The Revolution is here."

To our left, Del was turning a deep purple.

"I'm going to have to ask you to lower your voices," he said, "or leave the museum."

"I was about to leave anyway," snapped Jasmine and grabbed my hand. "Come on, girl, I'm about to choke in here."

Outside, she threw back her head and laughed aloud.

"What's wrong with Del?" I asked, torn. Del used to give me chewing gum when he was cutting the neighbors' lawn.

"He's a Tom, that's what's wrong. That man has kissed so much white ass I'm surprised his face is still black."

I felt sad then, for all of us—me, Jasmine, and Del.

"That's the difference between us," remarked Jasmine. "You're over there feelin' sorry for Del Washington. Well, he hates himself for being black. He's the most dangerous of all."

The summer dragged for me. Jasmine was busy with work and her college applications. She was applying for early admissions

to Fisk, Howard, Morehouse, and Spelman. She laughed when
Harvard wrote to her and asked her to apply. "Why do I want
to be some place where they either flunk you out or bleach you
out? I'm not going to be part of someone's nigga quota."

We were on Jasmine's front porch watching the rain and I
was greasing her scalp. A streak of lightning startled us both.
Thunder followed right behind. "The Temptations in A Mellow
Mood" revolved on the turntable just inside the door.

A phone call had put Jasmine in a bitterly rotten mood. Some-
one had seen Lamar at Rocky's Roller Rink Monday night, and
Cindy Pavelka had left in his car. The old wound was reopened.
"Why can't white girls leave our men alone?" Jasmine fumed.

I yanked her head a little to the left and carefully separated
the next section of hair with the teeth of the comb. I kept
the parts even, creating little irrigation canals into which I
smoothed fingertips of Royal Crown. Jasmine's scalp gleamed
like hematite. I pulled the hair on either side of the part straight
up into rows, like stalks of corn. Cradling her head in my lap, I
used the comb rhythmically like a lullaby. Her shoulders rocked
gently against my knee.

"Tish, I'll be honest, I've never loved a man the way I love
Lamar, and he's breaking my damn heart!"

With her right hand she guided my comb to a spot I'd missed.
Little white flakes of dandruff lodged in the teeth of the comb.
"Come out with Chick and Benita and me tomorrow night." It
was more a command than an invitation.

"Where?"

"The Boot Center," said Jasmine.

I felt mildly panicked. "You know I can't go."

"Oh, come on. Say you're spending the night."

I must have hit a soft spot in her scalp because her head

pulled a U-turn. The specks of amber in her eyes caught fire. "Watch it, I'm tender-headed."

"Well, don't mess up my lines." I tried to yank her head back into position, but she pulled away.

There was a long pause, marked only by the whirring of the fan from inside and the drumbeat of rain on the porch roof overhead. She reached her hand up to her scalp and felt where I'd left off. "You take too damn long." She stood up and paced. On one side of her head, where I'd been at work, her hair stood up in thick fist-shaped spikes. "I don't see why your parents think the Boot Center is so bad, except that it's full of *us*, a bunch of black boots. I bet if Kimberly and Marjorie were down there dancing to 'Turkey in the Straw' your parents wouldn't be scared to send you."

I ran my fingers down the greasy prongs of the comb.

"I'll try to come," I said, "but if my mother finds out . . ."

Jasmine bit her lower lip. "I'm telling you, if Cindy's there, I'm through with him!"

I felt the tension rise, along with the humidity and the smell of Jasmine's scalp oil on my fingers.

There was the unexpected sound of tires on gravel, and we both looked out to the road to see Lamar's Chevy pulling into the rain-soaked driveway. "Shoot!" said Jasmine. "Nigga knows he's in trouble." She grabbed the comb from me and began furiously to work her hair. "Tyrone's with him!"

My heart went heavy as lead as two figures splashed through the rain and up the steps. Jasmine kept her lips poked out sulkily when Lamar said, "How ya doin', baby?" I'd forgotten how tall Tyrone was, how good-looking. The combination terrified me.

"Mama and Daddy are down at their social club?" Lamar asked with a grin. "Thought we'd stop by."

Jasmine nodded. "I need to talk to you, Lamar. We can go

listen to records in the basement. Tish, grab that stack of 45's, would you, girl?"

She picked up the record player. Tyrone and Lamar both smelled of cologne. I followed them down the steps like a sleepwalker. Immediately "Ooooh, Baby, Baby" was on the turntable and Jasmine and Lamar were linked together, murmuring to each other. Obviously Lamar was denying whatever it was Jasmine accused him of. Convincing. Smooth. Jasmine was loosening up.

Tyrone reached for me and I felt myself melting against him, as he guided me slowly toward the furnace. The record finished and Lamar started it over again. I heard Jasmine say, "You're gonna wear that record thin as a dime," and I felt the vibrations of Tyrone's chuckle in his chest as he pulled me closer while Smokey moaned.

My first kiss happened there in Jasmine's basement with Tyrone, but the experience was disagreeable. The smelly old sewer pipe ran straight out of the floor at our feet, and so that moment was permanently framed in my memory by a rising, heavy, sour odor too awful to consider. But I was in love with Tyrone, my heart about ready to explode.

Later, after they'd left, Jasmine, who seemed to be in better spirits, asked me, "Tyrone say he'd call?"

I shook my head, still overwhelmed that just moments before a boy's mouth had been pressing against mine.

Jasmine sighed. "What's wrong with the Negro? You're my ace honky."

I hated her holding the other mirror to me like that. "Shut up," I said.

A shadow crossed Jasmine's face. "Maybe Tyrone thinks your father will shoot him through the phone."

"I keep telling you," I protested, "my parents don't care."

"Don't be so naive about your so-called liberal parents."
Jasmine frowned.

"My parents marched in Selma," I said, uneasy.

"So, then why don't you ask Tyrone to come by and have
dinner? Get to know your folks?"

She was mocking me so I didn't answer. I didn't know why.

"See what I mean?" said Jasmine smugly.

Anxiety marked my veins like medical ink. "You're wrong,"
I insisted.

"I'm more right than you realize. Your parents would lose
their minds if they thought you'd gone cuckoo for cocoa puffs."
She lit a Kool Long and French-inhaled so that the smoke
looped back through her nostrils.

We went upstairs where she heated up the iron to press her
uniform for work. Overhead, on hangers, the dashikis we'd
sewn hung like half-people from the light fixture. Jasmine's was
black and yellow and red; mine was blue and white and green.

She mumbled to the wall, as if enjoying a private joke, "I
must be outa my mind making a dashiki for a white girl." She
winked at me as steam rose from the iron. "I'll have it ready
for tomorrow night. You're comin'."

Jasmine picked me up on her way home from work. She was
still in her waitress uniform. My mother walked me out to
the black Ninety-eight. She pointedly asked Jasmine if we were
going out anywhere or if she could reach me at the Bonners'.

"We might go get Dairy Queen." Jasmine was sly!

"About what time would that be?" asked my mother.

Jasmine looked coyly at her watch. "Oh, maybe around ten."

My mother's eyes narrowed. "Jasmine," she said with mater-
nal clairvoyance, "you know Letitia is barely fifteen years old."

"What are you trying to tell me?" asked Jasmine.

But my mother had turned abruptly and walked back toward the house.

At Jasmine's I changed into a short skirt and the dashiki. Now I was edgy as we drove past the Baptist church to pick up the others. I imagined coming face-to-face with my mother's car at every corner.

"Will you just relax?" said Jasmine. "I'm the one who should be nervous, what with Daddy being so fussy about his damn stupid car and all. One tiny scratch and I'm dead."

Mr. Bonner'd said if we weren't home by midnight he'd send the sheriff out after us.

"Your Ninety-eight ain't no Cinderella," Jasmine had muttered.

"Yeah, and you ain't meeting no Prince Charming neither," Mr. Bonner reminded her meaningfully. It was no secret he wasn't fond of Lamar, whom he called a "scalawag."

Jasmine was wearing blue jeans, her dashiki belted at the waist. On her long slender feet were slave sandals, the latest rage. I instantly regretted my short skirt, ashamed of my knobby knees. We split up a bunch of her metal bracelets, and crisscrossed our arms like gypsies.

Maxine and Jasmine made small talk up front. I envied their big afro silhouettes, blocking my view through the windshield. I was stuffed in back with Benita and sourpuss Chick. Benita commented sweetly on my hair. "You sure have some pretty curls. They natural?"

I thought how long I'd futilely envied the straight-arrow cuts of the white girls, every hair in place. Jasmine had picked out my hair, and now it bloomed around my head.

Chick scoffed from the corner by the window. "It just looks like some of that old flyaway shit to me."

As I leaned forward to check my eyeliner in the rearview mirror my leg accidentally brushed Chick's. She jumped back as if I had a disease. "Please keep your body parts to yourself," she said and crossed her eyes at me.

You could hear the Boot Center before you could see it. James Brown blared from speakers lodged in the open window frames upstairs. Shadows of dancers rose long against the walls.

"Ooooh, my song," said Chick and jumped out, full of baby, and headed up the stairs. "SAY IT LOUD!" she bellowed along with James Brown, "I'm black and I'm proud!"

Jasmine came up beside me and dug her fingernails into my arm. She hissed in my ear, "You better pray Lamar's at work tonight."

"Don't worry," I said, but I had serious doubts.

We tromped up the outside stairs, just as if we were a club. Girls accustomed to one another, who hung together. The music swelled from the packed dance floor. Across the room, through blinking lights, I recognized the black vice principal from our school, Mr. Foster, who'd been called down to chaperone after some fights between our town and Elyria. Everyone knew he Tommed. From what I'd seen, Mr. Foster faked it on both sides, playing "brother this" and "brother that" when it suited him.

The air was so close I immediately broke into a sweat. My head felt thick. Maxine yelled over at Jasmine, "See what happens when you get a bunch of niggas together?" She wiped drops of perspiration from her forehead with the back of her hand as proof.

Jasmine pulled me through the crowd like a needle dragging thread. We were headed toward Tyrone, standing alone in the corner. Jasmine thrust me at him in a way that made me suspect she had planned this all along. "Here's Tish," she said as if delivering a package.

James Brown over, Nancy Wilson began a lugubrious "You Better Face It, Girl, It's Over." The moody bass pulsed in my veins. "I didn't come here to hug the wall all night. Would you like to dance?" asked Tyrone, the perfect gentleman. He took my hand in his. My fingers went cold.

I looked around for Jasmine, but she was nowhere in sight. Tyrone drew me close. "You feel good," he said. I went sleepy inside. Out of relief, I rested my head on his shoulder. His arms tightened around me and I closed my eyes. "Follow me," he whispered in my ear. "Keep the beat." An anonymous hand in the dark yanked my hair down to the roots, checking to see if I was or wasn't, but I played it off, a mistake, a miscalculation. I felt the sharp pain at the back of my head eased by the hypnotic movements of Tyrone against me.

But the trouble began before I'd fully regained my senses. The record was still playing when Tyrone gently nudged me and pulled away. I misunderstood at first. Then I looked in the direction in which he was staring. Just as Jasmine had predicted, just as she had known, Lamar strolled into the Boot Center with a bigger-than-life Cindy Pavelka. He was wearing a black fishnet shirt, a cap, and the gold medallion map of Africa.

Lamar's car keys dangled from his hand. He was trying his best to merge with the dancers, but Cindy hung close. When his eyes caught Jasmine's, his face registered first shock, then mild sheepishness. They stared at each other, moving toward that inevitable moment they'd created together. Tyrone murmured, "Uh-oh, my boy's in deep trouble," and gripped my hand tightly, as if to console us both.

Heads turned from all directions. Lamar kept moving. He gave the fist to several of his cronies, a forced smile across his face. Cindy wore a defiant look, like someone who'd won something. And the shameful thing was she hadn't even bothered to comb her hair, as if she'd just climbed out of his back seat.

Tyrone left me for Lamar. They clasped hands, grabbed wrists, then stacked their fists in the air, desperate to seem casual.

I found my way to Jasmine's side. Her features had all moved together in a mask of horrendous rage. She had known, hadn't she, all along, that this was why we had come tonight? Maxine and Benita and Chick stood over to one side, observing. Jasmine walked slowly toward Cindy. "You stupid white bitch." Her voice rose over the music. Dancing couples slowly parted, as more and more people caught on to what was happening.

Cindy's smile was forced and impudent. She heaved a bored sigh and put her hand on her hip, challenging. But the heavy pulse in her throat gave her away. "Get out of my face, Jasmine," she said.

Chick and Maxine and Benita closed around her like a fence. A murmur of "Fight, fight" rumbled through the Boot Center.

"Jasmine . . ." Lamar reached out. He tried to stop her, but Jasmine shot him a bitter look and struck his hand away.

"Don't you touch me!" she said and advanced toward Cindy. "Are you out of your mind?" A little push and Cindy looked startled. "Don't you know Lamar belongs to me?"

I squeezed in between Maxine and Chick. Cindy glanced nervously at me, then shifted all her weight to one side. "Look, don't you touch me again," she shot back helplessly. "It's none of your business what I do." She was losing her nerve.

Then Jasmine burst into tears, accepting defeat. I couldn't stand it. Before I knew what I was doing, I had drawn up my fist and pulled my elbow back as if stringing an arrow in a bow. At the moment my fist touched Cindy, the needle scratched like a scream across the 45. The music stopped cold.

Cindy stumbled back a couple of steps, her mouth drawing downwards. She looked back in hatred. Next to me, Jasmine grabbed a fistful of Cindy's hair and cried out like a wounded creature, "Leave Lamar alone, you honky bitch, leave him alone."

I started for Cindy again and would have shoved her against the wall, except that someone took hold of my shoulder, yanking me backwards.

"Have you lost your mind, girl?" It was Chick, her eyes dark and startled in her yellow face. "How can you?" she asked me. "How can you do that? This ain't none of your business."

Someone shoved me hard from behind. I heard murmurs of contempt. Mr. Foster broke through the crowd yelling, "Break it up, break it up. Disperse. Let's go." People began pointing, accusing. In the confusion, I turned to see Jasmine disappearing out the back and down the fire-escape steps, her body bent in the shape of heartache. Lamar threw down his car keys in disgust, as if inviting anyone to drive off in his Chevy. Mr. Foster's eyes smoldered as they came to rest on me. "Hey, you!" he said, starting toward me. There was nothing left to do except push past Cindy, the only person blocking my way, and get down those stairs as fast as I could to the street below where I wasn't sure what to do next.

SUMMARY IN DETROIT

Where's the crazy ole white lady?"
Franklin was out of breath. The screen door to his grandmother's sunny yellow kitchen snapped shut with the ferocity of
a firecracker. As a kid, he'd taken a number of switchings over
that door. Grandma Frieda, poised in fury, worn out from the
kids running in and out all day, bang, bang, bang, tracking in the
dust, the heat, the overripe scent of their heavy play, and holler-
ing at the top of their lungs.

"You do that one more time . . ." Frieda would warn, and
the kids would plead ignorance: "But the door got away from
me . . .," "But I *held* it . . ." or, worse, "But I didn't mean to . . ."
And then the sting of the flyswatter or the spatula, whatever
Frieda had handy, joining up with the backs of their dark legs.
Frieda's aim was impeccable.

It was pointless to protest; back talk earned only another
swat. Frieda had warned them all, over and over. Hadn't she
lined them up and explained the spring mechanism of the screen
door, pointing out exactly where to catch the metal with your
hand so it would close like a whisper behind you? And hadn't
they all nodded eagerly and agreed that they understood, that
they'd be more careful? But hours later, worn out from chasing
one another through the humid twilight alleys of Detroit, thinking only of making it home before nightfall, one of them would
forget. Snap! Bang! The deed was done. Frieda was all over
them, raging about peace and quiet, calling them hooligans,
swatting them all the way upstairs to the bathtub where she
dumped in enough Ivory Snow to make your skin peel off, and

then tossed them in, one by one, as if they'd been dirty socks.

Now Franklin stood huffing and perspiring from his run. He'd underestimated the warmness of this particular summer day, and he bent over to ease the knot in his chest. Then he stood up again and tore a paper towel from the rack above the sink and wiped the sweat from his head. He was running out of hair. He traced his ever-broadening scalp with the paper towel, then mopped the back of his neck.

"Shshshsh! You make too much noise!" For a moment, Franklin thought, it could have been Frieda herself, her red hair streaming down around her shoulders. But it was Dawn, in a dark housedress and red espadrilles, her voice shot through with annoyance. She was standing in the darkened doorway of the room that used to be what Frieda called the parlor, where she kept her sewing machine and a sofa and, as Franklin was growing up, a black and white television.

Now it was where they kept Frieda, because it gave her easy access to the bathroom and there were no stairs to climb. Because times had changed and Frieda was as fragile as the misty white heads of the dandelions that now ranged with a will through her back yard.

"Frieda sleep?" he whispered to the dark shadow in the doorway.

"Yeah, if certain loud folks don't wake her up!" Dawn stepped out into the light of the hallway toward Franklin. "What are you doing here?"

"I came by to see my grandmother."

"Hmmmmm" was all Dawn had to say. She made a deliberately wide arc around Franklin to get to the refrigerator for a cold drink.

The sight of her stirred something in him. He couldn't resist, what with Dawn still so long and tall and pretty. He lunged playfully at her and tried for a kiss on her cheek.

"Don't start kissin on me." Dawn pushed him away. "God, you're just like a child. And your timing's lousy. I just got Frieda to sleep and you come in here slamming the door. Some things never change."

She popped the tab on a soda. Franklin went to the sink and ran some cold water on his face. Then he looked out the window where the garden used to be. Silence reigned. Butterfly-wing silence, so quiet you could imagine the creatures' wings beating as they alighted on flower petals. At least that's what Frieda had told Franklin so long ago, when they used to stroll in that once-flourishing garden, there in the old part of Detroit, where grasshoppers sizzled in the white heat of summer in the long, tall grass growing along her fence. And always, always, the butter-flies fanning the air like so many orange, brown, and yellow angels. They vibrated over the brilliant flowers, touched down still trembling, then skipped lightly from cosmos to zinnias, the sun shimmering on their wings. As a child, Franklin feared the over-brilliant flowers might devour them. He had held his breath, believing the spell could be broken by the merest of exhalations. His heart swelled at the sight of swallowtails, the size of tiny birds, folded as delicately as origami, moving pur-posefully through the air like swimmers in water. And his grand-mother's hand, tightening on his with promise, would lead him to the arbor where she would pluck him sweet, black scupper-nong grapes the size of chestnuts.

"Mama said Frieda was having a bad day."

"Every day's a bad day, far as I'm concerned. She's so weak now," said Dawn, sipping her cold drink and staring almost irritably at Franklin. "Bonnie and them hardly ever come by anymore, and your mother won't visit after dark."

Franklin's mother Jessie lived over in Ann Arbor and refused to drive into Detroit unless she absolutely had to. She made no bones about it. "Detroit's gone crazy," she said. "Folks'll kill you for breathing the wrong way." A friend of hers had been carjacked outside a food mart. Jessie wouldn't leave her car parked on the street and she locked her steering wheel with something that resembled a lethal weapon. She carried Mace in her purse and always wore running shoes for quick escapes. When Franklin suggested she was letting her fear get out of control, she silenced him with a look. "And don't you start talking black power to me again," she said bitterly. "I've watched us killin each other off for years, just finishin the job white folks started. People so crazy nowadays they wouldn't think twice about knocking off a sixty-eight-year-old black woman just minding her business."

It was futile to argue. Franklin had tried pointing out that statistically she ran more chance of being killed in an auto accident than shot by a drug dealer.

"You can talk statistics til you turn purple in the face," Jessie said, "but my point is, what if *I'm* the one?"

Franklin gave up.

"Frieda has a lot of bad days," Dawn went on. "*And* she's talking all crazy again. She forgets what year it is, who I am . . . she still calls me 'Franklin's wife.' " She took another slow slip of soda.

"That must cut you to the quick," said Franklin.

Dawn didn't find it amusing. "I think it's the heat. It parboils her mind."

"Frieda, Frieda, Frieda," murmured Franklin. "Sweet, sweet old Frieda." He stretched his arms up over his head so that the black mesh tank top he wore followed upwards and exposed the tight stomach muscles he worked so hard to maintain. Another stretch and the top inched up to his broad chest.

Dawn gave his bared flesh a quick once-over. Not a flicker

of curiosity or interest, not even disapproval. She had a cool eye. "I see you're staying fit," she remarked wryly.

"Yeah, well," said Franklin, "not too bad for forty."

"Always wanting to rub it in, aren't you?" She filled a jelly glass with cold water and handed it to him.

"You look great for forty-se- . . ."

"Shsh! You don't need to say it." Dawn was laughing in spite of herself at her own vanity. "But you can't resist, can you?"

For a moment Franklin thought they might be friends, and he started to say something that would tie them together. But he caught the warning in Dawn's eyes, and he knew better. He turned to look out the window again.

He'd run the whole seven miles from his apartment, close to the junior high where he coached track and taught one class euphemistically called "Family Life." What it meant is that he, Franklin Breedlove, held forth to twelve-year-olds on the mysteries of human existence, trying to distill the complexities of passion and hormones into that weak solution known as testable fact, something you could quantify with a, b, and c answers and get a passing grade on.

He'd paired up girls and boys in his class and entrusted each "couple" with an egg, which was to be cared for as cautiously as if it were an infant. "Remember now," he said, "you can't just go dashing off without arranging for someone to watch your egg. And you can't forget it and leave it somewhere. You're responsible for keeping this egg intact until the end of the week. You can trade off caring for it, but as parents one of you has to be in charge at all times. Keep track in your notebooks how you divide your duties."

A smashed egg signaled failure. The kids took the assignment seriously. Some wrapped their eggs in cotton batting and carried them in slings around their necks. Some cradled the egg in their hands, moving cautiously from class to class as if they wore glass shoes. Each egg was carefully marked by Franklin so there could be no last-minute substitutions. When the week came to an end, he interviewed the egg couples one by one, helping them assess what was now being called "projected parenting skills."

"Hey, Breedlove, how can you teach us Family Life when you don't even have a family or a life?" wisecracked one kid named Rodney. A smart boy, growing up in the projects, where each day he was tempted by what everyone loosely called "the streets." He'd taken to hanging around a bad bunch, but so far showed up at school like clockwork. Franklin adored him, occasionally took him to see the Tigers and out for pizza.

"You trying to save me or what?" Rodney asked him once.

Franklin was so touched he came as close to tears as he had in years. "Naw, man," he said softly. "I can't save you. You have to save yourself."

Franklin had also resisted the urge to whack him. The kid didn't realize what he was saying, or maybe he did. He had Franklin figured out: a lonely man, without a family, and time on his hands to be worried about someone else's kid.

Now Franklin accepted another paper towel from Dawn and wiped his arms and legs. His shorts and the top he wore, even his own muscle and sinew, hung on him like weights, every inch soaked with perspiration. He badly wanted out of his clothes. But he knew, clothes or no clothes, his own skin would still be there to hug him like a tourniquet. There was no escaping. Not when he struggled so hard inside to free himself of all the years that had irrevocably changed him. But you can't untangle yourself so easily. Each choice chooses the next. Franklin kept moving faster, ducking and dodging, trusting that those thin cables holding up his life wouldn't finally snap and shackle him.

"I've got to go to the center," said Dawn. "I'm in charge of the music hour this afternoon. Can you stay and keep an ear out for Frieda?"

Franklin leaned over and stuffed the crumpled paper towel into the waste can. Coming back up, he had an attack of vertigo and breathed in slowly to steady himself. "Sure," he said, though he hadn't planned to stay.

Dawn wasn't even mildly touched. She leaned against the counter, long-limbed and angular, studying him with her fawn-like eyes. Her knee-length cotton housedress had big white buttons all the way down the front. The sunlight through the window fell on her face harshly, made her look tired. Her brown skin took on a hard, metallic cast. After all these years, she was back to straightening her hair. It had grown out to almost shoulder length. She wore it pinned in a clip, a small wisp of ponytail at her neck.

"You know," said Dawn, "Frieda's gonna die soon and it will be the end of an era."

Franklin bent down into a runner's stretch and felt tension shoot like electricity out the heel of his foot. "Don't be morbid," he said. He was breathing into his stretch. The toe of his fluorescent green and white running shoe was just in view. "That ole woman's got more life in her than you and me put together."

"Hey you just don't want to face the facts," said Dawn.

Franklin came up for air. The sweat broke out on his face in little drops. "Okay, okay, lighten up on me." He pulled himself up to his full height. His right hand hovered over the back of his head and then he stretched one long finger down through his thinning hair and scratched his scalp. "So I've been busy. Tell me what's going on."

"I just told you." Dawn moved around him and to the other side of the kitchen. "She's old and she's dying."

Franklin looked toward the darkened room where Frieda now stayed full-time. He hesitated, could already smell the rankness of old age in the air. Dawn was right. He'd let too much time pass again. He knew he should come more often, but he just didn't, mostly because he couldn't stand the way Dawn judged him, always making her sly comments about what he was and wasn't doing. Or maybe it was Frieda herself, prying and wanting to know about this and that, and was there a woman in his life.

He always imagined Frieda to be partial to Dawn's side of things. He could picture the two of them shaking their heads over him still. "Out of sight, out of mind," he'd heard Dawn remark with such finality to Frieda and Jessie one Thanksgiving, he knew without question that he had been the subject of that comment.

"Should I go in and say hi?"

Dawn shrugged. "Go on."

He wandered over the threshold. The drawn shades kept the room cool. As a little boy, Franklin had slept here in a four-poster bed wrestling against his younger sister Bonnie and his brothers for the covers, for space, for the right to stretch out his long body. There were all those times Frieda kept them when Jessie and Franklin's father Eddie were just too tired, too busy, and too poor.

Old Frieda and Grandpa Henry. An unlikely pair. Henry, dark and quiet, easy-natured, and soft on the grandkids; Frieda, big and overbearing, an irrepressible talker, full of opinions on everything, her pale freckled face alive under her gardening hat, her strong arms hoeing peas and corn and collard greens, as if she'd always worked under a strong summer Michigan sun rather than dark German skies.

Franklin eased his way softly toward her, the rubber soles of his shoes making light sucking sounds on the floor. Poking out over the bed sheet was her shrunken face, the wisps of red hair gone white, the shriveled hands clutched at her sides. Her eyes were closed in sleep . . . or, thought Franklin with a start, in death.

"Frieda," he murmured involuntarily.

The eyes flew open. Opaque blue, shimmering like water. All those years in the sun had wrinkled her badly. She had never darkened, just reddened slowly, her skin turning to the texture of tree bark.

She stared past him. Today she looked tiny and helpless.

"I didn't mean to wake you, Frieda."

"You didn't" came the gravelly voice. "I was just fakin it." She paused. "Dawn was in here earlier singin like to burst my eardrums and I couldn't stand it, so I just closed up my eyes and pretended I was asleep. Or maybe she thought I was dead. I think that's what you all think, that I'm layin up here dead, and now you think you can help yourselves to my stuff. All those colored people out there burning everything down. Tryin to take my stuff."

Hers was a funny accent, part German mixed with English she'd learned primarily from rural black people in southern Ohio where they'd first lived when Henry brought her back with him.

"Naw, naw, come on now, Frieda," said Franklin, settling himself on the edge of her bed. His huge frame dwarfed hers. He lifted one of her tiny gray hands into his and gently stroked it. "I was thinking of baking you a sweet potato pie, but it's too hot to turn on the oven."

"Boy, you ain't about to bake me no pie!" said Frieda.

"That's right, it's too hot," Franklin repeated.

"Hell's hotter," murmured Frieda. "But the flames don't touch the righteous."

Frieda had never believed in God, though Grandpa Henry had

been a devout Baptist, going to church regularly on Sundays while Frieda stayed home and baked heavy German dishes with gravy and sauces. This was Dawn's influence. Dawn with all her praying and singing: oh, the zeal of the recently converted! Franklin thought. She had told him once that finding Jesus was like growing a whole new skin. She described with a radiant light in her eye exactly how the smothering of the world had been pulled off her (those were her exact words) and she could breathe again, reborn into new flesh. How time had changed her, had changed them all. She had found an outlet for her grief, had finally put the past to rest. A crutch, Franklin told her. A drug to mask the pain.

"But you could too," she said. "Jesus will be a balm for your troubled soul. You can't keep going over the past in your mind. You have to move on with the spirit of Christ to guide you."

Franklin told her he didn't want to hear it.

"Dawn's upset with you," remarked Frieda, with a sly lowering of her eyelids. "Just a no-good nigger."

Franklin was shocked, even though he should be used to it by now. Frieda wasn't Frieda anymore. They all tried to make light of it; after all, it was just words pouring out of her mouth, wasn't it, the endless babble of a senile old woman?

"Isn't Dawn *your* wife?" asked Frieda, her face sinking into a shadow.

"She was," said Franklin, though legally it was still true. Even after ten years, he and Dawn hadn't bothered to finalize anything; why, he didn't know. Perhaps because he'd never really found another woman, and Dawn had found only Jesus.

"Tell me again who you are," said Frieda, peering at him. Suspicion: she didn't trust herself to recognize. One minute she was lucid and full of memories, the next her thoughts scrambled, and the ordinary had gone foreign. She made it sound as if her memory lapse was his fault.

"I'm Franklin, Frieda—Jessie's oldest boy."

"Well, you don't look like any boy to me," said Frieda. Then, to herself, she muttered, "Black niggers burning down my house and garden."

Franklin swallowed hard. Jessie and Dawn claimed Frieda didn't know any better, but he wasn't so sure the old witch wasn't taking advantage and getting back at everybody after all these years for the hardship of having been disinherited when she married Henry, and then being subjected to intense scrutiny by Henry's family, straddling for years the fine line between rejection and acceptance. "Henry's *white* wife," they used to call her. "Brought her back from Germany, couldn't find one of his own kind." Finally, after her fifth child with Henry, who was Franklin's mother Jessie, Frieda became, well, just Frieda, adored and honored, sharp-tongued and irascible. "I've graduated to matriarch," she jokingly told the family at her seventieth birthday party.

Franklin looked away from the old woman. He released her hand and shifted his weight. The bed exhaled slightly as he rose up. "Frieda, I sure liked you a lot better when you weren't like this," he said.

"I don't know about all that," said Frieda vaguely. "I don't know." She raised one hand. "You can still smell the smoke. I've been coughin all morning. Look out the window there, you can see them all, tearin up the streets like a bunch of wild animals. There've been sirens and police out there, and they say people have been shot. Dead people out there. Burnin down their own homes in this heat. Thank God Henry isn't alive."

Dawn appeared in the doorway, hand on her hip again. "Franklin, why'd you go and get her all worked up?" She let out a sigh of annoyance.

"Well, now, isn't that nice," said Frieda, all smiles, as Dawn crossed the room and plumped her pillow. "Isn't that real nice of you."

"Yes it is, considering what a crab you are most of the time," Dawn countered cheerfully, moving the light blanket off of Frieda. "Franklin, hand me that comb. I'm going to get her hair out of her face."

Franklin did as he was asked.

Dawn took a place next to Frieda's head. She unpinned the hair and began slowly to comb. In the semidarkness she glowed like a soft brown light, the way she had when Franklin first married her, when he thought he was the luckiest man in the world.

"You're a saint," he said to Dawn.

"Don't you know it."

Franklin smiled in spite of himself. Even after everything, he still liked Dawn a lot. She was a good soul, generally speaking. And she took good care of Frieda. She was family, more than she'd ever been a wife, Dawn was, as much or more of family than he, still hanging around his sister Bonnie's house three blocks over, playing whist and Scrabble, taking the nieces and nephews for the weekends, showing up at birthdays and Christmas with homemade casseroles.

Dawn carefully tugged the snags out of Frieda's hair and pinned it back up on top of her head.

"How can you stand the way she talks?" Franklin asked.

Dawn shrugged. "You mean the 'N' word?"

Franklin suspected she was poking fun at him. "Yeah, you're damn right I mean the 'N' word. I can't believe it's coming out of her mouth."

"She doesn't mean it," Dawn said gently.

Frieda perked up. "I'm not crazy, you know."

"See what I mean?" said Franklin. "She knows what she's saying . . ."

"She's remembering the riots," said Dawn softly. "What else? It gets hot and her memory gets confused and gets in a rut and she can't get out of it. She loses track of time, that's all. Last week she thought she was a girl in Germany again. Today she thinks it's the riots."

At that reference, Franklin felt the old pain ignite in him. "How can you stay here?" he asked. "You know, after everything."

Dawn looked up sharply. "This is my home."

Franklin got up and went back into the kitchen. He could hear Frieda talking to herself. It was more of the same; she was trespassing on dangerous territory. Dawn's voice was consoling. Franklin banged his fist on the kitchen counter and looked out the window at the ragtag garden. Where flowers had once bloomed, weeds reigned. The old arbor had fallen apart; the crumbling fence looked like another weed itself. He had a momentary thought that he could bring his tools over and set about revitalizing the place, plant seeds, till soil, but for what? Soon Frieda would be gone, he and Dawn and Jessie would split the sale of the house, and Dawn would probably move to wherever her daughter Julie wound up in for graduate school.

Dawn emerged from Frieda's room. "Why are you taking this all so personally?" she asked. "Have a little Christian love, Franklin."

"Christian love my ass! Those words come from somewhere. It's like she's stockpiled them all these years."

"She's almost ninety years old," Dawn told him. "Try to understand."

"What is she, senile?"

Dawn shrugged. "Franklin, even your own mother doesn't hold it against her."

Franklin gritted his teeth, feeling his cheek muscles tense and untense. "When did you turn so good?" he asked.

"I've always been good. You just didn't notice. I've got to get going. See you in an hour or so."

It occurred to him that Dawn had not bothered to ask if he had anywhere to be this afternoon. She was just assuming he didn't. He could call Beverly later; plans hadn't been definite, and he was wearying of her anyway. Beverly was only for the moment; before her, there'd been Sabra, then Linda, Marquita, and Debra, a patchwork of women from beige to bronze, none of them ever managing to get it right. And he, Franklin, having to face himself the morning after, disappointed at the ease of trading one warm body for another, but pretending that was freedom.

For a moment he imagined that he and Dawn were still living together in Frieda's house, that any moment she would emerge from the kitchen with the scent of red beans and rice trailing behind her, and she would be brushing against him with her long limbs, and her dark wild braids would slap across his cheek as she bent to pull him against her. She always smelled clean, her skin giving off a strong scent of something close to pine.

Franklin closed his eyes and listened for her breathing, the soft whispers against his neck that assured him of his rightful place in the world. "I believe in you, Franklin," she had said to him one night shortly after they were married. And he had thought that was all it took.

He turned and watched Dawn walk away, taking in the backs of her legs, or what he could see of them, still firm under her cotton dress. He longed for that familiarity, now out of reach and impossible.

II

Franklin sat on the screen porch with a glass of sun tea and thought of those early years when he and Dawn struggled on a shoestring in their falling-down gray shingle house, just three blocks from Frieda's, where they slept on mats on the floor and gave more potlucks for causes than a hen has feathers. Their friends from those years, dashikied and afroed, their collective rage spiraling toward the Revolution, all culminating in one fateful summer, had over the years softened. They now followed careers around the country: attorneys, doctors, teachers, business people, one minister, and two jailbirds. Before the smoke had cleared, they'd all deserted the heart of the city, apologetic but firm in their resolve to give their children better lives. Yes, as soon as the opportunity presented itself, they opted for private schools and suburbs and what Franklin laughingly called "Maul Land." Holidays, Franklin was amazed by the arrival of their cozy family snapshots: kneeling children, dogs, sectional furniture, fireside hearths, nose rings and African trade beads replaced by modest button earrings and pearls, little newsy updates like "Teddy was made partner last year," or "Kwasi is president of his senior class."

The only one with any integrity left from the old days was Ollie, teaching poli-sci over at Wayne State, still riveting the next generation of students with his invocations of the times, the heat, the anger, the history that must never be forgotten. He scheduled walking tours every semester, and dragged his flock out there, black and white alike, poised over their notepads and pencils, moving awkwardly like elderly tourists on a nature walk through a bird sanctuary. Franklin had gone once and was struck that day by the irony that HONKY KILLS scribbled on the walls had simply been replaced by CRACK KILLS.

"Same dog, different collar," Ollie had mused to his students, most of whom didn't understand and might as well have been on an archeological dig after dinosaur bones.

Franklin skimmed through a magazine lying on the table in

front of him. He was restless, uncertain. He read an article about sailboating on Lake Erie. The article claimed that more people sailed in the Cleveland area than in sunny San Diego. A woman he'd once known, Angela, was from Cleveland, and now she worked in administration at the museum. At the last minute Franklin had changed his mind about her, counting on that deep feeling in his gut to keep him safe from entanglements.

"You're stuck in the past," Angela had told him, not unkindly. "Things change but you don't."

A year later she phoned and announced she was three months pregnant and marrying someone named Cedric. Most likely someone more progressive, Franklin thought bitterly, someone with a huge bank account and a Mercedes. This was pure speculation on his part, but it made him feel better. Cedric be damned! Franklin didn't go out all that weekend. Instead he sat in his living room watching old reruns: *I Spy, Bonanza,* the whole lot, with a vengeance.

III

It had been years since Franklin had been alone in his grandmother's house. With Dawn there, the place was usually overrun with relatives, kids mostly, nieces and nephews, people dropping by, church friends and neighbors, and Dawn's daughter Julie home from college with some of her friends. Franklin got up and went to look in on Frieda. She was snoring.

He walked back down the hall to the living room where Dawn's piano took up one whole wall. On the mantel above the fireplace were framed photos of Frieda and Henry at their wedding: young and expectant. Frieda wore white lace and a veil; Henry, a dark suit. His hair was parted on one side and pressed and greased into submission. His ears were too big, her nose too pointed. There was the photo of their first house outside of Toledo, Henry's first car, Franklin's mother as a little girl with her brothers and sisters, the house before the screen porch was added, then Franklin and Bonnie and the boys as children posed stiffly on the front steps, dressed for Sunday. Jessie had them all confirmed Catholic, why, Franklin never really knew. Off in the corner was a snapshot of Franklin and Dawn that brought a smile to Franklin's lips: what Jessie had called their "African phase," when Dawn and Franklin had briefly joined the Black Muslims. Dawn wore a print head wrap, and Franklin's head was shorn.

The past always made him uneasy. He had a sudden urge to look around upstairs. He wanted to see what all had changed. Quietly he mounted the steps. Dawn still slept in the first room to the right. He walked past, and down to the end of the narrow hallway where the door to Dawn's daughter Julie's room stood partially open. Franklin peeked inside. It was pretty much as he'd remembered. An empty suitcase lay open on the floor. It had been several months, he knew, since Julie had been home from college, and the room had a slightly musty, unaired feeling to it. He closed the door. To his left were the narrow, steep stairs that led to the attic. In the summer, it was like a steambath up there. Franklin recalled the way the squirrels ran through, their scrambling claws as noisy as hail overhead. He pulled the attic door open and stared up the steps.

Dust motes danced before his eyes on a shaft of afternoon sunlight from the window at the top of the stairs. He imagined the vague figures of a small boy and a girl standing above, and he pictured himself and Dawn playing up there together as children in the sweltering heat, although that never could have happened. It was some other girl, a neighbor girl named

Chloe who moved away shortly after he'd kissed her, and the two events had always stayed linked in his mind.

He closed the attic door and roamed back down the hallway. A fist of apprehension tightened in his stomach. With the tense purpose of a trespasser, he moved into Dawn's bedroom and stood squarely in the center of the floor. The room was neat as a pin, but that came as no surprise. The quilt on the bed was smoothed tight, the surfaces of the furniture carefully dusted. He recognized her old dressing table, from their days together, where she would sit and painstakingly outline her eyes in kohl and pick out her giant afro with a cheesecutter. When he first met her she was in her mid-twenties—he was nineteen—and she wore her hair in a tall shellacked missile on top of her head. A year later she took the straightener out of her hair, grew an unruly natural, and donned army fatigues and black body suits.

Franklin parted the lace curtains at the window and stared down into the street. Below him was the slowly deteriorating neighborhood that had never been able to recover, growing more and more run-down as the city deserted its own soul. Sidewalks were broken, yards were overgrown with weeds, porches sagged, and houses were badly in need of paint. An old Chevy sat on blocks in the middle of what used to be the lawn of the brown house on the corner. There is a particular odor to despair; Franklin breathed that in, wondering just how far it extended. These streets had once burned and smoked, but the phoenix never rose from the ashes. Instead, he thought ruefully, it lay on its back, wings broken, claws stretched hopelessly upwards.

Across the street a family of poor whites, looking as if they'd just arrived from the mountains of West Virginia, crowded on the front stoop. Three fat teenage girls each held a round-faced infant. In front of the boarded-up storefront on the corner a group of young black men stood drinking something from a brown paper bag they passed around. There were no more neighborhood stores, just one Arab-run place two blocks over where you paid twice as much for a carton of milk as you would at a grocery. Dawn refused to go there, said she couldn't afford it. A brown-skinned woman strolled by in skin-tight pants and a short tank top. She was barefoot, and was hauling a toddler by his hand. As she passed, the men stopped drinking long enough to whistle. One stretched out his arm as if he were going to touch her. Franklin realized the woman couldn't have been more than fifteen. She yanked the child against her and snapped sharply at the men. They hooted loudly and stared after her.

Several children roared down the street on bicycles and skate-boards. There was a toughness to them that Franklin couldn't remember himself having had as a child. He wondered how they had managed to make it this far in their short lives, and how much farther they would make it. His throat thickened. He turned away from the window, knowing what he was about to do.

He went straight to Dawn's closet and pulled open the door. Her clothes hung neatly on hangers. Most of them were new things he didn't recognize. She still kept her shoes packed in their original boxes, stacked one on top of another. On the top shelf were several more boxes, one which contained a wide-brimmed hat she had loved years ago but no longer had reason to wear. Franklin inhaled slowly and breathed in Dawn's familiar scent. Though he knew he had no business doing what he did, he ran his hand across the top shelf, feeling for the shoebox he knew she must still keep. She had promised, hadn't she? She had said she would safeguard it, he hadn't wanted to. What he hadn't told her was that he didn't trust himself with it.

The box wasn't on the shelf as he'd expected. He bent down then, his knees cracking, and explored the floor of the closet, taking care not to let his hands brush against Dawn's dresses. In a moment he found what he was looking for: a blue canvas duffel bag slouched in the corner. He pulled it out into the light. Inside was the small shoebox, bound loosely with old string and taped lightly along the sides. Over the years the tape had yellowed and cracked around the edges. He lifted the box out and set it cautiously on Dawn's bed. An ordinary child's shoebox, with the words "P.F. Flyers" in red written on the side. The box had once contained brand new sneakers that belonged to their son Phillip. Franklin could remember even now how he and Dawn had fussed at each other over buying those sneakers. Dawn thought they cost too much. He had insisted. He pulled off the string and carefully pried back the tabs of yellowed tape. The sound of his own breathing filled the room. Sweat stood out on his forehead. He peeled back the top of the box, too easily, he thought.

With a mixture of relief and anguish he stared down at the jumble of snapshots inside. Some lay face down, others only partially exposed. He caught a glimpse of a half-hidden face, a fragment of a Christmas tree, a child on a sled. He poked one index finger inside the box and flipped over a snapshot. He was startled by what he saw. It was himself, a young, hopeful man, leaning without a care in the world in a doorway he didn't recognize. He was shirtless and held a beer in his hand. Franklin pushed the snapshot aside and went further into the box. He came across an old pacifier with a red handle and a small ring of colorful plastic teething disks that made a clicking sound as he touched them. At the bottom of the box, in a brown wooden frame, was a black and white studio portrait of a small boy with Franklin's eyes, hair slicked back, obediently posed in white shirt and dark jacket on the edge of a large chair. There was a fierceness to his expression, a determination that struck Franklin like a blow to the gut. "Little Man," he murmured, but whether the words were actually spoken or simply stirred in his head he wasn't sure. He quickly covered the photo with the rest of the contents of the box as if he had just done something terribly wrong. He shoved the top of the box back on abruptly. He had meant no harm, he only wanted to be sure that Dawn had kept her promise. That she hadn't forgotten the pictures or lost them or, worse, thrown them away. He hoped that within her act of safekeeping there was forgiveness.

Funny how over the years his memory of that day had only sharpened, and now came into focus through the tropical heat of this day, not unlike the stifling heat in the streets over twenty years before when the National Guard, young white boys armed for war, poured through the same streets Franklin had played in as a child. How little anything really changes, Franklin thought. How long those summers could be. How long they still were.

He pressed his hands along the side of the shoebox, ironing the brittle tabs of tape down with his fingertips. He readjusted the string. He had a momentary urge to leave the box on Dawn's bed for her to find when she returned, but he was afraid she would misinterpret his gesture and finally accuse him of all the things she had never spoken about. He thrust the box back into the duffel bag, closed the closet door, and left the room quickly, breathing fast as if he were running uphill behind his house. Running as if he were trying to outrun something. Breathless.

His mind was knitting together the fragments of that day: the streets awash with heat and frantic people, clubs coming down on black heads, and the sound of breaking glass and screams, and he, Franklin, running among his neighbors and friends, carrying Phillip on his shoulders.

What exactly did Frieda remember from where she had huddled inside her house while angry neighbors tore through her garden out back, and down the alley, to escape the clubs and tear gas and gunfire? For when it finally came down to it, she was a white woman—not Jessie's mother, nor Franklin's grandmother, but a stranger here in Detroit, suddenly afraid for her life and property. Without Henry, Frieda seemed to forget she belonged. She had turned fearful and angry, a foreigner who could never comprehend the fearsome truths forcing the heat to the surface.

When she looked out of her window through the smoke, she saw Franklin running toward her, Phillip limp in his arms, a rag doll. Except then he hadn't realized Phillip was dead. He only knew that Frieda was moving toward him on her porch, a small shape in yellow, crying out, "What have you done? How could you take him out there?"

No one in his family but Frieda had outright accused him; how could they when they were able to comprehend his confusion and fear that day, as he zigzagged through the streets? Franklin's face and hands were streaked with blood, but he hadn't noticed when it happened. He remembered thinking only how his life and the lives of those around him no longer mattered. Smoke mixed with the muggy air. Glass seemed to shatter everywhere. He knew he was witnessing the death of a city, but he hadn't realized right away that he was also witnessing the death of his son. Phillip, the "Little Man," had loosened himself from Franklin's grip and charged off the curb. He ran headlong into the street, something he knew better than to do. For what reason, Franklin would never know. The car that hit Phillip never stopped. Franklin pulled the child up off the street as if he'd merely stumbled. Around him people yelled and pushed. Police were using bullhorns to order everyone off the streets. Franklin did the only thing his instinct told him to: he began to run, the boy's body tucked up tight against his chest.

Only Frieda continued to denounce him. "How could you take him out there? How come you take a baby into those streets?" Because that was her fear. All he could do was stare at her in disbelief as he held Phillip's lifeless weight in his arms. He had cried out to Frieda, "Because those are my people out there!" But her question haunted him long after.

In prison, where he subsequently spent three years for assaulting a police officer who refused to call an ambulance for a dead boy, Franklin grew impatient when the other inmates talked about the riots. He could silence them with a look and the cold reminder that none of them had sacrificed their own sons to that week of tempest.

Dawn visited him faithfully in the prison. At first she was hopeful, assuring him the lawyer would have him out any day now, that the appeals looked good. All those hours she put into his release, which seemed to grow more and more elusive by the day. Ollie and the others came too at first, full of talk and condolences. Then hope began to wear thin. Slowly Dawn wearied of his absence. She got busy, started missing visits. After all, it was a long way to come and Franklin had become impossible to talk to. Once he even slammed his fist against the glass window separating them. She stared at him long and hard, then murmured that the window between them had existed long before prison. That was the closest she ever came to admitting what she surely must have felt in her heart. Cautious not to ever blame him, there came a point when she could no longer see him.

When Franklin finally did come home, and it was to Frieda's that he first came, the world had changed. Vietnam was in full swing, King was dead, and Dawn was living with some black South African guy named Winston, a Ph.D. engineering student who claimed to be a direct descendant of Zulu warriors.

After that day, Franklin's life never really took hold again. He moved in a surrealistic blur from one blunder to the next. After prison, he went briefly to his mother's, then to jobs that never lasted, prison again for violating parole, a degree that took him seven turbulent years to complete, and finally his current life of solitude, the only way he saw himself fit to live: in an ascetic apartment, dirty clothes in a heap on the living room floor, bed unmade, garbage stacked in bags by the back door, books scattered everywhere. It was as if by surrounding himself with decay he was safeguarding himself against the falling away of his own flesh. No woman to interfere for long. No limits. Without limits, he would die soon, he could feel it, just the way Frieda would.

To her credit, Dawn had tried sticking with him out of pity or duty, he was never sure which, but finally she'd had enough. He read it in her face and eyes, and when she finally left him, it was the way a visitor steals quietly and hopelessly from the bed of a dying relative. That same look was reflected in Dawn's daughter Julie's face when she was growing up. She added her own little sour twist to it, refusing to look him in the eye and calling him "FRANK-lin," without the slightest care, as if he were merely an annoying classmate who had pulled her braids.

IV

"Dawn!" Frieda's voice was surprisingly strong. It resonated through the house.

Franklin found her sitting up in bed, her bed jacket open across her thin chest. He bent over and kissed her cheek.

"Where's Dawn?" she demanded.

"She went to the center. She'll be back soon."

"I finished my nap."

"You want to come out and sit on the porch? Get some air?"

Frieda nodded. Franklin folded back the sheet and helped arrange her nightgown over her legs. She could sit up on the edge of the bed, but couldn't trust her own legs to stand. He placed her arms around his neck and lifted her. "Don't drop me," she cautioned. He carried her out to the screened porch and set her down on the chaise with thick foam pillows. She peered up at him, childlike and expectant.

"I'll get you a drink."

"No ice," said Frieda.

Franklin went to the fridge and poured juice into a glass. He diluted the juice with water. He found tea biscuits in a metal canister, and set three on a plate. When he returned to the porch, she was staring out at the yard. He placed the drink and biscuits next to her as an offering. Outside, the sky was clouding over. The air was thickening.

Franklin sat down in Henry's old wicker rocker. Frieda continued to stare at the wide back yard, as if searching for something. From her expression, he gathered she was disappointed. He wondered if perhaps she had forgotten there was no garden anymore. And the arbor, once full of the sweetest grapes and blooms of sweet pea, now stood like an old weathered skeleton missing knuckles and joints.

"You never come see me anymore," she remarked without self-pity.

"I get busy," he said. "I'm sorry, Frieda."

"Shoot, busy don't mean a thing." Her mind was momentarily sharp again. He saw the color rise in her face. She took a cautious sip of juice, holding the glass in trembling hands.

"Remember how the garden used to look?" Franklin said. "Remember the first time I helped you plant flowers?"

"I don't remember," said Frieda. When she inhaled, her breath crackled like paper. She had always suffered with asthma. As a child, Franklin used to listen to her wheeze and snort at night. It was almost comforting when he woke in the night to be able to locate her in some distant part of the house, to hear her moving around, a nocturnal creature keeping everything safe.

"Sure," said Franklin, "I took your shovel one morning and got out there and tried to dig you a hole for your tomato plants and instead I ended up tearing up a bunch of your flowers. Boy, you whupped me good that day!"

"I don't remember any such thing," murmured Frieda. "It sure is a mess out there. Look what they did to it."

"Nobody did anything to it. Time has done that," said Franklin.

"No," said Frieda. "*They* did that, runnin through here like a bunch of crazy folks. Nothin was ever the same after that." A breeze stirred at one end of the porch, then moved gently across them both.

"The rose bush still blooms," said Franklin. "I could get out there and trim it for you." It had long ago outgrown the trellis and was now pushing pink and yellow blooms over the top of the garage where Henry's '63 Buick LeSabre was still parked. Franklin had asked Frieda about that car more than once, even asked her outright to let him have it. "You must be outa your mind," she'd responded. "That car was Henry's pride. It doesn't have a scratch on it and it's staying right where it is."

She peered suspiciously into her juice glass.

"There's no ice in there," he said.

"Okay then," said Frieda almost contritely, and she took another cautious sip. Her hand trembled over one of the tea biscuits, but she got it up to her mouth and chewed off a tiny corner. Thunder rumbled faintly in the distance.

Franklin sighed. "Remember how you showed me when to plant and how far apart to put things, and how to tell when vegetables were ready to be picked?"

"That was Henry showed you," said Frieda, her voice warming. "Henry knew everything that was worth knowin. He had farmin in his blood, you know. Never belonged in the city, not Henry."

Thunder rolled boldly along the horizon. Phillip's face lit up with firecracker quickness in Franklin's mind. A pain, a headache. Funny, he'd go for months without getting a clear image like that. Sometimes he'd forget about it altogether. Phillip was the only person he'd ever really missed. Not Dawn. Not her daughter Julie. Not his mother Jessie. Not even his father when he died. Not his sister Bonnie or his brothers. When he'd served time, he stopped caring about those who were alive, and longed only for the dead child crumpled from the blow of a stranger's car.

"Henry," murmured Frieda uncertainly. Her eyes searched the blackening sky. "Henry sure knew how to make things grow."

"Tell me all about how you two first met," Franklin urged feverishly, as if he hadn't heard the story many times before.

"Oh, I don't remember." Her eyes went filmy.

So Franklin seized upon the story himself and told it the way she had told it so many times when he was growing up. Frieda didn't interrupt, but listened quietly. When Franklin had finished, he saw that her eyes were closed and her chest was still.

He mistook her for dead. And then, he realized, he didn't want to try to wake her. But because he knew it was the right thing to do, he leaned over and gently touched her arm. That was when he saw the imperceptible heave of her thin chest, and in the corner of her eye was a glimmer of blue between her lowered lid and cheek, marking the narrow distance between sleep and death.

Franklin whispered, "Frieda!"

Slowly she opened her opaque eyes and stared out with a face vacant of expression. It was the look of someone who has stumbled into foreign territory and now is uncertain whether she stares at friend or foe.

"I'm Franklin, Frieda."

A very small, almost saucy, smile played in the corners of her mouth. Her eyes closed again, but her mouth was turned upwards.

"I know who you are," she murmured coyly. She reached one long white finger out and tentatively touched his dark brown arm. Franklin felt no more pressure than if it had been a raindrop. "You remember how my sweet peas used to climb way up over the fence?" she asked. "All over there, red and blue and white and pink."

"Yeah, and those hollyhocks you had. I loved those hollyhocks." Her grip tightened on his arm.

Round and round on the brick walkway they would go when he was a child, hand in hand, discovering the secrets she never shared with any of the others. "Just for you, don't tell nobody," she'd say as she popped open a pea shell and fed him straight from her palm.

Now he took her hand and drew it tightly into his, as if they could protect each other from whatever it was that would eventually claim them both. It suddenly mattered to him that she would soon be gone. He found reassurance in the warmth of her flesh. In the collecting darkness of the afternoon, a faint memory of happiness pulsed softly against his face like butterfly wings.

DEAD WOMEN

Just when I'm convinced night will never end, it's dawn. The air outside glows with a frosty fierceness that belies the flat, gold Castilian plains glistening on either side of the speeding train. To my right, in the autumn sky, an icy sun begins a long, cold climb away from the horizon.

The other three women in my couchette are French. Very French, I might add. We've all had a rough night of it, only they don't show it. Looking remarkably rested, they sit primly on their seats in their unwrinkled clothes. One wears a scarf with tiny red flowers. It is a peculiar trait of French women to appear eternally composed and well coiffed. Two of them are now elegantly sharing a small box of *petite beurre* biscuits, without dropping so much as a crumb, and staring placidly out the window as if we hadn't all spent a horrid night on Procrustean beds. Over and over our sleep was disrupted by the nightmarish shriek of brakes, followed finally by the slow jolts and grinds as we changed tracks at Hendaye.

I glimpse myself in the small mirror hanging above and quickly begin to work at my hair. I use my fingers to smooth out the skin on my face. Nothing to be done about the wrinkled blue jeans and T-shirt I slept in; nothing to be done about my stained socks. I work on tucking and zipping myself together, accepting a sympathetic smile from the thin brunette in the eggshell skirt-and-sweater set. When, I wonder, did she manage her makeup and hair, unnoticed? Now she sits nonchalantly peeling an orange, as we rattle and tumble along.

She told me last night she has a fiancé in Madrid, a French-man studying at the university. She herself works in a Paris bank in administration. "*Et vous?*" she asked so sweetly I didn't have the heart to explain I no longer have a life, that my old one is an empty skin hanging up in someone's attic catching cobwebs.

I never mention my pending divorce. Not to people I meet in my travels and not to Paloma at the Barcelona agency where, when I passed through a month ago, I was hired as a live-in governess for the Amado family in Madrid. María and Andreas Amado, Paloma had told me, would be back from vacation September 1. How quaint, I thought at the time, a governess. Like Jane Eyre. They still have such things here. "You'd be per-fect," Paloma explained. "A real teacher. Let's see, you taught for three years . . . . Now, they had hoped for an English girl, but I told them you had a lovely American accent. Where are you from?"

I had been wearing my one dress that now lies rolled in tissue paper at the bottom of my duffel. My hair was neatly yanked back in a severe barrette, and I had squeezed my feet into the one pair of pumps I carry with me.

"Michigan," I'd said. "My accent is Midwestern American."

Paloma made more notes. "And you want to live in Madrid?" she asked.

"Very much," I said, without having a clue as to why. I was only passing through, I thought, and it was really Barcelona that caught my eye, but then . . .

She quoted the salary, which was hardly enough to feed a mouse, but I would be out of money soon and, besides, I was travel-weary. I added as an afterthought, "I'd like to learn Spanish."

This seemed to please her. "I think you will get on with this family very nicely." She smiled. "They are very literary. See you in September."

Spain has arrived this time around much too quickly, and I am expected to adjust in a matter of moments. I have had no time to get out of Paris.

In the Madrid station people are already swarming. Madrileños even look different from the French, who have over the last month actually become familiar. The severe faces strike me as frigid as the wind now polishing the air like glass. Countenances merge: a sea of long, angular El Grecos and round, stubby Goyas. I am in Spain, I keep telling myself, dragging myself past other travelers. I am in Spain. I say it over and over, in disbelief, like a child on the first day of school. It is my habit these days to remind myself where I am, or I will make a mistake and speak the wrong language or seek out the wrong places.

María Amado assured me she would be at home to meet me and pay the cab driver. I throw the driver a confident smile and wonder, if I suddenly ran off, how far he would go to chase me down. And what would María think, her new governess simply vanishing without a trace?

Ever since arriving in Europe, I walk everywhere, skip meals, sleep on lumpy mattresses in cheap *pensiones,* and wash out underwear by hand. I am a saver, not a splurger at all, and the length of this cab ride begins to work on my nerves. It's not my money being spent, I keep telling myself, watching the buildings flash by. But I'm as uneasy as if it were.

Autumn leaves swirl through the streets. Aproned shop owners are out already washing down the pavements in front of their *tiendas* with blasts of water from garden hoses. Madrid is repressive: rows of wrought-iron balconies and shuttered windows; at eye level, broad boulevards and plazas full of monuments. The city is big and unwieldy, not old at all.

The driver points out Retiro Park with its thick explosion of fall colors to my right. Two more turns and we lurch to a halt in front of a skinny plaster building the color of an old peach. The driver has, surprisingly, brought me the most direct route, and yet I think, if María has not kept her promise . . .

But she is waiting for me, or at least I assume it is she, standing three stories above on a wrought-iron balcony. She is not at all what I expected: much younger than her forty years, thin, tall, with one of those distinctly European faces that speak of centuries of tradition. Beautiful, not exactly, but sensual and natural, yes. Hers is a face that haunts. Besides, she is dark, with big eyes, long lashes, a hint of pout, a glimpse of Moorishness, and I have always envied dark women.

"Well," she says, after she's paid the driver.

She turns to me. "Welcome, Diana. I am so pleased you have come to my house." She states this as if my arrival were by accident and not design. Or as if I am a guest, which I am not, and we both know it.

I follow her up the scuffed and peeling linoleum steps. She makes small talk, cautiously testing out her English, which is less good than I expected. She speaks haltingly, with long pauses between words.

"So, you are a professor?"

"A teacher," I quickly correct her and explain the distinction in English.

"You look too young." She keeps turning around and studying me, Orpheus to my Eurydice. I now wish I'd changed clothes in the train station.

"I'm twenty-five," I tell her. "I taught high school in Detroit."

Already she is doubting me, I can see that. I know I will never tell this woman that I am still married, that I left my husband only four months ago, someone I now hardly remember who still calls me "wife."

At the top of the stairs she ushers me through an open door into the most chaotic jumble of a room I've ever seen. I set my bags down and follow her into the kitchen.

"Come, come, you must be hungry."

Before I can say I'm not, María pours powdered cocoa from a packet and turns on the flame under the teakettle. With a knife she assaults half a pallid Spanish omelette partially draped in Saran Wrap, and squeezes out a slice for me onto a plate. I collapse in an uncomfortable metal chair at the uneven table and take in my new surroundings.

I try to imagine myself in the disappointing light in which María must see me. I am an American, and not the fancy British governess she'd asked for: a far less evolved human being with a flat Midwestern accent and slovenly clothes.

María sits down across from me as I take perfunctory pokes at the omelette; she exudes a tremulous sort of humility, staring from dark, expectant eyes. Her long black hair is thick and loose. She has a habit of lifting it with her hands over one shoulder and then letting it fall down her back. She does this over and over until her arms grow tired or she gets distracted.

"So you're a writer," I say. It is my first stab at deference. I, too, am a writer: an avid writer of letters, postcards, and aerograms. I take notes, stash ideas in tiny notebooks. I write things no one will ever read.

A cautious smile spreads across María's face. Or is it self-complacence? Paloma at the agency told me how María had recently been catapulted to fame with an important collection of short stories called *Cantos de amor por las mujeres muertas,* for which she won the Spanish equivalent of the Pulitzer Prize.

I say boldly, "I'd like to read your book."

She waves her hand at me. "Boof! It is a small book. You cannot understand it. It is much, how do you say, surreal."

I persist. "I like surreal writing. I've read a lot of Latin American writers." But she is not listening, because she really does not care if I read her book or not.

I finish the cocoa and omelette, both of which conspire to turn my stomach. I am not completely present, but perhaps my air of preoccupation will appeal to María, who strikes me as only vaguely present herself.

"Come!" she says wearily. "I show you around." I have the sense that she has already tired of me, and wonder if I've done something to offend.

María and her husband Andreas rent a pair of second-story adjoining flats on the third floor of this building. María keeps everything padlocked—doors, cupboards, even the three boxy powder-blue telephones scattered about the main flat. She wears a number of keys on a bracelet around her wrist. "Because of the servants," she explains, referring to the two teenage girls, Cello and Isabel, who share a room just off the kitchen. "They are ignorant, silly girls from the provinces."

Cello and Isabel sleep on two mattresses shoved together. They are cousins, poor girls from the country, one skinny, the other as round and doughy as a biscuit. They are napping together when we poke our heads in, curled up like babies together under a dirty sheet. They have adorned their plaster walls with posters of American rock stars, all the way up to the high ceiling. A tiny black and white television teeters on top of an old dresser with mismatched drawers.

"They always sleep for an hour in the morning," explains María, as we withdraw ourselves. "They awaken at five-thirty to make breakfast, they clean, then sleep."

She begins unlocking and locking doors, carrying out her duty with the authority of a convent abbess.

She talks to me about my charges, her two sons, Tomás and Horacio, now off at school. I am to eat breakfast and speak English with them Mondays through Fridays. Evenings, they receive formal English instruction, an hour apiece. Saturdays I take them on a half-day, English-speaking outing. Sundays I have off, to do with as I please or, as María says, "To see friends," oblivious to the fact that I know no one here. In theory it sounds reasonable, certainly no less worthy than other things I could be doing. I'm certain she sees this as a favor to me, my living here with her and Andreas and the two boys.

We pause in the doorway of the boys' darkened room where the shades are still drawn. I make out the silhouettes of a set of bunk beds rising above a heap of dirty clothes thrown on the floor. A sour odor assails my nostrils: unwashed bedding and damp pajamas. María claims they are *lovely* children, and repeats this assurance at least half a dozen more times.

Andreas's study is the best room in the whole place, the only one unmarred by careless renovation. Andreas's absence is most conspicuous, perhaps because of the reverence María seems to hold for the empty room. Her voice pours like liquid over his name. "Andreas." Two of his walls are solid books, mostly in Spanish. I try to imagine Lady Macbeth crying out: "*Mira,* Macbeth!" How would one say "Screw your courage to the sticking place" in Spanish? When I stand on tiptoes to read titles, María gives me a look and informs me gently the *estudio* is *privado*.

"Andreas writes here," she explains deferentially. "Even the children do not come here." When we leave, she checks the lock twice.

What I know of Andreas from the agency is that he is a

poet of some repute, currently finishing up a week of lectures in Barcelona. He will be home in a few days. Like María, he teaches at the university on the outskirts of Madrid.

In both flats, the ceilings are twice as high as a person, and the rooms are spliced together haphazardly, creating odd sizes and shapes. There are all the awkward mismatchings of a place that has been the victim of careless occupants: a useless faucet jutting from an alcove wall; half a room painted royal blue, the other half a sickly pea green; a runner of dull brown carpet ending abruptly mid-room, like an unfinished sentence, and so on. María's mismatched furniture only adds to the lack of coherence. It is illogical: odds and ends stacked together, upholstery ripped at the seams, a broken table leg propped at an angle, bookshelves stacked with unsorted papers and manuscripts in battered folders.

"I'd really like to read your book," I try again.

"You may find it—how do you say—*aburrido*—uh—bored."

"Boring," I correct her companionably.

"Ah, yes, boring!"

"No, no, I'd find it very interesting." Why I persist, I'm not sure.

We move across the hall to the second flat, where my room is. The first door leads to the small filthy bathroom I will share with Cello and Isabel. Undaunted by the grime, María points out tub, shower, and toilet. We do not linger, and I make a mental note that my first task will be to scrub down the bathroom. Down the hall, she summons me into what appears to be a laundry room. The floor is littered with islands of sour-smelling clothing. About this, María muses, with a puzzled expression, "I must remember to tell Cello and Isabel they must wash the clothes soon."

A door through the laundry leads to a small unused kitchenette. It smells of stale coffee grounds left sitting in the electric
pot on the counter. The room is a haphazard space that doubles
as María's office. The floor is covered by cracked linoleum
with one scatter rug shoved into the corner. Stacks of papers
lie strewn across a tabletop. In the center is a Royal manual
typewriter. Two beat-up bookshelves run from the floor to the
ceiling, stacked with books and loose papers and cleaning materials. There on her desk are four more copies of *Cantos de
amor por las mujeres muertas*.

"May I?"

With a shrug, she hands me a copy. The cover is stained with
circular coffee-cup rings. I flip the book over to the black and
white head-and-shoulders shot of María on the back. She wears
that dreamy gaze often urged on subjects by well-meaning pho-
tographers hoping to capture the essence of artistry.

"Come, I'll show you your room." I clutch the book in one
hand and we traverse the entire length of the hall to a room
which, in comparison to the others, is surprisingly pleasant. A
large window looks down into a small cement courtyard. There
is a firm mattress with a stack of clean linens piled invitingly on
top. María points out the antique armoire for my clothes. Just
opposite is a writing desk. Someone has laid a dark blue throw
rug on the floor to take the autumn chill off the linoleum.

"I think you will like it here," she says with certainty. "Our
last governess was very happy."

"Thank you," I tell her, and am so startled by the relief of
her warm smile that I don't bother to ask why the governess
left. I'm not sure it would matter.

That afternoon I unpack slowly, spurning the drawers, keeping
everything right where I can see it. My head is thick with dis-

orientation. I keep feeling the most recent hands on my flesh, Marcos's warm breath on my cheek, his slender arms draped around me. He is a vague presence now, no longer real, but a postcard image from Paris, reduced to one dimension, a series of snapshots caught at various angles. I can smell his warmth and taste his mouth, but cannot remember what he looks like. It happens so fast, these things, and I wonder how long it will take for him to blur with the next one. Kevin is light-years away, a thing of the past. My marriage is over, even if not legally. There was a Greek fisherman and then an Israeli art student; before that, a Belgian biker, and preceding him, an architect from Argentina I met in a hostel. They all begin to collapse into one fragmented body which I have possessed over and over.

Outside in the hallway Cello and Isabel are giggling. But I don't open the door and soon they go away, murmuring about "*la señorita.*" I sit down at the desk and look around me. This is it, I think. This is what I've rushed off to. I take a peek out the window and down into the courtyard. There is the vague, incessant murmur of voices from neighboring open windows, but I can see no one.

I flip through María's book. The print job is awful, even faded in places. I scan the table of contents and then, with the help of my *diccionario,* begin to read. The first story focuses on an ill-fated love affair between an arrogant young man and a much older woman. Stumbling on idioms, I still manage to get the gist: the young man falls for another older woman, the first woman ends up committing suicide and haunts the young man for years after, tormenting his conscience and causing him to be impotent until his new lover abandons him.

The voice is passionate, the language feverishly erotic. Marcos's face suddenly reappears; he is the young man in the story, passionate, fearless, and cruel. I am drawn into the blur of romantic parables that make up this new fiction called my life. María's words, in a language I don't know well, invoke our parting: my train pulled out of the Paris station and Marcos ran alongside, striking the window with his fist and turning his stricken face, wet with tears, toward me. Just that morning he had dutifully confessed to me how he loved me, and I obediently reciprocated, knowing it wasn't true. But the words came easily, predictably. Arm in arm we strolled through Père Lachaise Cimetière and finally sat gloomily on Modigliani's tomb. The hour of my departure loomed over us. We both pretended to be sad, or maybe we were. One of us was crying. His vacation from law school was almost over, he was probably more despondent about returning to his books than my leaving.

"You must come back," he told me, but even then I was picturing the handsome Spaniard I was sure to meet in Madrid. I simply shrugged, the old restlessness rising in me, Marcos a thing of the past.

I finish María's story with only the slightest of pangs, wondering how long it will be again before I can't breathe, can't sleep. It was how I awakened that one night next to Kevin, sitting upright in bed, panting like a long-distance runner. I heard myself say, "There's no air in here," and then I knew. He knew too. "I could open a window," he told me, "but I don't think that's what you need." I put a coat on over my nightgown and went down into the street, just like that, and sat on the curb until Kevin came out and told me he was worried I'd catch cold.

María's boys, Tomás and Horacio, are twelve and eight. We are introduced just before they go to bed. The older, Tomás, carries a small marionette that he controls with strings attached to a wooden cross. He manipulates the doll to make it dance wildly. Tomás is tall and blond, almost Nordic. He looks unlike either of his parents. He wears an icy expression of privilege and superiority. When he shakes my hand, he treats it as a joke.

"It is a pleasure to meet you," he says with exaggerated courtesy.

Horacio is small and brown-haired, a nervous, giggly, bird-like boy. He wears soft wrinkled cotton pajamas with bunny rabbits on them. His two front teeth have grown in crooked and overlap each other.

María hovers, expectant and pleased.

"So, you are from America?" asks Tomás. He allows the marionette to hang limply from the cross. It is a clown with mismatched shoes and a pointed red cap.

"From Michigan."

"Michigan?" says Tomás sharply. "And where is that?"

"It's the mitten-shaped state."

"The what?" he asks curtly, as if I am the one who doesn't understand.

I draw a mitten in the air with my hand and repeat, "Mitten-shaped." María looks on approvingly.

"I don't know what you mean," he says petulantly. He jerks the marionette around.

"I'll show you on a map." I pretend to be conciliatory. I want María to see how you handle such a boy. But he has turned away, fiercely thrusting the marionette into the air.

I look at María, expecting her to address the boy's rudeness, but she seems oblivious.

"They are lovely boys, aren't they?" she says, and smiles with enough appreciation for both of us.

Over the next few days, María asks me about myself. Frequently, when I eat, she sits at the end of the long table and studies me, toying with the fringe at the end of her red scarf.

"You have a nice American accent," she says encouragingly.

"I asked for a British girl, but the agency recommended you. And I see how you are with the boys. You make them laugh."

I can tell she is trying to reassure herself that she has made a good choice.

"You are well educated," she continues. "You are like me."

"Not exactly," I explain. "I taught high school, you teach college."

"No matter, you are still young. Oh, by the way . . ." She moves cautiously over that expression, which she has picked up from talking to me, "I mean to tell you that Tomás uses a how-do-you-say, uh, a potty in his room, and every morning you must now empty into the toilet." Her eyes remain unblinking on me.

"Tomás? But he's twelve."

María's face tightens. "Yes, that is correct." An awkward silence comes between us, and then she reinforces, "But you have not been empty his potty." I don't answer, and she stands up with a sigh. "I must prepare for the university."

She is barely out of the room when the front door opens. I can hear the scrape of footsteps and the sound of a throat being cleared.

Andreas, back from Barcelona, pokes his face into the kitchen. "*Hola,*" he says and then enters.

He is not tall and he is frail in a too-sensuous, Byronic kind of way. He drops his satchel to the floor with a thump and removes his jacket.

He looks exactly the way a poet should: his pale olive complexion almost consumptive; dark curly hair and a mouth that is too carnal. He wears oversized corduroy pants, a battered sweater, worn Italian shoes, and a wool scarf around his neck. His eyes are wet and mournful, his expression one of eternal exhaustion with the world.

"Ah, and you must be . . ."

"Diana." I stand up, still chewing a mouthful of omelette.

"Andreas." He extends his hand. I grip his in mine and feel it go limp. "Welcome," he says, withdrawing his hand slowly. "You are all arranged here?"

His smile is angled sideways like a fish's.

María appears suddenly in the doorway behind him. A dark flush rises in her face. "Andreas . . ." She looks as if she has seen a ghost. "I heard the door."

He is breezy and unconcerned, unwrapping his scarf from his neck. "Busy trip," he says, and she stops short of embracing him. I realize they are speaking English for my benefit.

"You have met Diana, of course," she says, her eyes firm on his face.

Andreas smiles. He gives María a quick kiss on the cheek. There is something distinctly cold in his expression, and I suspect he is capable of great indifference.

"Diana is a very pretty girl, don't you think?" says María. Her tone has a stony control, but underlying it is a trace of anguish. Their eyes lock and I feel myself vanishing. Andreas's face goes blank, the way I have seen men do with women they no longer want.

"I'm very tired," he says. "Barcelona exhausts me." He crosses the room and disappears toward their bedroom. María gives me a wan smile, then picks up his satchel. She follows her husband like a hopeful child, her long legs and arms moving rapidly.

I throw the rest of my omelette in the garbage. I've lost my appetite.

I've just returned from walking the boys the four blocks to school to find a letter addressed to me on the hall table. It is too early for today's mail; I wonder when it came. At first I think

Kevin has found me. But the postmark is Paris, and the writing is unfamiliar, a tiny cramped hand. I carry the letter into the boys' room, turning the envelope around in my hand. Tomás's chamber pot awaits me like a wild creature about to spring. It is full of urine, a rich, dark orange color with a stench at once so sweet and pungent that it catches in my throat in that stuffy room, and if I don't hold my breath, I find myself tasting it over and over in my imagination.

I leave the chamber pot unemptied and wander out to the balcony. A heavy gray overcast hangs on the skyline. The letter, I realize, is from Marcos. Someone has lined through the agency address and forwarded it to Madrid.

The first paragraph is perfunctory; he's back in school, he's *très occupé*. But then he begins to describe walking in the Luxembourg Gardens where we had walked together, and how he was startled by a ray of sunlight through the clouds, which reminded him of my smile. He misses me. He misses the long afternoons in his stifling room, shades drawn against the outside world. The details are buried in the French words he has scrawled on the blue paper. It is only with great concentration that I move beyond the dreamlike foreignness of his words to the smells, tastes, sounds of our bodies together. Slowly the words disappear altogether. I close my eyes. Marcos and I first met beneath the gargoyles of Notre Dame. It was raining lightly, and neither of us had an umbrella. Within that first hour he had pressed his mouth against my damp neck, then onto my hair. His hands were inside my jacket, then under my shirt. Suddenly we were falling, fast, and he was no longer a stranger murmuring over and over, "*Viens, j'ai envie de toi.*" The voice seemed to come from inside me. By now my hair was soaked by the rain. We got under an awning and he told me I must come home to his place, that he would dry me and feed me.

The whole time he kept one hand wedged under my shirt, his fingers roaming warm over my bare skin. He was impatient, Marcos was, and I read it as passion. It was urgency I wanted, what dragged me out of my lethargy.

I finish the letter and turn the envelope over and over in my hands, repeating aloud his address from the ninth arrondissement as if it were my own.

"*Ma cherie* . . ." I start again. There is even more I have missed in the first reading. By the end of the second page I feel the heat in my face and the emptiness of longing. Marcos writes incautiously and beautifully in a language that belongs to neither of us. Marcos is from the Dominican Republic, and his native tongue is the language I hear all around me now in Spain. Marcos speaks no English.

I am back in his sparse room, with its single bed shoved against the white walls, the unburned candle by the bedside, and the view of the street from his window when the shutters were open. "*La semaine perdue.*"

He told me after we'd finished making love the first night, "No one knows we are here." This seemed to give him immense satisfaction.

He would be returning to law school after a two-week break; but where would I be returning to? I purposely told him all about Kevin, to make him jealous, and it worked. Marcos dubbed Kevin "*la pierre,*" the stone. And Kevin, poor gentle Kevin, came to represent all that was boorish and all that we detested, and Marcos spent the week proving to me he was everything Kevin was not. "I, too, had a stone," Marcos told me the second day we were together. Her name was Anne; she was French. He told me that at first she had offered him entreé into Parisian life. Bit by bit she had strung him with so many bourgeois expectations he began to feel like a puppet. "I can never be French," he told me wryly. "She wants a Frenchman

in public . . ." He paused. ". . . and a black man in private."
Only, in French what he said was "*un homme noir*," and for
some reason we both laughed.

So I became the antithesis of Anne, just as Marcos was the antithesis of Kevin. We often joked about introducing the two of
them. As we lay sweating against each other at night, Marcos's
hand moving between my legs, he would whisper, "*Je suis pas
Kevin*," and I would murmur, "*Je suis pas Anne*."

María walks out onto the balcony. She wears a blue silk
blouse, black corduroy jeans, the red scarf, and a wistful expression.

"Good morning, Diana. Did you sleep well?" She peers down
at the street below. In one hand she has a small piece of dry
biscuit, something they call toast, and in the other, a cup of
cocoa. "I'm late for the university. I overslept again. I stayed
up with Andreas, just the way we always do, talk, talk, talk,
talk, talk. He is finishing an important book of poetry."

I am not sure why she tells me these things, for I am not her
friend. Perhaps she wants me to envy their complex creative
life. Perhaps it is a warning of sorts. She peers down at the
envelope on my lap and then at the letter in my hand. She looks
at me, as if I owe her an explanation, and settles into the metal
chair next to mine.

"From France? Who writes from France?" she asks so sweetly
that I break down and confess.

"A friend."

"Oh?" Her interest is pathetically girlish. "A man?"

I don't know how to explain Marcos, or any other men I've
known, for that matter, but I suspect María is not so easily
satisfied. "*Mi amigo*," I say, because it sounds less dangerous
in Spanish. But I have instantly formalized whatever passed
between Marcos and me.

"Oh, you have a French lover!" María cries, delighted as a

child. She picks up the envelope and turns it over in her long fingers. She stares at his return address. "Oh, that is so wonderful he writes you! And in French too!"

Marcos is not at all what María is imagining, but I say nothing. His mother is actually Haitian and his father is Dominican. His parents never married, and he grew up poor, alone with his mother, in a small ugly house near fields of sugarcane. Starting when he was ten, he made monthly visits to his father, in Santo Domingo, a rich man with servants and many other children. It was on his father's money that he'd come to France to study.

"You know," María says earnestly, "passion is so precious. And young passion is the very best. You must miss him terribly."

Again, I recall Marcos at that last moment, how he ran along the platform next to the train. He kept up with me until the train groaned out of the station. In the frosty air his breath smoked. I could make out his parting words, "*Je t'aime, Diana,*" his face constricted in the cold. He wore a blue hat on his head that struck me as oddly comical, but now I cannot recall his face. It was only appropriate that he should say he loved me, I thought, as I leaned my head against the leather upholstery. They all have, and I've loved them, because it is actually very easy to fall in love. People talk about how hard love is, but they mean something else. Marcos grew smaller and smaller on the edge of the platform until he was just a speck. A moment later he was invisible, and I was on my way to Spain.

"You are so lucky," says María wistfully, as she stands up. "Your poet—Emily Dickinson—she said, 'Love is all there is, is all we know of Love.' Isn't that lovely?"

I nod. I want to say, "Love's stricken 'why' / is all that love can speak," but I don't.

"I am very glad for you," she persists from the doorway, "about your French lover."

"Thank you," I say and realize María has just assigned Mar-

cos a place in my life. I get up and go to the kitchen for a cup
of cocoa.

Andreas shuffles by me in his gray-and-red flannel bathrobe
and pours cocoa mix into a mug. His sleep-stiff hair stands
erect on his head. "Good morning," he murmurs grumpily in
my direction, then casts an annoyed glance toward Cello and
Isabel's room. The television blares. A woman's voice wails,
"*Mentiras! Solamente mentiras!*" Violin music soars. Having
been invited to their room a couple of times, I know fat Isabel
and skinny Cello are slumped together on the mattress, their
eyes riveted on the seductress La Rubia.

Isabel has a real boyfriend, scrawny, with hair like shoe
polish, who meets her in the bushes downstairs and takes her
for walks so they can smooch. Cello, on the other hand, is
lonesome and probably a virgin.

"*Déjame sola!*" screams the tormented female voice. Andreas
yells at the open door and the woman's cries dissolve into
silence. I hear giggling, then Cello emerges earnestly with a
mop in her hand and heads for the other flat.

Andreas settles down in a chair to drink his cocoa. "Stupid
girls," he mutters to no one in particular. His bathrobe has
risen up over one white leg, exposing coils of hair springing
along his calf and thigh. I think of Marcos's milk-chocolate
skin, the very smoothness of his hairless limbs, and wonder
why Andreas doesn't cover himself up, he is revolting. I remain
standing, leaning against the kitchen counter.

"María has left already?" he asks.

I nod.

"She likes you very much."

I don't answer.

"You know María is a famous woman." There is a hint of
mockery.

"I know that."

"Very clever, very beautiful," he tells me. "An irresistible combination, don't you think?" I don't know what he is getting at, but his air of superiority hangs over him like mist.

"I finished one of her short stories last night. It was wonderful."

"Oh, good," he says. "Very good that you like her work. You must tell her. María is most insecure about people who must like her work. You know María was a student of mine. She was not yet a writer then, and certainly not a poet. She was young and very serious, and very—how do you say—uh, talented. I told her she must be a writer." He pauses. "You are very intelligent, Diana. I can tell, by your eyes. You understand much. You are good for María."

"Well . . . I don't know . . ." Uncomfortable, I turn and set my empty cup in the sink. There is an awkward silence and I can feel Andreas's stare.

Isabel appears from nowhere and begins stacking dirty breakfast dishes, giving me little conspiratorial winks. I've managed to piece together some of the less-than-flattering descriptions she and Cello use in reference to "*el senor*." They have declared him "*muy feo*," and "*flaco*," stuck-up, and so on, but much of this is class warfare. The servants are expected to hate the master, and the master despises them for their subservience. Andreas plunges back into the newspaper, reading rapidly aloud and swinging his naked leg carelessly. There is a smirk on his face.

I take Marcos's letter and go back out on the balcony. It is turning into a smoky, smoggy day, the air choked with the smell of diesel. I read the letter through three more times, discovering more I've missed. With each reading, Marcos comes more clearly into focus, but it is not the Marcos I knew in Paris. I sit for a while staring down into the street. I have nothing else to look forward to except the return of the boys from school in the afternoon and the resumption of our ridiculous English lessons in which Tomás insists I am wrong and he is right.

Later, I take an aimless walk, the letter folded inside my sweater pocket. I've picked up a habit of studying people's faces, as if I could decipher a strange country by the countenances of its inhabitants.

I find the cafe several blocks away where I've come twice this week to sit and write postcards to friends in the States, detailing with crisp vanity my latest romance with Marcos and my new life in Madrid. My notes are breezy, written at the quick, careless pace I wish my life were actually traveling. The coffee is dark, served in a small white cup, Turkish style. I sit by the window and watch people pass. The women are haughty, stylish, and enviably dark. They walk quickly, with purpose. María has told me most Spanish women my age are married and have children. I am conspicuously American in my jeans and sweatshirt and sneakers, undignified to say the least. But I have no money for clothes, and I grow despondent, imagining how foolish I look. When I left the U.S., I just left. Kevin kept the apartment and all the furniture, not that it was much to speak of, and I took two suitcases and my duffel. We were both pretending, I suppose, that I might actually come back. I had my books and clothes stored at my parents' house. My mother made no comment, seemed to almost take the split for granted. "Of course you want to see Europe," she said, and that was the closest she came to discussing my divorce.

Today I read the title story from *Cantos de amor por las mujeres muertas*. It is told from the point of view of a woman who has died of breast cancer and now reflects sadly over her faithless husband's escapades during her illness. Now that she is dead he is unable to love anyone else. When he makes love to others, it is always her face that appears. When he finally finds someone he thinks he loves, he discovers it is his wife's decaying body he holds in his hands.

The following week passes slowly and I'm afraid I've made a terrible mistake. Each day in Madrid feels like Sunday, as if my life has closed down, windows shut, curtains drawn. I struggle against loneliness. I carry on conversations with myself in my head. I steer clear of Andreas, whom I have caught staring at me. I keep hoping that María will invite me to one of the social events she and Andreas always seem to be rushing off to. Hearing her in the hall one evening, I boldly plant myself in my door frame and smile brightly.

"Going out?" I ask.

"Yes, and you?" she responds cheerfully.

I shake my head.

"Oh, poor thing, you're thinking about *him*." She heaves a sympathetic sigh. "You must go out more," she says, as if I had somewhere to go, and disappears on down the stairs.

I am desperate to go out, but where, in a city in which women do not seem to go about by themselves much? I cannot afford to eat a leisurely dinner in one of the plazas downtown, hoping someone will take an interest.

On Wednesday two more letters arrive from Marcos. Each one accelerates in passion. I cave in and allow myself to believe.

You must write me. You must return to Paris. The fragile script has acquired a fever. *Diana, I must have you again. Why don't you answer my letters?*

Our letters have crossed in the mail. By now he should have received two from me, written with great pains and a lot of help from my *Petit Larousse* for *le mot juste*. Like María's dead women, I have invented hindsight, brought about by distance, ignorance, and my own absence. And all the time in the world, which Andrew Marvel lacked, to leisurely compose my romance in a borrowed language. I admit to him I am unhappy in Madrid. But I make no mention of returning to Paris. Instead, I speculate about heading down to Segovia, where it is warmer. I have heard it is a beautiful city, I tell him.

I write my third letter to Marcos in Spanish, as a surprise. *Mi amor.* I say things in Spanish I would never say in English. I borrow a line from María's book and forget to put it in quotes. So be it, I think.

I head down the street for a mailbox, returning with a heightened sense of my own importance in the world. I am loved. And I am sick of emptying Tomás's piss pot and cleaning up after Cello and Isabel. I have found blood on the toilet seat and dirty tissue wadded in a corner on the floor. Cello combs her stringy blonde hair into the sink and leaves bits of it there to clog up the drain. Isabel forgets to pick up her dirty underwear after a shower.

I plan to register these complaints with María as soon as possible. We are developing a friendly rapport born of mutual respect. After all, she often asks me about English literature, and we compare notes on things we've read. We occasionally sit and discuss books we've both liked. She seems pleased I am struggling with *Cien anos de soledad,* even though I'm cheating, because I already read it once in English. She tells me she's read Shakespeare only in Spanish, and I have offered to read her some of *Macbeth* in English. I want her to hear the rhythms, the sounds of the words themselves. She seems to like the idea, but never mentions it again.

Still, she often seeks me out, either in my room or on the balcony. No matter how the conversation starts, it inevitably turns to Marcos.

"Your French lover . . ." she remarks to me today, her voice thick with interest. "He has been writing you often?"

"Four letters. Four letters in *two weeks*."

"Ah," she sighs. "He is very much in love."

"Yes." I manufacture in my mind the moment Marcos and María actually meet. I am stuffing the widening gap in my daily life with the presence of Marcos.

"That is so wonderful." She runs her long slender fingers along the wrought-iron railing. "Love is everything. Will you go to visit him for Christmas holiday?"

"I suppose," I say. "I suppose I have to." I have not even thought that far ahead. But Christmas in Paris! Of course, that's it! The Amados will be off to the country for two weeks, and I have no desire to be left alone in Madrid.

María sits down next to me. There is sweet smelling oil in her dark hair. I resist the urge to reach out and stroke it. María is a child, someone who requires care.

"I was very much in love with a boy once—at university. Before I meet Andreas of course." She pauses, then adds, "He was the only other man I was *with*."

I try not to register surprise.

She continues in her plaintive voice. "It is very sad. His family wanted him to marry another girl, someone they choose. He was fighting, fighting with them all the time about me. And then I matriculated—into a class in Latin American poetry. Andreas was my teacher, and he seemed so . . ." Her face takes on a dark despair; her voice fills with hopeless yearning, as if she were speaking of someone who has recently died. Andreas is a brilliant poet, she informs me intently. Eight years older and, oh, so wise about life. Many women have loved Andreas, but his work always came first. But with her, things were different. He sought her out after class. They were married when she was not much older than I am now.

"We are the same, Andreas and I," she muses softly. "It is not always so good to be the same. We understand too much about each other." She pauses. "Sometimes," she adds, as if testing me, "I still remember the boy, but he is dead now."

"I'm sorry," I say, feeling a vague sense of my own losses, whatever they are. María has located hers, given them a name and a focus. I have never grieved over anyone, not Kevin, my husband of five years, not the boy I once loved who drowned in a lake just outside of Ann Arbor. But I feel for María.

Her eyes light up. "Oh, no!" she protests, as if I've misunderstood. "I am very happy to be with a man such as Andreas. He is a very important thinker, you know. I had never knew a man like him before."

Her eagerness makes me uneasy.

"I am happy you are here." She reaches out impulsively and touches my arm. "I hope you are happy too."

Sensing the time is ripe, I move our talk to the household sources of my irritation. I choose my words carefully. "María, I wonder if Cello or Isabel could empty Tomás's chamber pot in the mornings. It's a difficult thing for me to do." I pause. "Also, the girls leave a terrible mess in the bathroom and I am tired of cleaning up after them . . ."

María's smile fades. Her mouth stiffens and thins. "I don't know what you want me to do," she says coolly.

"I just thought . . ." I catch myself. Of course we're not friends. I am María's employee. I exist somewhere between the two boys and the two maids, someone she can confess herself to precisely because we are not peers.

I excuse myself and go to my room, where I lie down on

my bed, hands folded under my head, and consider how, after three months of travel, I have reached a dead-end. My thoughts cannibalize themselves.

I hear Marcos's words, "You must come back, Diana." I feel the strength of his desires, a balm for my present unhappiness. How stupid of me to come to Spain when I could have done so many other things.

I am awake most of the night, and the next morning when I rise to get the boys up in the still-darkened flat I find myself completely disconnected from my surroundings and wishing I were in Marcos's tiny room, his naked body against mine. I want to be touched again. It suddenly occurs to me just how lonely I have allowed myself to become.

I take up walking. I invent destinations for myself. I spend hours in the Prado, seeking companionship as much as the art. I did not leave Kevin merely to dead-end in dreary Madrid. I wonder if he has been taking good care of the cat I gave him right before I left.

One afternoon in a coffee shop near the Prado I spot a red-haired woman sitting across from me reading a bodice-ripper in English. The cover of the book shows a wild black-haired woman with a ruffled blouse open down to her navel. She is being seized from behind in lustful embrace by a shirtless blond man with an earring in one ear. The title of the book is *Savage Desire*.

The woman reading the book is a heavy person in a dress, probably younger than I, but very matronly, so that she appears older. Her dress is ankle-length, and she wears black clogs. She has caught me staring at the book.

"Are you English?" she asks.

"No, American. And you?"

"Australian. From Sydney."

She sets down her book and invites me to come sit with her. "Would you like another cup of coffee?" she asks. When I hesitate, she orders it, then insists on paying.

She is an au pair for a Spanish family who live on the outskirts of Madrid, and this is her day off. Once a week she takes the bus into the center of town and drinks coffee and reads trashy novels in English.

We introduce ourselves; her name is Jennie.

"Have you made friends here?" I ask.

"Oh, not at all," she says cheerfully. "I'm not really interested in making friends. Spanish men are so dreadful and Spanish women are too standoffish. I was friends with an English girl who worked for some neighbors, but she left. She had a boy-friend back home."

The second cup of coffee goes to my head. I find myself telling her about María and Andreas and the two boys, Cello and Isabel, and even Marcos. Funny I don't mention having been married. Somehow it just doesn't seem like anyone's business.

Jennie is so good-natured I take to her immediately, and it is sweet relief to speak English with someone so easily. She's lived in Madrid almost a year, but hasn't bothered to learn Spanish.

"I have no knack for languages," she says, "so I don't bother." She says the family she works for speak varying degrees of English.

The afternoon begins to merge into twilight, and I am suddenly horror-struck that I will be late for tutoring the boys. Jennie and I quickly agree to team up and take a day trip to El Escorial or Toledo. She insists on paying for my two cups of coffee and a biscuit I ordered, and leaves a generous tip. I envy her ease with money, and wonder if she has generous parents.

As I board the bus I catch sight of Jennie flagging down a cab. She doesn't see me, but I wave frantically anyway, the caffeine swarming in my head like gnats.

The following day María knocks on my door and invites me to come hear her lecture at the university on women writers of Latin America. We drive out together in her car and I mention how much I am enjoying her book. She seems pleased. I want to talk to her about the women in her book, to know why she uses dead women as both images and characters in her stories. But to my disappointment I see she is not listening at all.

"Anyway," I say to the passing scenery on my right, "I look forward to the rest."

At the university she deposits me in a seat in the back of the room and assures me I must not feel obligated to stay to the end. She even goes so far as to tell me which bus I might catch, and where to transfer. But I do stay, I remain the whole hour, taking pleasure in what I am able to understand, even jotting some notes in my notebook about Gabriela Mistral, Marta Traba, and María-Luisa Bombal, whose work I have read only in translation. Afterwards, María is so busy with students she doesn't seem to notice I am finally preparing to head off. Two girls about eighteen years old smile and I eagerly smile back. But then they put their heads together and begin a private conversation in Spanish too rapid for me to follow. Their intimacy, their youth, their shared experience, all serve to exclude me. I am an outsider.

I wander the campus outside, but it is unremarkable and gray. It has been almost a month since I've made love to a man, and I realize I could be as easily captured as the woman on the cover of Jennie's *Savage Desire*. I'm actually hoping to catch someone's eye. But the men here are all so young, and Jennie is right, Spanish men are not attractive.

I wander over to the bus stop to return to the center of town. María hadn't even acknowledged me when class ended. I think about this, wondering why she would go to the trouble of inviting me. She has extended herself in unexplainable ways and encouraged my connection to Marcos. I am not a maid, yet I am not an equal. She has allowed me to go only so far. This is her signal to me: this is why I still dutifully empty Tomás's chamber pot in the mornings and wrestle with his verb tenses in the afternoons, even though María will bring me tea and biscuits on the balcony and talk to me about love.

From the bus window I watch the bleak university campus passing. The bus makes a stop just on the edge, where half a dozen or so students wait. The girls are all dark-haired. They look like young Marías in their dark jeans and sweaters, scarves casually tossed around their necks. Their skin has a high color, their eyes flash. They begin to board, talking and laughing.

That is when I see him. He is coming up alongside the bus on the sidewalk, his curly hair tossed and windblown. It is Andreas, strolling intently down the sidewalk, but he is not alone. His arm is wrapped tightly about the shoulders of a tall, thin girl with long black hair. I recognize the carnal expression on the girl's face: it is passion at its most furious. I have never seen such a look on my own face, but I must have felt it, sometime, somewhere, in order to know it. Every few steps Andreas presses his lips against her neck. Her face is flushed and whipped by the wind; I catch a glimpse of her shining eyes, the curve of her full mouth. She is beautiful because she is so young, her hair spiraling downwards to her waist.

I am mildly unnerved by the coincidence, but not at all surprised by what I have seen. Of all the stupid luck, I think, being assigned the role of Andreas's secret sharer.

The bus starts up again and rounds a corner, leaving Andreas and the girl lost in a cloud of exhaust. My annoyance with María turns briefly to compassion. My first instinct is to protect her. María, with her nervous pacing and erratic gestures and plaintive eyes. María, whose heart bleeds like an open wound on the badly printed pages of her book. She writes so beautifully, I think, yet her life is such a mess. Two reckless and rude sons, slovenly maids, a messy flat, and now, a faithless husband. And I suspect Andreas is no stranger to faithlessness.

Now I know something for sure. I've suspected it, but now I know. María, I think, must be the better writer. But it pains her, because she loves Andreas, still views him as her mentor. How jealous he must be of her. The bus thunders through the center of Madrid and screeches to a halt. I get off and cross the street. I think of the young girl, pressed against Andreas, still radiating the afterglow of sexual enthusiasm. She is probably like María was years ago when Andreas first saw her in class, before María grew so sad.

I go to a cafe. I begin another passionate letter to Marcos. María would approve, I think. I write furiously, reaching for images: sun-drenched trees in the park, the smoky rose of dawn, the steamy gray of evening. I wonder with a pang if he has gone back to seeing his old French girlfriend Anne, and then I am sure of it. I think of the two of them now, sprawled across his bed, his hands working over her body as they worked on mine. I am consumed by utter jealousy, or desire, or maybe they are the same.

I know, as I finish the letter, my heart fattening on its own desires, that I can never tell María about Andreas's girl. He is the reason, I think, that she writes about dead women. He may even be the reason she writes. Anything I would have to say would be superfluous, a disruption of the balance they've managed in their lives. For María probably already knows, and it is that which drives her.

That evening, lessons go poorly with both Tomás and Horacio. I am irritable, in no mood for foolishness. Horacio plays distractedly with his pencil, poking holes in the paper. He is impatient with my corrections, and switches to a rapid Spanish I cannot keep up with. When I patiently work with him on idioms, he argues in a loud voice, then stabs his paper with the pencil. Finally, María drops in and sends him off to watch television.

"He is tired from school," she offers as an excuse. "Horacio has worked hard enough." There is maybe the implication that I am too hard on the boys, but I ignore it.

I don't mention to her that he hasn't worked at all. She sends Tomás in. He is in an equally foul mood. It is as if the boys' instincts are so finely tuned that they anticipate the uneasiness lying just beneath the surface of it all.

"Why do you say 'super' that way? It's pronounced 'supah,' " Tomás sulks.

"That's British, I'm American."

"You're stupid," he informs me. "Everything American is stupid." He produces a pen from his pocket and uncaps it. A mischievous smile plays on his lips. I watch him rolling the pen back and forth in his dirty little fingers. He has chewed his nails to the quick and the skin around the edges looks gnawed on.

I try to distract him. "Look, would you like to learn some American slang?" I suggest.

"I don't want to. I hate all this."

I keep my voice patient, half suspecting that María is poised just on the other side of the door. I am hoping she will overhear

Tomás's rudeness, and will come to my rescue. But when the door opens, it is Andreas who enters. He wears the same impatient but self-satisfied smile he always does. As he unwraps his scarf, I can almost imagine the smell of the girl wafting off him like a breeze. I look away, not wanting to meet his wet gaze.

"Good evening," he says, including both Tomás and me in his glance. "Is work going well?"

I take a chance. "No it's not, Tomás doesn't seem interested in anything."

Andreas grins at his son. "Are you giving Diana trouble?" He shrugs at me and says, "Boys will be boys, you know."

I can't help myself. "Sometimes men will too."

He doesn't hear, or else he doesn't understand. Instead he asks where María is.

"I don't know," I say, just to be stubborn. To myself I think, I can't keep all your doors straight, all the locking and unlocking that goes on in this household. I want to ask Andreas why he doesn't keep track of his wife himself.

Tomás pipes up, indignant. "She's in her bedroom."

He doesn't say "your bedroom," he says "her." I wonder if Andreas has noticed, but he only grunts and leafs indifferently through the stack of mail. He holds up an envelope to the light, peering at it closely. "Here's something for María," he says and opens it. He pulls out a letter and scans it. "Hmmmm," he says, as if pleased with something. "María has been invited to lecture in Sevilla." He folds the letter up, then saunters in his Italian shoes toward the bedroom. A moment later the door closes behind him, and Tomás looks at me triumphantly.

"I knew she was there," he says. Then, without warning, he points his pen at me and shoots ink all over my sweater, like an octopus.

I am too stunned to react immediately, but instead watch the dark ink stream like blood down the front of my sweater and onto my jeans. All I can think of is how I have no money for new ones. Tomás begins a demonic cackling, clutching his sides and rocking back and forth with laughter. The sight of the ink stains both outrages and depresses me.

"You little bastard," I say, sitting very still.

I imagine him running to María and repeating what I have just said, but I don't care. I want an excuse to leave Madrid, to be driven by some compulsion. I happily imagine boarding the train that night and heading back to Paris. I'd go to Marcos's, simple enough, and his bed would be empty, waiting for me. And from there?

Tomás doesn't budge. He looks at me as if I've pulled the plug on him, with an expression that borders on pity. "It's not real ink," he says softly. "It's the kind that disappears. It hasn't hurt you one bit. Watch, it will go away."

I look down at my stained sweater and, sure enough, as if by magic the ink begins to evaporate and the stains it has formed begin to shrink.

"End of lesson," I tell him. "Go do what you want. I really don't care."

I stand up, shaken.

"How can the lesson be over?" he challenges. "It's not even six yet. And the ink went away."

"The lesson is over," I repeat firmly and pick up my books and leave him sitting there. I go directly to my room and sit down hard in the chair by the writing desk.

I spend the next hour penning a letter to Marcos. I press down hard on the paper. I can no longer separate frustration from ardor. Marcos has become a goal, a place to return to each evening after I've faced my dreary tasks. When my wrist grows tired, I turn to María's book and finish another story of hers about a young village girl who has a passionate affair with a rich married man in town and is later found drowned in a well. The man's wife finds out and leaves him and the man is left alone to recall the youthful girl's beautiful body, which he may no longer have.

There is a knock on my door. I half expect to be punished for having called Tomás a bastard.

"Come in."

"I hope I am not molesting you, Diana," María says cautiously from the doorway. She holds her head the way a wounded animal will, slightly to the side.

I wait for her to mention my spat with Tomás, but she says nothing.

"I spoke to Cello and Isabel about the bathroom," she tells me earnestly. "I insist they clean more—for your sake." She labors over the words.

"Thank you." She makes no mention of Tomás's chamber pot.

"And about your trip to Escorial tomorrow. I hope you have a very nice time with your new friend Jennie."

I nod. María lingers in the doorway, peering at the letter I have written to Marcos. I do not ask her to come in and sit down, as I have done in the past.

"You are writing to *him* again."

"Yes."

Her features soften. "Ah, you are so in love. How many letters he has sent you now?"

"Seven, eight." I point to the stack, neatly rubber-banded on the corner of the desk.

"He is a poet?"

"No, just a law student, but he writes beautifully."

"Very good," María says approvingly. "And you write to him in French?"

"Yes. Sometimes I try a little Spanish."

She doesn't ask why. "Perhaps I should speak to you in Spanish, so you may practice."

"I couldn't ask you to do that. I speak like a child."

She looks at me gently. "You are . . ." She pauses. "You are a breath of fresh air." She says this with the speed of someone reciting a poem. I can tell she has rehearsed this line, something she has read somewhere. "I hope," she adds, "that you and your French lover are as happy as Andreas and I are."

The words fall like a curse on my head. She excuses herself to go in search of Andreas, who is late for a dinner engagement. I sit inside my tiny room and listen to the sounds from the courtyard, the voices rising up from below, the sound of dinner plates and chatter, of other people's lives. I realize now María has never asked me what Marcos's name is. And I realize how foolish it all is, my being here, that is.

All night I toss and turn in my bed, longing feverishly for Marcos and feeling terrified that this growing anxiety is the way real love feels. What if I never see him again? In my dreams I confuse him with Andreas, wrapped in the arms of another girl, and the next morning I awaken disoriented, in a frenzy of nerves. I confess to María at breakfast that I haven't slept well. She brings me a sleeping tablet for the next night and lays it on my writing desk.

"This will help you," she promises knowledgeably. "It will destroy the *diablos*." And she pulls her long hair back up into her hands behind her head and looks down at me with sympathy. I put the tablet away in the desk drawer.

The next morning I awaken late and take the bus down to Plaza del Sol, dropping my letter to Marcos into the mailbox on the way. The day is so warm I discard my sweater. I am relieved to be away from the dismal flat where Cello and Isabel listen to the endless parade of soap operas and María wanders about nervously locking and unlocking, searching for Andreas, and he for her, in that odd dispassionate ritual of theirs.

Jennie is prompt, and as cheerful as she was the other day. Today she carries a book called *Tawny Embrace*. We drink enough coffee to rattle my nerves, and I find myself feeling careless about everything, even Marcos who, now in the light of day with the promise of adventure, strikes me as remotely silly.

On the train to Escorial my earlier mood unravels into something close to ecstasy, and I realize it is the sound of the wheels on the tracks and the forward motion of the train that has shrunk my anxiety. Urged on by Jennie, I talk about Marcos. He is a good story, and our meeting and subsequent week together have all the requisite qualities of a good romance. She lays *Tawny Embrace* face down on the seat and listens. Seated across from me, she is taking most of the breeze on her pale, freckled face. Her red hair blows full and thick. She wears a long skirt and a neatly ironed long-sleeved blouse. I feel as if I am on an outing with my mother.

The train ride is nothing short of spectacular. The warm fall air blows in perfumed gusts through the open window. I stare at the countryside rolling by. Jennie has brought cheese and bread for us to eat, all neatly sliced up and wrapped in cloth napkins.

"I'm here for two years," she tells me, stretching out her thick white legs on the seat opposite. "I'm so glad to have gotten out of Sydney for a while. It was making me sick and I needed a big change."

She tells me about the wonderful people she is staying with and working for. She calls them her family. The mother is Swedish ("I'd never work for a Spanish woman," says Jennie) and the father is Spanish. There are the three children Jennie is quite attached to. The Swedish woman's English is excellent, Jennie explains, and the two of them have become very close. "I tell her everything. We're very open with each other." According to Jennie, her life here is perfect.

We wander through the church at Escorial. I want to see the art collection, Jennie has no interest. The palace is closed for repairs, but we sit outside nearby and eat an overpriced lunch for which Jennie insists on paying. I am overwhelmed by her generosity and offer to buy her coffee, but she won't hear of it.

"Save your money," she says magnanimously. And then she begins to tell me about Bill, the man she left behind in Australia. Bill is rich. He owns a yacht, he has flown her in a plane to Bali, he has even offered to leave his wife for her.

"His wife's name is Cynthia," Jennie tells me. "She's a model. I tell him not to leave her. She needs him and I don't. I mean, the sex is incredible, but you don't need to be in love to have good sex." For a moment I think she is making fun of me.

She lingers over her coffee and dessert, slowly licking the icing from her fork.

"Bill writes me just about every week," she says. "He's thinking of coming to visit at Christmas. Will you be around?"

I'm at a loss for what to say.

"I'll show you a picture of him." Jennie digs deep inside her purse. She produces a wallet bulging with stuff. She pokes around in it. "Ah," she says, "here's Bill," and she pulls out a small photo from behind plastic and hands it to me. It looks to me like a passport photo of a clean-cut, handsome man with dark hair. He is wearing a jacket and tie. I stare at it perfunctorily and return it to her. "He's quite good-looking." I look at the people walking by.

"Yes, isn't he?" she says with triumph. She smooths down her skirt over her wide lap. "He's an incredible lover. He likes to lick me all over." I don't look at her when she says this. I keep my eyes averted, but I am certain her expression is smug. She is lying, and lying badly. I desperately want to leave Escorial. I don't want to sit here with Jennie any more. I suggest we catch the earlier train back. I feel as agitated and nervous as María. I want to get away from Jennie. Suddenly Marcos is the bright light in my head and the burning in my body. I close my eyes. When I open them, Jennie has paid for my meal, against my protestations. We walk back to the train station.

"You know," says Jennie, interrupting my thoughts as the train glides along, "there's something I haven't told you about my family."

"What?" I brace myself for something awful about the Swedish woman and her Spanish husband.

"I take stuff from them," Jennie says quite calmly, as if testing me. She is cleaning her perfect fingernails with a small orange stick.

"What do you mean, you take stuff?"

"I take stuff." She smiles. "You know, a watch here, a ring there. I have a whole bag of stuff." She opens up her expansive purse again and produces a large plastic pouch. I say nothing and she begins to spread things out on the seat between us like prizes. There are rings and watches and necklaces, even a beautiful pair of gold earrings.

"What if they catch you?"

"They won't," she tells me confidently. "They have so much. They won't even notice."

"What are you going to do with it?"

"Sell it. Pawnshops or wherever. My family hardly pays me enough to make ends meet, so I figure I deserve it."

"I thought you liked the family. You're stealing from them."

She looks at me almost sympathetically and shakes her head. "They expect me to. That's why they barely pay us anything.

You mean to tell me you live off your measly 3000 pesetas a week?"

I regret having told her what I made.

"Well," she shrugs, folding up the bag of stolen paraphernalia and tucking it back inside her purse, "it's your loss."

I think of María with all her keys. I'd always assumed it was Cello and Isabel she suspected. Jennie and I fall into silence.

The train crawls back to the Madrid station where the winds have come up again. At the bus stop in town I lie and tell Jennie I'll call her the following week to see about walking in Retiro Park. She smiles patiently at me, her round face doughy around the edges. She knows I'm lying and she's enjoying it in a way I can't understand.

"Say hello to Marcos," she tells me in parting. "I'll tell Bill you said hello too."

María is waiting for me, pacing like a cat. At first I think I've gotten my days mixed up and there is some appointment I've missed with the boys.

"You've had a phone call," she tells me. I've never seen her smoke before, but she smokes now. "Your Frenchman telephoned. He speaks excellent Spanish."

I don't tell her why.

"He is at a friend's. He awaits your call. I have the number here." She hands me a slip of paper. "Andreas is very late again," she tells me, inhaling the cigarette smoke. But smoking seems to irritate her and so she stubs the long white butt out in a flowerpot on the table. "It is terrible of him to keep me waiting. I am getting an award tonight."

"An award?"

She doesn't answer. "He wants you to call him," she says, "right away," and for a moment I think she means Andreas. "Come with me."

She takes me to Andreas's study and unlocks the door. She flips through the keys from her wrist and finds the one to unlock the blue telephone.

"He will be here at this number until eight o'clock," she says urgently, "waiting for you."

"But this is Andreas's phone."

María nods vehemently. "You must not be disturbed." Then she proceeds to stand there as I pick up the phone to dial.

It has now been six weeks since I've been with Marcos in my arms, but the memory of his shape has been worn into them and reinforced by what I believe to remember. I cannot, though, remember clearly his face, or even how tall he is.

I dial the unfamiliar number with clumsy fingers, trying to piece together in my mind a reasonable likeness of the Marcos who emerges from those rainy nights in the words on blue paper.

María's arms are folded tightly across her chest, as if she is trying to keep them under control.

It is going to be difficult enough for me to speak to Marcos, let alone in French, or should I try Spanish, no not Spanish with María standing so close by. What I really want to speak is English and put an end to all this pretense. Yet speaking English all afternoon with Jennie has not yet cured me.

The phone line erupts into short spasmodic beeps. The line crackles with distance.

A man's voice answers, deep and rich.

"Marcos?" I say eagerly.

"*Un moment.*"

There is a clatter, a shout, a patter of feet. I hear male voices and then the phone is picked up again.

A voice, so high-pitched and unfamiliar I am taken aback, addresses me with excitement. "Diana?"

"*Oui, c'est moi,*" I say softly, hunched over the blue telephone. I feel relief at those words; a connection is made.

Marcos tells me I must come immediately to Paris. He can't stand how unhappy I must be in Spain and he is so unhappy in Paris without me. And how awful that I must try to teach such horrible boys.

"*Tu me manque,*" he says over and over. "*Je t'aime, Diana. J'ai envie de toi.*"

When I hang up, I am uncertain what I've just committed myself to. My chest constricts. María paces on the periphery of my awareness. She turns to me, stricken.

"He is coming here?"

"No," I say. "I am going there."

"You are going there?" María pauses, her face pensive. She turns to the window and parts Andreas's heavy dark drapes with her long fingers. She stares out into the harsh light. For the first time I notice how tired she looks. "He loves you so, Diana. Yes, you must go to him."

I say something that makes almost no sense. I ask her, "But what about you?"

We both hear the key in the lock at the same time. The sound echoes down the hallway. María bolts for the door and flings it open. "Andreas! At last you are here! We are late!"

He looks puzzled as we emerge from his office. His expression demands an explanation.

"Diana had an important phone call," she says in English for my benefit. Then in Spanish she begins to chide him for his tardiness.

"Yes, well," he says sheepishly, continuing in English. "I was—uh—detained, you know, at the university. I'm sorry. I know it is late."

"Hurry," María says, "you must get ready. Hurry, please."

She turns and locks the telephone behind us, then slides her wrist back inside the key ring as if into a manacle. We walk out together into the living room where María turns and says to me, eyes swimming with tears, "I wish you luck."

That night I take María's sleeping pill and fall into a black drop. I don't awaken until noon, and then it's to a clatter of plates and silverware from one of the open windows across the courtyard. It means I've missed getting the boys up, but no one bothered to remind me. I dress quickly, my mind blackened and singed by a hot, dreamless night. No one is about; María and the maids are out, and the boys are off at school. María has let me sleep.

I stand on the balcony watching the traffic below. I hear Marcos's voice, tinny and anxious. Higher-pitched than I recall. Back in my room, María's collection lies open on the desk. I'd begun something I hadn't finished. I sit down and read the last pages of the story before tucking the worn book into my duffel. Most finished books I simply discard to keep my travels light. But there is no place to toss this book that María wouldn't find it.

I have no regret saying good-bye to Tomás and Horacio. They barely notice, they are occupied with a board game. The night I leave, Andreas is out. María insists on helping me carry one of my bags down to the taxi. She seems almost relieved to see me go and presses cab fare into my hand.

"Go quickly to him," she says dramatically. "*Buena suerte.*" And she stands back wistfully on the curb and waves good-bye with one spidery hand.

Night trains are surrealistic, illuminated by garish compartment lights. The aisles are astir with travelers boarding and searching for their seats. I am overcome with a sense of panic, realizing I have no idea what I am going to. The couchettes are cramped. I step to one side while a steward stands in his sock feet to make up the linen on the top bunks. I share the sleeping compartment with five Spanish women who agree to watch my bags while I wander up to the dining car. Two of the women are already in nightgowns and stretched out on the upper bunks.

In the dining car a short, stocky Spanish man smiles at me from across the aisle. I have a sudden impulse to change my destination. The weeks of yearning for Marcos focus themselves in a new direction. Just like that! With the man grinning at me, my anguish is relieved. I splurge and order *merluza* and *arroz,* and flan for dessert. I drink two glasses of wine. The meal costs me half the money in my pocket, but I don't care. I am relieved to feel the motion of the train and I think how I never want to stop. The Spanish man invites himself over and takes the seat across from me. He speaks little English, and is willing to talk slowly in Spanish to accommodate me. He is amused by my awkward constructions, my foreigner's use of metaphor when vocabulary fails me.

Two shots of whiskey and my Spanish seems to have improved, or at least my impression of it has. The man's name is Diego. He's thirty-five and he's traveling to Paris to see his fiancée who works at a clothing shop. The dining car closes and Diego invites me back to his car to play cards with two of his friends. More whiskey is produced and I sing them all the old song "Passengers will please refrain / from flushing toilets on the train / while passing through the station / I love you. Every night just after dark / we goose the statues in the park / If Sherman's horse can take it, why can't you?" They have no idea what it means, but they laugh and slap me on the back. I try to teach them "Found a Peanut," but they tire of the repetition.

The groaning and clanking sound of the changing of the tracks at Hendaye signals the border crossing. I press the palm of my hand against the window and feel the chilled glass. Diego's friends leave the car one by one, and suddenly everything is very dark except for someone breathing low and soft against my ear. I keep hearing María's words, "If you love him you must go to him," and I think how they easily could have emanated from one of the soap operas in Cello and Isabel's room.

I consider getting off the train in some small town along the way, but it is dark now. I weigh the facts: with the little bit of money I put aside in the weeks at María's I could last only a week or so in hostels. Marcos would come down to the station and find I wasn't on the train, but he would get over it. I would go on to Barcelona and then Rome, maybe even Greece and Turkey.

But I have made a promise of sorts, one that should be seen through to the end. I am not going to get off the train, even though I know how things will be. At dawn I will meet Marcos as planned and go to live with him for as long as it will take us to tire of each other and for me to discover that the French girl named Anne has not gone away at all. She will arrive dramatically at the door one night when Marcos is studying at the law library and she will tell me in perfect English, with a defiant tilt to her beautiful head, that she intends to marry Marcos and I should get lost. But I don't and we sit and wait together. When Marcos gets home, we confront him. He is surprisingly unaffected. He escorts Anne out. He's back almost instantly, explaining that she is crazy, that she is suffering for no reason, and that he will end it once and for all tomorrow. But I leave, within minutes after, despite the fact that he hands me a straight razor and begs me to kill him. I throw the razor to the ground, disgusted with the whole business, and for the first time I have an unexplained pang about my ex-husband. I leave, teary-eyed more from weariness and anger than any real disappointment. Anne can have him, and good riddance.

I will wander hopelessly down through the Marais until I meet a Vietnamese hotel clerk who speaks good English and offers to let me sleep in his room while he works. He will show me how to double lock the door, and then leaves me the only key to the room to assure me I will sleep on clean, white sheets, undisturbed. In the morning he brings me fresh croissants and a paper, and then busies himself at the hot plate making me coffee. He pulls "Sergeant Pepper's Lonely Hearts Club Band" from a collection of Beatle albums in mint condition and puts one on the phonograph. I am thrilled by his kindness, but am already thinking how the world is full of generosity, if you know just where to look.

Now, as the train lurches along the tracks to Paris, I find myself, at two in the morning, urged on by the alcohol and my open-ended desires. I strain against Diego's presses as the train screams around curves and shudders through dark tunnels. After, I sleep briefly against the cold leather seats and awaken alone to a flat, gray dawn. I return unobtrusively to my couchette, where I fall into a deep sleep for another hour. I am worn out, and sorry to be heading for Paris. I check, but there are no more stops.

Diego buys me breakfast in the dining car, and I smoke a cigarette. "*No te preocupes,*" he teases, reaching over to flip my hair. "*Sola una broma?*"

I readily agree. "*Una broma.*"

Diego leans over and kisses me on the mouth. "I like you. *Qúe lástima!*" We grin at each other.

As we pull into Paris, the mist is so thick I mistake it for snow. I wait nervously until everyone gets off the train, wanting to avoid Diego. He has slipped me his address, invited me to come visit.

I find myself half hoping Marcos won't be here to meet me, and thinking how much easier it would be to hoist my bags over my shoulder and wander off penniless through the streets. But the conductor has come along and poked his head into the car. "Finished!" he announces, making a cutting gesture with his hand across his throat.

I pick up my duffel and knapsack, heave a sigh, and head for the exit. I spot Marcos before he spots me. He is not the same.

This is how I remember it all. He was the last one on the platform, small and agitated. I hadn't realized how frail he was, a brown mouse in his blue cap drawn over his ears, his shoulders dwarfed by the bulk of a red parka. His nose was red and swollen from the cold. He was anxiously searching the train windows for some sign of me, his beloved.

Of course he must have also been preoccupied by how he would eventually explain me to Anne, but at that moment I decided to believe, and so did he, as I stepped off the train, that I had returned to Paris for love, that what we had written each other was true. Even then I knew it would never work, but I came at him full force anyway, wrapping my arms and legs fiercely around him, burying my mouth in his thick, wiry hair. He spun me in the air just as Diego walked through the station hand in hand with a pretty young Spanish woman. I could have sworn he turned and winked at me. What did it matter? When Marcos whispered, "*Je t'aime,*" against my ear, I knew he was

228

lying. But I'd come all this way, hadn't I, backtracking no less, to find him. I searched for his eyes, but caught instead the back of Diego's retreating head and the platform where the train track ended. I put my cheek against Marcos's and murmured back, "*Te amo*," but it was not for him at all. It was for María, who believed in such things.

Alyce Miller won the 1993 Flannery O'Connor Award for Short Fiction for *The Nature of Longing*. Her work has been published in *Story*, *Los Angeles Times Magazine*, *Glimmer Train*, *Southern Review*, and *New England Review*. In 1991, Miller won the Kenyon Review Literary Award for Excellence in Fiction. Born in Europe and raised in Michigan and Ohio, she spent most of her adult life in San Francisco. A professor of English in the creative writing program at Indiana University, she now lives in Bloomington with her husband.

Available in Norton Paperback Fiction

Edward Allen, *Mustang Sally*
Aharon Appelfeld, *Katerina*
Rick Bass, *The Watch*
Richard Bausch, *The Fireman's Wife and Other Stories*
Stephen Beachy, *The Whistling Song*
Simone de Beauvoir, *All Men Are Mortal*
      The Mandarins
      She Came to Stay
Anthony Burgess, *A Clockwork Orange*
      The Long Day Wanes
Mary Caponegro, *The Star Café*
Fiona Cheong, *The Scent of the Gods*
Stephen Dobyns, *The Wrestler's Cruel Study*
José Donoso, *Taratuta and Still Life With Pipe*
Leslie Epstein, *King of the Jews*
      Pinto and Sons
Montserrat Fontes, *First Confession*
Jonathan Franzen, *Strong Motion*
Ron Hansen, *The Assassination of Jesse James by the Coward*
      Robert Ford
      Desperadoes
Carol DeChellis Hill, *Henry James' Midnight Song*
Janette Turner Hospital, *Dislocations*
Siri Hustvedt, *The Blindfold*
Ivan Klima, *My First Loves*
Lynn Lauber, *21 Sugar Street*
Thomas Mallon, *Aurora 7*
Bradford Morrow, *The Almanac Branch*
John Nichols, *A Ghost in the Music*
      The Sterile Cuckoo
      The Wizard of Loneliness
Manuel Puig, *Tropical Night Falling*
Jean Rhys, *Collected Short Stories*
      Good Morning, Midnight
      Voyage in the Dark
      Wide Sargasso Sea
Joanna Scott, *Arrogance*
Josef Skvorecky, *Dvorak in Love*
      The Miracle Game
Rebecca Stowe, *Not the End of the World*
Barry Unsworth, *The Rage of the Vulture*
      Sacred Hunger
      Stone Virgin